MADE FOR YOU

A SMALL TOWN MILITARY ROMANCE

VETERANS OF SILVER RIDGE

CLAIRE CAIN

Cover design by Jess Mastorakos - Jess@jessmastorakos.com

EBOOK: 978-1-954005-43-3

PRINT: 978-1-954005-45-7

For the readers who've been patiently waiting for Bruce, and for the people like him, who've been holding it all together.

CHAPTER ONE

Nikki

If I didn't know better, I'd say my dearest, prim little Gram was spying on the neighbor.

From my seat on the couch, I craned my neck to see what could have captivated her so but couldn't tell anything from my acute angle. Her silver hair was twisted low at her neck with a clip, and she was already wearing a smock— must be a painting day. She stood so still, morning pottery mug full of coffee in hand, gazing out as though in a trance.

Evidently, nothing would be happening until after she'd taken in whatever it was that had ensnared her. She used to be into bird-watching, but memory and logic both said a mere bird wouldn't entrance her quite this much.

"What are you looking at, Gram?"

Her head snapped a sharp ninety degrees to the left like she'd forgotten I sat just eight feet away. "What? Me? Just, uh... Bruce is outside."

I raised a brow. I'd heard a bit about *Bruce* since he'd moved in next door a year ago or so. Apparently, he was now one of my great-aunt turned grandmother's good friends and she sometimes helped him out with his daughter. I didn't have all the details, but I did know the name.

I also knew Gram thought Bruce was a *total babe*, as she'd once said. I hadn't yet caught a glimpse of the dreamboat neighbor since my arrival less than twenty-four hours ago, so I didn't want to miss a chance to size him up. What kind of man would catch her attention like this?

At first, I'd imagined a silver fox situation. She'd mentioned once, when I told her she should ask him out, that he was too young for her—before she'd told me about helping with his teen daughter. Still, my curiosity had been piqued, and I'd likely meet him eventually. Might as well see what all Gram's fuss was about.

Hauling myself off the royal blue couch, I tucked my hip-length cardigan around me and padded toward the kitchen in my slippers. September tended to be fairly warm still, but Gram liked to keep it glacially cool with her air conditioning until the weather cooled off more sharply in October. She stood in front of the deep farmer's sink, still peering out of the picture window framed with carefully painted vines of flowers she'd done decades ago, one hand pressed to her chest and her head shaking back and forth slowly like the beat of a metronome.

"*Mercy*," she muttered right as I arrived, dipping her face into her mug without tearing her eyes away from whatever view she enjoyed.

Tucking my lips between my teeth to stifle a laugh, I glanced out and could only see a line of trees, then a ways past it, the side of the neighboring house. A bit more modern than Gram's but by no means a new build, it'd always been there from what I remembered, though Gram's house had been here before the neighborhood *was* a neighborhood. Her place stood out from the rest thanks to her eclectic yard, her bright yellow door, and the various artsy sculpture-ish details. Oh, and the hand-tiled sidewalk, which somehow withstood Utah winters.

"I don't see anything." A wisp of a worry that maybe she was imagining things spiked into my mind. She'd insisted she needed my help, and though I hadn't seen any signs of her age catching up with her, maybe this was it.

She whipped toward me, only now realizing I'd joined her. Instead of a little blush or anything like embarrassment brightening her still-high cheekbones, like I might've expected to see on her at having been caught red-handed playing peeping Rosie, a gleam entered her eye. "You have to stand right where I'm standing to get the best angle. Hear the ax?"

The muted *thunk* reached my ears as her hands on my shoulders guided me into place and her finger pointed over my shoulder to—

My gasp sounded loud and squeaky. Heat hit my cheeks in an instant and burned a path up to the tips of my ears and down into my chest as my heart rate shot straight through the ceiling. Words were zinging in perpendicular lines and crashing at intersections in my brain, and my mouth dropped open with nothing more than stunned silence coming out. I'd never seen anything like it—never in my life had I imagined an actual person could look like *that*.

What a sad, sorry little imagination I had, apparently.

A man—Bruce, evidently—was cutting wood with a red-handled ax. Jeans rode low on his hips and he wore dark, outdoorsy boots... and no shirt. *That's right.* No. Shirt. And this guy had detailed tattoos splaying across muscular pectorals and drawing the eye down to a six-pack—possibly eight. Maybe he'd imported a ten-pack from a metric-based country? There was something so far superior about the metric system. I'd always thought so—felt it in my gut. *And now, ladies and gentlemen, exhibit A.*

I'd need a closer look to be sure of the count, but the heat from his magma-hot body would probably melt my corneas if I got any closer—because watching him swing an ax overhead in a perfect, satisfying arc and bring the tool down to split a log in one fluid motion wasn't ever something I thought would make me feel so inexplicably *aware* but wow. Wow.

The muscles in his torso shifted as he pulled the ax with one hand and set it down, placed a new log on the stump in a move that did glorious things for his well-developed biceps, and then picked the ax up again. The swing overhead stretched him out, displaying every bit of his glorious torso for a flash before his razor-sharp movement used what had to be incredible momentum to slam the bladed edge into the wood, and another *thunk* rang out.

My math-loving brain scrambled for a tether to something familiar and reverted to its base mode as I wondered at the potential energy there in that swing. What actual kinetic energy did he use each time? The ax had to weigh six pounds, maybe eight. What kind of force was he generating to split the log, at what kind of velocity? I had no reference for this—I'd never once thought about it. Yet, my mind launched into calculations of how many newtons of force one might need to get an edge into a log let alone split it, of the kinetic energy expended each iteration. The path of his swing would be a huge factor as well. Clearly, he had superb technique, likely honed from much practice to get just the right impact.

Did people really *do* that—split wood manually? And with no shirt, really? Did they actually look like *that* when they did it? Or could this be some weird fever dream my brain had manufactured from Gram's couch, brought on by the incredible series of failures my life had become in the last year and now culminating in fantasizing about the arc of an ax swing and fictional men outside my grandmother's house?

"Rather impressive, is he not?"

My mouth snapped shut, and I turned to see Gram's Cheshire cat grin, then blinked back into the reality that *no*. Or, *yes*. Or—whatever. Bruce was a real person, and evidently, *this* was what he looked like.

Mercy, indeed.

"He—Gram!" I'd nearly agreed to just how *impressive* he was, and it only hit me now she'd wanted me to discover this truth from the minute I'd come nosing around—I'd nearly played right into her hands.

"Nikki!"

"You just stand here and watch the man cut wood topless?" I asked, more than a little scandalized but not entirely sure why. Gram and I were honest with each other, and she'd never been shy about appreciating men. Something about subjecting them to the female gaze. Was there harm in her enjoying the view?

Well, probably. If roles were reversed in any way, it certainly wouldn't seem okay. Would it? No. Probably not.

Definitely no.

"I didn't tell him to take off his shirt. Plus, he doesn't always. I think the sun's hitting just right..." She faded off as she rose on her toes to peek out the window again.

"Gram. Seriously. You have to stop. What if he looks up and sees you?" The horror of the thought made me swallow hard, and I shuddered against the deep discomfort even imagining such a scenario caused.

"Oh, he waves sometimes. I always give him a little lift with my coffee or wine or... you know, whatever beverage I'm drinking."

I coughed out a laugh. "He knows?"

She shrugged. "I'm not sure he knows I made it a point to notice when I hear that ax hitting the stump, but he has witnessed me standing here watching. I will say he doesn't always end up completely shirtless," she said, then if I heard right, mumbled, "*unfortunately*."

So many thoughts. So many, many things we needed to sort through. "Wait, this is Bruce? The Bruce whose daughter you watch sometimes? The Bruce you've called a 'dear' more than once?"

She held up a finger. "Sister, not daughter. And yes. He *is* a dear. He's downright adorable."

I sputtered. "Um. *Yeah.* I know sometimes we have differences of opinion, but that man? Not someone I'd ever call *adorable*."

The word was so deeply misused in reference to the stunning specimen out there—a literal ax-wielding, topless Superman look-alike. Adorable was sleeping kittens and babies napping and a freshman passed out from studying all night for their first applied and computational mathematics exam... other small things in repose.

That man?

Dangerous.

Lethal.

Potentially hazardous.

"Don't be fooled by the physique, Nikki. You'll meet him soon and you'll see." She took one more sip of coffee, then tipped her wrist and dumped it before setting her mug in the sink.

Ignoring the way Gram saying *physique* made me want to squirm, I acquiesced to the point. "Guess I will if I'm going to be here a while."

And thanks to the pep talk I'd given myself the entire time I'd driven from California to Utah, I didn't let the statement send me into a doom spiral. Sure, the prick of unease registered yet again at my neck and between my shoulder blades, triggering the clench in my stomach at the vast, gaping maw that was the incalculable ahead, but no. I would not panic. I would not cry any more tears.

My hand found its way into my pocket to feel the small stone there, seeking its reassurance, the tether it provided. Funny how it'd gotten so smooth. Last time I'd been here, when I'd taken it, it'd been sharp and brittle.

Gram had welcomed me with literal open arms and hugged me tight when I'd rolled in around six yesterday evening. My fifteen-year-old Corolla hadn't faltered—well, not too terribly —I'd made it up the winding canyon climb to Silverton okay.

It felt like one part home, one part foreign country, all topped with a little sprinkle of shame. Even though I'd given myself one heck of a pep talk, it still coated my insides —the shame. All my plans and years of work, the life I thought I'd have... gone.

Laid off from my job of over eight years, broken up with a boyfriend I'd thought I loved until he left and I felt more relief than heartache, and generally feeling like I had no idea what I was supposed to be doing now that everything I'd done to stay on track had faltered.

But I had this soft place to land. Gram was more than willing to let me stay with her while I found my way, and she'd insisted she needed help with day-to-day life more and more, though so far, she'd shown no signs of being worn out like she'd mentioned. In fact, the only reason I was here came down to her nearly begging me to come help her, and it'd been just the excuse I needed—a way to make a decision that meant something to me. Take care of Gram—*of course*.

Was part of me doing it since I knew my parents never would've, never had? Even though my great aunt Rosie had functioned as my mom's surrogate mother for a few months after my grandparents passed when she was a teen, my mom had never seemed loyal to her. I'd only known Rosie existed because my parents had complained she was stingy and didn't like anyone who wasn't exactly like her.

The reality I'd discovered years after their deaths was so much more complex, but the heart of it was that Rosie hadn't been willing to let them destroy themselves with her money. She was generous and open and loving, but she'd learned to have limits, and she'd had to develop them because of my parents.

Their perspective on the whole mess meant that they felt she owed them. They never would've shown up to help her unless they thought they could get something out of it.

Or maybe I was selling them short. Who really knew? Not me, since I didn't like to think about that.

I'd always loved these mountains, and the pull to return had been instant once the option opened up. Ties cut and most of my worldly goods sold off in California, the move here had been obvious, even if the "now what?" in my mind loomed large. In what had to be the worst betrayal of my life, there was no mathematical proof to solve and find x for what came next.

For now, I'd work on helping Gram and see about finding a job—the numbers in my bank account were quite clear on my priorities. Maybe I'd add focusing on making some friends. And just maybe... enjoying the view. It wouldn't hurt. And men like him? They existed in a realm even quantum physics couldn't penetrate, let alone mere mortals. So enjoying the view is all it'd ever be.

With a secret laugh as Gram bustled out of the room, I snuck one more glance out the picture window—to my own peril. My stomach dropped at the sight again. Good glorious grief, *what a physique.*

CHAPTER TWO

Bruce

Lunches packed, water bottles filled, coffee—*shoot*. We were ready to walk out, but if I didn't bring my own, I'd end up drinking the swill Kenny had been making the last few months. A shudder hit at the thought—high time to get a new admin since Sarah had been on maternity leave for a while now and it didn't seem like she wanted to come back.

"I'm leaving! See you tonight," Kiley hollered from the front just before the sound of said door closing reached my ears.

I jogged after her out to the driveway, knowing full well her ride would be squealing out of here before I reached the car if I didn't move it. "Dude, you're forgetting your stuff."

She turned and shot me a peeved look. "Bro, you know *dude* makes you sound like an aging surfer, right?"

"Sorry, *bro*, I forgot the kids these days are too cool for dude." I held out her lavender lunch box and reusable water bottle—both items she'd insisted on after reeling back in horror at my suggestion we use paper bags. Apparently, protecting the environment was all the rage and I happily complied.

She snatched them before cramming the box into her backpack and hooking the water with a finger. "I call you bro because you're my brother, dummy."

My mouth hitched up in a half-smile. *This kid.* "I know, bro, but then you call everyone else bro, so..."

Her eyes widened, her silent signal for me to shut the heck up before I embarrassed her any further.

Message received, I nodded, holding up my now-empty hands. "Have a good day, Ki."

She scowled, tossing her bag onto the floor of the back-seat while three other disaffected youths gazed out the front windshield like they weren't listening. She pulled the door as she stepped one foot in, but before she disappeared inside, she whispered, "You, too, Boo."

I winked, and she returned it before the door shut and she was buckling, my heart warming at her use of the old nickname. She'd called me "Boos" when we'd first met, but eventually it dropped to Boo, and I hoped I turned a hundred and still got to hear her call me that name. It only came out every so often these days.

Since I'd received a fairly stern talking to a few weeks ago after standing there watching her get carted away by the carpool driver, Jeremy, and I wasn't about to risk that again, I turned back to the house. I'd been feeling particu-larly protective of her thanks to her dad calling her a few times in the last few months, but I'd tried to tamp the impulse down.

In reality, I had no time to stand here musing. I had

approximately six minutes before I had to get to work, and my phone was already ringing.

"Saint, to what do I owe the pleasure of your voice before eight a.m.?"

Wilder Saint, the world's happiest broody veteran and my best friend, never called unless a text wouldn't cut it, so this had to be bad—or really good. Still, given the realities of life, probably bad.

An unknown vehicle over at Rosie's sat parked at an odd angle in her driveway. *Huh*. Hadn't seen it pull up yesterday, and I certainly didn't know Rosie to have overnight guests. I could get a little overprotective of the nice older lady next door, who'd welcomed us with open arms.

"Bad news. Kenny's got food poisoning." Wilder's voice had an apologetic tone already.

I pushed inside the house, knowing what this meant. Tristan was on assignment. So was Theo. Literally every other personal-security-qualified person was occupied. Eddie would do the job, but her fiancé had just gotten back from a trip and I knew she needed time with him. That only left Dorian, who was still insisting he wasn't available to work even though he'd been showing up for monthly meetings coming up on nine months now. He didn't take a paycheck, so he owed us nothing, especially if he wasn't ready to work yet, but I could've used him.

So it fell to me, and I wasn't about to complain. I owned half the business and had flexibility. Jogging back inside, I grabbed my stuff, then bolted to the car as I spoke. "Already on it. See if you can get Beast to come in a few hours early for his evening shift so I can get Ki settled and—"

"I'm sorry I can't help. This is stupid," he said, clearly in misery at causing me to scramble.

Gruff though he was, Wilder Saint didn't want anyone doing a job he could do. I understood because I worked the same way, albeit we had our own fortes. But Wilder, his wife, and their tiny baby had all had the flu. They were coming out of it, but he still needed another few days before I'd ask him to step in like this.

"Don't apologize, just get better. And get ahold of Beast while I get over there, okay?"

He acknowledged, and I hung up just in time to pull out of the driveway. I had to stop by the office and pick up a few things before going up to the hotel. The press junket for the upcoming movie festival would take place later today, the town already crawling with celebrities, no one more in demand than Jack McKean. We were guarding him, too, but today, we had some guy named Damon Crade on the docket. Didn't know him by reputation nor had I reviewed the files, so I needed a quick refresher. I'd stick with this kid until afternoon, when Beast could take over. Pretty sure Kenny was guarding till midnight—I'd ask Rosie to watch out for Kiley and then I'd head back before the evening schedule began. No problem, no stress.

As a typically practical yet sanguine person, when things didn't go my way, I handled it. I'd had a lot of practice spinning negative situations into manageable ones. Sperm donor of a father beating up on me? Join the Army and get out. Mission going to hell? Solve the problem. Teen sister wanting to date?

Shove all my feelings deep down and pretend it's fine

and I wasn't once a teen boy myself and therefore deeply mistrusted this *Marcus*, who'd been coming around more and more.

But none of those issues were the reason I found myself currently on the verge of breathing fire. Today, from the time I entered the office—no, before that—until this moment, every single thing that could go wrong had.

I'd forgotten the coffee I'd meant to get before leaving, so I had the displeasure of drinking whatever sludge Adam had left in the pot earlier this morning. Then Damon Crade? An absolute waste of space. And I really wasn't the kind of person to judge—I genuinely didn't find it bothersome when people were jerks or entitled. But that guy was a walking lawsuit. It only made me gladder I hadn't asked Eddie to take the work, because she would've been harassed unendingly, no question. Granted, she would've put him in his place and made him fear for his life if he continued his crap, but still.

Beast had been fifteen minutes late and could only cover for an hour because of something I hadn't fully absorbed at the time, much to my chagrin, and now, I had twenty minutes until I had to leave again, and I still needed to get ahold of Rosie and see if she could hang with Kiley when my sister got home from math club.

I banged on Rosie's bright yellow door one more time, deciding I'd give up and start calling her friends' parents if she wasn't home. The little junker still sat in the driveway, which might mean she had guests and couldn't help.

Irritation surged through me. I needed to eat something and get back, and I needed to do it all *after* finding someone to hang with Kiley. I'd already messaged her to let her know, and she was unfazed, as usual, but would I be able to tell if she was bothered over text? No.

I knocked one last time, and just as I was about to turn away, the door swung open. A woman I definitely hadn't seen before peered back at me, blinking at the early evening sun just starting to fade behind me.

"Uh, hi. Is Ms. Rosie in?" I asked, mildly annoyed this person was answering my neighbor's door. This meant more time lost—time I didn't have.

"Um... she...." Her big light-brown eyes blinked back at me like I might hold the answer to a question I'd just asked.

I exhaled, willing the impatience thrumming in my veins to chill. The day going to the garbage wasn't this woman's fault, and me standing here huffing and puffing like an angry bull wouldn't solve any problems.

Checking my watch, I gritted my teeth and pressed my mouth into a smile because apparently, finishing that sentence wasn't going to happen without prompting.

"She...? Is she in?" I didn't normally push people like this. I was actually pretty good with them, but right now, I had no time and this girl was... was she intoxicated?

She gave a slight shake of her head. "Sorry, no. She should, um, be back in a few. Can I help you?"

She tipped her head to the side and seemed genuine—the clarity in her words and those eyes banished any question of her sobriety. Shame on me for jumping to quick, erroneous conclusions.

"No. It's fine. I'll figure it out." I was already turning and jogging down the sidewalk, wishing I could restart this day as I searched through my contacts for Kiley's friend's mom's number.

"I'm happy to help if there's anything I can do," the woman called out before I'd reached the street.

"I don't know you." I dialed the number and it instantly hit busy. *Crap.* Turning back to the woman, I gave her a chin nod. "I'll give Rosie a call. Don't worry about it."

She shrugged and lingered for a moment before shutting the door. And because it felt like I was out of options, I did dial Rosie, who answered immediately.

"Bruce, honey, to what do I owe this pleasure?"

Her warmth glowed through every word, even over the phone. I took a breath, her presence via the line easing a touch of the tension winding its way through me. She was one of the most welcoming, genuinely kind people I'd ever encountered, and I considered myself very lucky to have bought the house next door to Ms. Rosie Renwick.

"I'm sorry to bother you, but I'm in a pinch and was going to see if you'll be around later to hang with Kiley? I've got to head back to work and she's been... well, I want to make sure she's got company since I might be late." Silently praying, I made my way back up the street to my house.

"Of course I will. You know I'm always available to you two. I'll be home within the hour and we'll have a great evening. Did you have a plan for dinner or am I allowed to order pizza?"

I snickered, gratitude swallowing up some of the ire pulsing through me. "Pizza and whatever else you want. Kiley has my card, so let her buy. And I'll owe you one."

"You will not. Also, I wanted to mention—"

My phone beeped, alerting me to another call. I swore under my breath and returned it to my ear. "I'm so sorry, Rosie, work's calling me."

"No problem. We'll talk later. Leave it to me."

With that, I ended with Rosie and accepted the call from Beast, bracing for it because I already knew it'd be something bad if he was calling.

"Sorry, boss, but this guy's about to get himself arrested."

I scrubbed a hand over my face, then jogged into the garage. At some point, I'd eat a solid meal and not sub in a protein bar for dinner. Sometime soon, I'd take Kiley out for a nice dinner and catch up on her life without either of us distracted by our phones.

But for tonight, I'd be babysitting a drunk idiot with too much money and too little self-awareness. As inglorious a job as it came in this line of work, and yet, it was all for a purpose. Right?

Right.

Or so I kept telling myself.

CHAPTER THREE

Nikki

Gram slipped in the door a little before one in the morning.

"I know you said you'd be late, but does he work this late often?"

Don't ask me why I was asking about Bruce the Un-adorable at way-past-my-bed-time o'clock, but I couldn't help it. My mind wouldn't shut off, nor could I sleep until I knew Gram was home. I'd camped out on the couch watching *Gilmore Girls* reruns and done my level best not to think about the neighbor or the fact that Gram was *at* the neighbor's house.

Why would I be thinking about a way-too-handsome man who was kind of a jerk and routinely chopped wood shirtless? I wouldn't, obviously, and so I wasn't. That'd be like expecting two parallel lines to meet. Illogical. Not my style. *Not happening.*

But Gram out so late had my concern, had my mind wandering from Lorelai Gilmore's hijinks to the house next door.

"He doesn't unless he needs to, then he does." Gram arched a brow.

I shrugged like it didn't really concern me. And it didn't, obviously. "It just seems weird, I guess. His sister's fifteen, right? She could probably spend a few hours alone and then you wouldn't have to be over there standing guard."

She tutted. "Sixteen. You'll learn that Bruce always has a reason for doing things. And soon enough, you'll see that I don't normally go to bed before midnight anyway."

With a wink, she strolled out of the room without a backward glance, then padded up the stairs, leaving me with an undue amount of irritation.

After hours of thinking about how I needed to make sure I was refreshed and ready for the day at a normal time tomorrow, I finally passed out around three. I hadn't shifted the hour to mountain time yet, and mornings were proving to be tough on my body and brain stuck on Pacific time. But today, I'd be starting my new life—I'd find a job and soon, everything else would fall into place.

Gram was still in bed by the time I shuffled out the front door and walked the path to my car. With a small folder tucked under my arm and my purse slung over my shoulder, coffee mug in hand, I hustled along the mosaic walkway and nearly jumped out of my skin when a tall, dark figure appeared in front of me.

I flailed, the folder slipping out from underneath my arm, and nearly dropped my coffee but managed to keep hold of it.

"I'm sorry. I didn't mean to startle you—" He bent to pick up the folder.

No need to look up to see it was Bruce Camden, apple of Gram's eye, because his voice sounded just as smooth and distinctive as it had yesterday, if a little less annoyed and more apologetic. Not much of a difference where I was concerned.

I scrambled for the papers and stood right as he did.

My stomach flipped at the sight of him, yet I shifted my eyes away from that face for my own well-being. Good freaking grief, the man was stupid handsome, and I didn't have time or space or energy to accommodate whatever request he'd make of me. Presumably something about his sister again. I could imagine caring for a teen proved no small task. Still, I'd tried to help last night when I did have time, and even though I understood his disinterest in my offer since he didn't know me, I couldn't help now with no spare time before my interview.

"Truly, I'm so sorry. I snuck up on you—I shouldn't have. I hope nothing's ruined."

He handed me the folder, and I reluctantly met his eye.

My insides swooped. Dark brows, pure brown eyes, good hair with a little lock that arced over his forehead, cut jaw, somehow perfect nose, ridiculous lips, strong chin... incredible symmetry. Of course. Because traditional beauty was all about symmetry and the illustrious Golden Ratio— 1.618 times longer than wide and perfectly proportioned in every way. And like the most basic of all people, I happened to really, *really* love symmetry. Not just in nature and on a handsome man's face, but in all things. One might say all of math was about symmetry—balancing one side of an equal sign with the other. And here he was flaunting it.

I cleared my throat. "I'm sure it's fine."

"Do you have a minute?" he asked as I fumbled for the

car door. "I know not long—you're clearly leaving. I just need a quick moment of your time."

I dumped my purse, set the folder onto the seat, and shoved my coffee mug into the cupholder, mind unable to parse through what he could need from me. My pulse had climbed into my throat, and dual responses of incredulity and anticipation had me slamming the door just a little too hard. I straightened, internally bracing myself to look at him and not react.

"Sure. I have just a minute."

"Thank you. I just wanted to say I'm sorry."

I blinked. "It's fine. I know you didn't mean to startle me."

Half of his mouth kicked up into a smile—a.k.a. a deadly weapon.

"No, I mean about yesterday. I was rude and I apologize. What I should've done is introduce myself, ask you about yourself, and, well, really anything other than be a jerk like I was."

I blinked again, because really? My heart rate accelerated at his heartfelt, genuine apology. Yes, I'd thought him a bit of a jerk, but I could also tell he was distracted and worried about something. I wasn't upset so much as just kind of... surprised. Gram had gone on about what a good man he was and I'd kind of wanted him to rise to the occasion. What a lovely thought that her neighbor would be both a glorious specimen of manhood *and* a decent human being. Then he all but dismissed me, and sure, fine—he didn't know me. It deflated the old idealism balloon a bit, but these things happened in the light of day.

But now? Now, he was apologizing and thoughtful, not making excuses for anything. In all my life, I couldn't think of a time I'd encountered a man who'd behaved this way, and it made me oddly giddy.

Gorgeous neighbor Bruce was helpful and *not* a jerk and might actually be kind of shockingly… nice. *Huh.* The way this pleased me could not be overstated.

"It's fine. You needed Gram and you weren't expecting me."

He nodded. "No. I wasn't. But, hi." He extended a large hand. "I'm Bruce Camden. I've lived next door for a little over a year."

On reflex, I took his hand like I would anyone else's, but the second our palms pressed together, our fingers gripping just enough to hold on and not be weird, everything in me stopped. Eyes on our hands as they shook up, then down, I had no coherent thought beyond this wild, fleeting thought that went something like, *I can't wait to know you.*

What the heck?

My usual thought when confronted with strangers flitted something along the lines of reluctant acceptance that meeting new people was a necessary evil in life. And though I'd promised myself I'd make an effort here, I had never felt *eager* to get to know someone.

None of this made sense, but we'd already released hands from the brief shake, and I still hadn't spoken, so I responded. "Nikki Hastings. I'm Rosie's great-niece, and I've lived here for less than forty-eight hours."

When I met Bruce's gaze, my pulse jumped at the soft, perplexed look on his face. Before I could think much about it, though, he blinked a few times as though to clear his mind and then grinned.

"It's nice to meet you, Nikki. I'm sure I'll see you again, and thank you for giving me a minute to apologize. I hope you have a good day." With a small nod, he turned and walked back toward his house.

I admit, I watched him go in a daze. I couldn't put my thumb on it, but I felt markedly different after meeting Bruce, like shaking his hand was the key that unlocked a door I hadn't seen standing in my way or the answer to an equation I hadn't even realized had been on the blackboard of my mind.

What is wrong with you?

Logic had short-circuited. *Huh.* I shook off all those fanciful thoughts and got into the car, doing everything I could to push Bruce Camden from my mind and focus on my upcoming interview. This was the biggest and best accountancy firm in the small city and the closest to an obvious workplace for me as it got. I couldn't afford the distraction of a gorgeous man who was nicer than he should be and way too close for comfort.

I slumped down into the booth and mumbled, "Coffee" without looking up. If I caught a sympathetic gaze, I'd probably lose it and cry right here in this diner apparently cleverly named *Diner*. Hard no. I would not be the weepy new resident. And no, the town wasn't that small, but it sure felt it. My hand curled around the small stone in my pocket like it had a hundred times today. A feeble effort in finding comfort, and frankly, completely senseless. And yet, this little stone had been with me since I left Silverton years ago, and like a talisman reminding me I wasn't alone in the world, I never left home without it. Living in the house I'd taken it from didn't seem to dim my need to have it with me.

"You new here?"

I looked up at the softly spoken words coming from the woman setting a mug of steaming coffee in front of me.

Couldn't very well ignore her, could I? "Sure am. That obvious?"

She smiled in a warm, friendly way. Her dark hair was pulled into a high ponytail, and she had creamy skin with freckles across the bridge of her nose and cheeks. She was around my age, in her early thirties give or take, and if I wasn't mistaken, she was blushing.

"It's probably less that you're obvious and more that I observe people a lot, and I also happen to know Ms. Rosie." Her head swiveled to the pickup window and she held up a hand, then hustled to go get whatever was waiting there for her.

I sipped from my mug, my mind veering to its preferred default, thus estimating the number of steps she took in a day between any given table and the pickup window. I hoped she liked being on her feet, because I'd bet within a standard deviation of a thousand steps it was well over ten K based on her being the only waitress on the floor.

As draining as the day had already been, it felt good to talk to someone who knew Gram, even if I didn't know this woman. She felt like less of a stranger since she knew someone I did. It made the town feel smaller, which was both good and bad, I supposed, but I chose for that to be a good thing right about now.

The scalding coffee cooled quickly, and the waitress returned before it'd lost all warmth and topped it off. I'd forgotten how hot food and drink seemed to cool down faster thanks to a lower boiling point at higher altitudes.

"I'm Catherine, by the way."

"Nice to meet you. I'm Nikki. And obviously, you know Gram, so you know why I'm here." Or at least who I'm staying with. Hopefully, Gram hadn't shared the real why with anyone. Not quite the impression I wanted to make to start with my miserable failure in California laid bare in front of strangers.

"I guess I do. It's great you could come help her out. Are you staying for a while, or just passing through?" She pulled a pencil from behind her ear and slipped it down into the pocket of her apron. Her nails weren't manicured and looked a bit dry, likely from all the hand-washing required by the job.

Nudging the coffee mug out of the way, I sighed. "I think indefinitely, though the job prospects are looking pretty slim." I mumbled the last part, not exactly enthusiastic to share the status of my working life, especially to someone clearly used to hard work. Maybe one dead-end interview wasn't cause for this level of discouragement, but I had fully loaded my expectations into the tidy little basket of that one job.

"Oh, good. I mean, not about the job prospects, of course, but the staying indefinitely. And not to be the weirdo local who's too excited for you to get here, but this is my phone number. If you ever want to grab a coffee or"— she eyed my empty mug and her blush deepened—"a margarita or anything, let me know. Everyone needs a friend in a new place."

"Thank you. Seriously, that's so nice. I'm sorry to ask, but can I grab the check? I'm actually meeting Gram— Rosie." I hated to rush, but my alarm had just gone off, and I'd feel better once I shared the news with Gram. Maybe she'd show me around town and distract me.

"Oh, don't worry about it. On the house for your first visit." She gave me a shy smile. "I'll see you again soon, I hope."

"Thank you, you're so kind. And yes, definitely." As miserable as I felt, knowing I had at least one *prospective* new friend was not nothing. It was something. And I needed to collect those like diamonds.

With one last wave, I dragged myself out of the diner and across the street, right past the scene of my disappointment and a little farther down. I was supposed to meet Gram at a restaurant called Guac, which I vaguely remembered had excellent chips and guac, but stumbled upon her standing on the sidewalk just outside it, chatting animatedly with someone sitting at a table in front, in the little sidewalk café area.

With a gigantic cackle, she leaned over and patted the person on the shoulder right before I caught her eye.

"Nikki! Perfect timing. Come meet Bruce."

Because of course she was talking to Bruce Camden. And of course he was sitting there looking airbrushed and perfectly, painfully handsome while I strolled up with a chest full of disappointment and cheeks bright with humiliation.

But that was fine. What was one more instance of embarrassment after the last year, anyway?

CHAPTER FOUR

Bruce

I stood and extended a hand, bracing for contact. "It's nice to see you again, Nikki."

My stomach clenched as our hands slid together, a brief, business-like shake before dropping. It'd be a matter of minutes before the tingling awareness of having touched her wore off if this morning's encounter was anything to go by.

Rosie's brows climbed high. "You've met? How did I miss that?"

Nikki nodded. "Bruce came to introduce himself this morning."

Her eyes flicked up to meet mine, and a whip of electricity lashed through the air.

When she'd answered the door last night, I'd been in problem-solving mode. Sadly, I'd been a jerk to her, but she'd seemed willing enough to accept my apology. I hated the idea of being overtly rude to anyone, even while dealing with a mild crisis, and I especially hated the idea of being discourteous to Rosie's family.

Rosie had been there for us at some key moments this last year. The fact that she now had someone around to help her was a good thing. The fact that the person living with her happened to be the manifestation of everything I thought of as physically beautiful?

Not ideal.

This realization had hit me when I'd finally, actually *looked* at the woman this morning. I'd startled her, we'd juggled her papers and folders, and then we'd shaken hands, and everything had stopped.

Literally, it felt like the low-lying buzzing in the back of my head reminding me I wasn't doing quite enough to establish our lives here had paused. The wind rustling in the branches of the oaks nearby had stilled, and the rotation of the earth had halted in honor of our hands meeting. Exaggeration, yes, but I couldn't describe it any other way except to say it'd been weighty. I'd felt it in my chest like a blast at close range, jarring my insides and everything around me.

The same heady sensation snuck in and gripped me again, and though I dropped her hand a little too quickly, it lingered.

"I was a jerk last night when I was looking for you, and she was kind enough to forgive me," I explained to Rosie.

"I can't imagine you being a jerk, Bruce." Rosie patted my arm and shot a significant look at Nikki.

Did she have to be so glaringly beautiful? Missing it yesterday only showed just how preoccupied I'd been last night. The auburn hair, the large light-brown eyes, the pretty blush climbing her cheeks... it made me stupid.

"It's true. But she was very gracious." My eyes found Nikki's, and my gut tightened.

"You were busy, and I was a stranger. Now you know I'm not a threat."

She fluttered her lashes, and it hit me just right.

With a chuckle, I gave her that despite it being patently false. "Fair enough."

"Well, Bruce, honey, we'll let you wrap up your lunch. Is Kiley joining us tonight?" Rosie looped her arm through Nikki's as though they were about to promenade into the restaurant together.

"If it's still okay. I'm sorry to ask two nights in a row. I can skip book club, if it's at all—"

Rosie waved me off. "Nonsense. Of course you're going, and of course she's coming over."

"Book club?" Nikki asked, and if I wasn't mistaken, a note of interest colored her question.

"Yeah, it's a local group of some friends. You're welcome to come sometime, if you like reading. We meet once a month, sometimes twice, depending on what everyone has going on. It's casual." It was also a lifeline, and I felt nothing but relief that Rosie had insisted I go tonight. I'd canceled before, and missing it felt awful.

I wasn't a particularly needy person. I'd been independent since I could remember. I'd left home at seventeen and never looked back—hadn't even visited my mother for the first decade after I joined the Army straight out of high school. She'd actually told me to stay away. I'd enlisted since living near a major Army post had made that look like an easy way out, and the natural course of the job had taken me away until I'd finally ended up stationed back with EMU at Fort Liberty. When I did go back, I met Kiley, who was five at the time and the cutest little thing I'd ever seen in my life. And she was my sister.

She was mine, and I'd missed out on loving her for years. It might've seemed like an unnatural thought for a twenty-seven-year-old kid to think, but I'd never felt like I'd belonged in my family. My own mother had encouraged me to leave—to get away from the abusive sperm donor known as my father. He'd never touched her and that was the only reason she'd wanted me to leave—to protect me. It'd been noble, and maybe it'd even been right. Then, I'd stayed away, only calling every once in a while so as to avoid stoking the ire of my father, only to find out he'd walked out on her not long after I'd left and she'd had a child with another man. Kiley's dad.

The story between then and now was a long, winding one, but I'd learned one thing very quickly. I needed a small group of trusted people in my life, and after leaving the built-in family of my unit in the military, I needed it even more now. I'd only been out for a little over a year and the crew at Saint Security was like a family. Occasionally, the odd element of being boss made that dynamic stretch in new ways, and we were still building rapport as we grew.

But book club? For some reason, I'd kind of fallen for everyone in book club. Maybe because they were all book nerds like me, or maybe because the usual host, Jane Saint, was my best friend's mother and a woman I greatly admired. Each of the people involved brought something to the table, an interesting history, and incredible capacity for warmth and love. I suspected this was something engendered in readers, yet they were all exceptional humans at their core, full stop.

"Sounds nice. I'll look forward to meeting Kiley," Nikki said.

"You two enjoy your lunch," I said, trying my best not to creep her out by looking too closely at her eyes or lips or the curve of her jaw and *definitely* not lower. *No.*

"You, too, honey. We'll see you later tonight."

Rosie patted my shoulder and pulled her great-niece along with her. I stayed standing as they passed, then sat with a heavy sigh.

I needed to focus on work today and then getting to book club where I could ask Jane and Quinn for tips on how to get Kiley to talk a little more. I needed to get through this film fest and the long hours coming this weekend and then get back into the routine.

And I did *not* need to worry about the next time I'd see Nikki Hastings.

Jane Saint hugged me tightly, hard enough to push a bit of the breath from my lungs, then pulled back. "You're doing a good job, Bruce. Don't doubt yourself so much."

I huffed, not sure what to say. Moving into the world of being my sister's guardian over the last two years had meant my new part-time job was doubting myself. "Thanks, Jane."

"I say keep doubting yourself, but keep it in check." Quinn Darling, whose daughter was nearly eighteen, always had contrary and yet super helpful advice.

Jane rolled her eyes. "You're going to give the man a complex."

"More than the hero complex he already has? I don't think there's room for that." Quinn winked at me, then her sly little smirk settled into something more somber. "But seriously, part of this is the situation, yes. Part of it is what happens when the mutant genes of puberty overtake a child. There's only so much you can do, and stressing yourself out about it isn't going to change things."

I swallowed hard, recognizing the truth of it. In any other walk of life, I managed stress well. Black ops missions—hunting terrorists, retrieving kidnapped Americans, rescuing hostages... I'd done it all with relative calm. But that life was behind me. Saint Security had primarily static jobs, and most all of us were glad for the breather the change offered as we built the clientele.

"You're doing a great job," Dahlia Wallace said, her gentle words reassuring despite the doubts in my head.

She was a good friend and a sensitive soul who'd recently found her happy. I couldn't have been more delighted for her, or for myself, that her husband had embraced me as a friend, too. John was as good a human as they came.

Yet, it still felt off. Not that I didn't believe their words—something still didn't click. Like all this was stuff they were supposed to say. I ran a hand over my face. This whole situation was weighing on me like an overstuffed rucksack I couldn't off-load.

Everyone sat around Jane and Darcy Saint's living room, the matriarch of the Saint family and the local bookstore owner making an adorable hosting duo. I'd only known Jane for a while before she and Darcy had gotten hitched, but I hoped someone looked at me like Jane did him someday.

Thoughts like that are why you're feeling guilty.

Probably true. And I didn't need all this attention on me —they'd done a very thorough job of reassuring me. "When did this turn into console Bruce about his potential brothering failures? Let's get back to choosing the next book."

Everyone laughed, then launched back into conversation, and I sank into the moment. Embraced this moment now. It wasn't something I excelled at, especially lately, and I wouldn't get another one like this for a month.

An hour later, I wandered home to find the kitchen light on. Kiley tended to hang out downstairs when Rosie came over, but otherwise, she spent the vast majority of her time in her room, and increasingly more since she'd started dating the little twit from high school.

Fine. He wasn't a twit. Maybe I was grumpy. Maybe I needed to find a therapist here. I hadn't been able to shake this dread and anxiety lately, and that wasn't me. Not usually, anyway.

When I walked in from the garage, I halted in place. Kiley, Rosie, and Nikki sat at our little table, heads all ducked over something Kiley was writing.

"Perfect. Exactly. And then, you do the same thing next time," Nikki said, a beaming smile on her face.

If she'd tip her face up just a bit, I could see it full-out. I hadn't seen her smile like that yet, and the hint of it, the tease, sent an instant, cutting *want* down my spine.

Ki's head slowly turned, and she looked more excited than I'd seen in a long time. "I think I actually *finally* get this. Thank you." She flung her arms around Nikki, who returned the gesture with a startled expression before she caught my eye and flushed.

"Don't mind me. Just crashing the stats party, I guess." I waved awkwardly like this wasn't my own home.

"Boo, she just broke it open for me. Can she please tutor me or something? She needs a job, anyway, and—"

"All right then, honey, get up to bed so your brain can cement all of this in place. We'll see you soon."

Rosie's interruption left me a little surprised, and the deepening flush on Nikki's face explained it.

"I—we'll talk about it. Rosie's right. Get to bed and have a good sleep."

Kiley wandered past me with her armful of books, her dark hair sticking out at odd angles from her bun. She nudged me with an elbow on her way by. "Night, Boo."

Affection burst open in my chest—that easy. "Night, Ki."

The three of us watched her go, then I walked the ladies to the door.

"Thanks for hanging with her, and thank you for breaking open the mysteries of statistics. I'm pretty hopeless with math."

One of Nikki's brows raised. "I wouldn't have imagined you being hopeless with anything."

Rosie's grin spread across her face in a flash, and she flared her eyes at me with a chuckle. "Nighty night, Bruce."

"Good night, and thank you both," I said, then shut the door before I could say what I really wanted to say. "*Oh, yeah? How* have *you imagined me?*" I wondered how that would've gone over, even though I knew I shouldn't give it any more thought.

CHAPTER FIVE

Nikki

Bruce appeared on my doorstep the next day looking like he'd barely reached consciousness before he'd rolled out of his house and arrived at my bejeweled doorstep. Or, Rosie's doorstep, rather, but since she wasn't awake yet, it was me who swung open the door to reveal him in all his glory.

"Uh, hi."

He gave me a nod with that ridiculous face of his leading the charge, and I swallowed hard. Exhausted or no, the man was outrageously good-looking.

"I wanted to get here early. These are to say thank you." He handed me a pink box with white twine tied around it.

"What's this?" I saw no hint of its contents, though I smelled something slightly sweet.

"They're from Glazed, a little donut shop. My buddy's

sister, the owner, just opened it. You went the extra mile with Kiley last night, and I wanted to say thank you."

His dark eyes pinned me in place, and the quickening pulse racing through me since the minute I saw him at the door doubled.

"This is so... unnecessary," I said, more than a little baffled by the gesture. Not only had I enjoyed the time with Kiley, the interaction had given me the germ of an idea, and it'd taken root overnight. Fledgling still, and it'd take some time to percolate and develop, yet it had popped in to stay.

He huffed a laugh. "Well, you helping my sister understand a mathematical concept that is entirely opaque to me is a debt I can never repay, so let's call it even. Oh—" He pulled a small envelope from the pocket of his jacket. "And these are for you and Rosie."

I took the small packet and raised my brows.

"They're tickets. To the film fest. There's a pretty big screening tonight and—"

I gasped before I could stop myself. I'd just read an article about this in the small-town weekly paper Gram got. "Is it the Jack McKean movie?"

His lips pressed together, and his eyes narrowed. "McKean fan?"

Making no attempt to hide the truth, I grinned. "What a tautological statement..."

He blinked.

I cleared my throat, ignoring the familiar awkwardness and trying again. "Is there anyone who's not?"

Recovering perfectly, he pressed a hand to his chest. "I can't imagine."

With a chuckle, I attempted to lift an edge of the box, but it was secured too well. "How do you have them? I just read an article saying tonight's event has been sold out for months."

He glanced away, almost like he was... embarrassed? Or, no, that wasn't it. I couldn't tell, but then he spoke.

"Saint Security is covering the event."

"The screening?" I asked.

Gram had made clear his business was doing quite well, especially for only being a little over a year old, but I imagined an event like this was quite a contract. Numbers filtered across my mental screen, the possible count of attendees and the potential revenue from a weekend like this for both the premiere and likely his business, too. Of course, I wouldn't comment on such a thing because I'd learned long ago how commenting on probable taxable income struck people as inappropriate.

He glanced down, then up through his lashes at me. "The festival, the event, and for a few of the attendees as well."

My mouth opened, then shut. I'd imagined door security at most. "Wow. That's... impressive."

He chuckled, all good nature and humility. "We know the right people and got the contract because of them, but thanks. I hope it gives a little context for why I'm more edgy and stressed than usual."

"There's a lot on your plate." Everything I learned about him pointed to how remarkable he was. *Great.*

He ran a hand through his hair. "We've ended up being a bit short-staffed. I promise I'm not always running off at the last minute."

"I didn't think you were. Though..." *Hmm.* Maybe I shouldn't voice the thought out loud when I didn't really know him. I'd often experienced impatience or even offense when I verbalized my curiosity. I understood when the subjects were personal, and this certainly qualified as such.

Still, too late, because he tilted his head. "What?"

I shifted from foot to foot. "I guess I'm wondering why you want someone staying with her. She seems responsible and she's old enough to stay home alone, right?"

His face morphed to something like regret. "She is. And she's very trustworthy, high school boyfriend aside. But Kiley's had a tough go and... well, it's just a different situation." He checked his watch. "Listen, I've got to run and check in before I head to the venue. Let me know if you guys have any trouble getting in. I'll be there, but I'm not sure whether I'll be floating or on someone—depends on the staffing situation."

I didn't know what half of that meant, but okay. "Sure. Yeah, and... good luck."

He flashed a smile. "Thanks. See you soon, Nikki."

I held up my free hand as he turned and shut the door before caving to the temptation of watching him walk away.

"Well, how very generous of him."

Gram's voice coming from the kitchen startled me enough I nearly dropped the box, but I clutched at it to save whatever delicious-smelling treats lay inside.

"Yes, it was. And totally gratuitous." I hadn't done anything unusual, though obviously, he didn't have any great affinity for math. Sometimes, basic familiarity with a subject someone else found intimidating or confusing caused the smallest thing to expand beyond its actual value.

"Mm. Yes. But I'm not sure he's used to people doing things for him without reciprocating. I suspect that was one of the biggest adjustments to small-town life he'd had to make." She cupped her mug and took a sip, then nodded at the pink box. "What's in there?"

"Let's find out."

I snipped the twine with kitchen shears as she wiggled next to me like an excited child. We both sucked in audible breaths as we took in the large donuts nestled in the box. A half dozen—four with a combination of pink and white frosting, looking so perfect I hardly wanted to touch them, and two plain glazed.

"Oh, those look like a sugar coma waiting to happen," she said, then snatched a pink and white confection and shoved half into her mouth. "Thank God I never did get diabetes."

A laugh burst out of me, and I followed suit—no point in pretending I didn't want to eat the entire box. I wouldn't, especially if I was about to show up at some fancy screening of a movie later, but still.

Good. Glorious. Grief. This was the best donut I'd ever tasted. Sweet and slightly yeasty. Fluffy but enough give, enough resistance, to feel it in your teeth as you took a bite. Sugary but not so your teeth hurt. A touch of strawberry flavor in the frosting.

I should purge my brain of this moment. If not, I'd be liable to pledge my devotion to whoever his buddy's sister was and become her devotee in order to never go a day without experiencing this moment of heaven on earth. *Wow.*

"Are we going?" Gram said, mouth still full of her giant bite.

I loved how she didn't insist on being proper. Donuts this good didn't ask for proper. They asked to be eaten with gusto, with vigor, with delight. "To the premiere?"

She nodded, lips barely containing her next bite.

"I think we owe it to ourselves and all of humanity to go," I said, completely straight-faced.

She grinned, still pressing her lips closed over the donut. Once she'd swallowed it and a sip of coffee, she winked. "Then we, my dear, better go shopping."

Quite possibly, this was all a huge mistake.

Generally speaking, I didn't feel like a fraud. I was smart, good at what I did, and I knew it. Sure, I had a long history of people leaving me like a bankrupt strip mall, and I'd struggled with attachment since my early teens, but I'd functioned well, all things considered. I'd never met a number I didn't like, and I'd never considered the fact that showing up to a movie premiere would make me feel so deeply self-conscious and out of place.

The sunset lit up the western sky with streaks of pink, orange, and purple. The mountains hadn't quite faded into hulking shadows, and the heat of the day had burnt off enough that I was glad I'd left my jacket in the car, because I'd need it on the way home.

"Stop fidgeting." Gram nudged me, her silky pantsuit in a menagerie of colors somehow looking classy and artistic all at once. She wore low heels, her hair pulled back into a neater version of her usual low bun and pinned with a turquoise clip. She had bangles on either side of her watch and chunky necklaces she'd likely made or purchased from a local artisan. Overall, she had this air of mature artsy style that made me jealous.

That said, I did feel freaking great. I rarely dressed up beyond a suit for work—or, my past work—and tonight I was fully embracing the moment. My hair was down, and I'd done a classic wavy look in the vein of the 1940s and makeup to match, with a red lip and smoky eyes. My dress was a deep teal color, which I never would've had the boldness to wear except Gram made me promise to wear it. When I saw the price tag and decided I shouldn't spring for it without having a job no matter how well paid I'd been in the past, she'd snatched it off the rack, slapped her credit card onto the counter, and completely ignored my protests.

Honestly, I was glad she had, and I'd pay her back. The fit was perfect—sleeveless two-inch straps that dipped into a vee interesting enough but not revealing in the front and far lower in the back. Thankfully, it had built in padding, so undergarments weren't an issue. The bodice fit close and tucked in at the waist, then flowed out in a lighter-weight fabric and fluttered all the way to the floor.

Maybe someday, I'd get married in this dress. I never had any illusions marriage was in the cards for me, but if it ever happened, I wanted *this* dress. It was beautiful and flattering and felt more than a little bit like something out of a dream.

I'd never been the kind of girl to dream of wedding dresses and ballgowns. I'd been more preoccupied with unraveling whatever mathematical theorem I'd recently discovered and surviving my stints in foster care. If I had envisioned such an event, it would've been wearing something like this dress.

When I'd agreed we should attend tonight, I hadn't realized we'd be dressing up like this, but thank goodness, Gram knew exactly what to expect. As I looked around at everyone in black tie attire, the men in tuxes and the women in dresses of varying lengths and all levels of formality, it felt more like I was attending an event in Hollywood than here in the small town of Silverton.

Perhaps it was the steady stream of A-list stars smiling for cameras as they walked the red carpet—and yes, they'd laid out an actual red carpet over the wide steps at the entrance of the Egyptian Theater.

The theater itself was historic and had been built in the 1920s, an odd little piece of history still standing in this town and a vestige of the old tradition curiously established in Utah back then. There were only a small handful of Egyptian theaters left, as I'd discovered when I'd fallen down the rabbit hole of history while waiting for Gram to finish readying.

I saw a handful of familiar faces, including a comedic actress I loved, Jenna Halter. She hugged famed pop star Miss Mayhem, and they turned to laugh with none other than arguably the most famous pop star to come out of the US in decades, Bri Williamson.

"These are all the locals. I think the out-of-towners will be popping in any minute, though, so we better get inside." Gram looped her arm in mine and guided me up the stairs to the side of the flashing lights.

Locals? I hadn't visited Silverton since leaving years back, and I certainly didn't remember anyone famous wandering around in the past. Granted, I hadn't been here since it'd blown up as a luxury destination, and before that, I probably wouldn't have noticed. I mentally considered how this raised the town's tax income and extrapolated the rise in per capita income, the increased tourist and industry traffic—so much of the growth in this town made more sense now.

We slipped in a side door, and a docent inspected our tickets. "Oh, very nice. You'll be down front, though Bruce asked me to let him know when you're here. One sec."

The man smiled, dark eyes sparkling, and Gram stood

straighter. *Oh.* Hello. He was probably a few years older than her but seemed fit, healthy. I didn't remember her ever telling me she was dating, and I honestly hadn't really thought about her being interested in such a thing. She was so fiercely independent and hadn't ever mentioned it.

But this man? His name tag said Amir, and he winked at Gram. I eyed her, and she gave me a narrow-eyed glare that said *knock it off* without words. *Interesting.*

"If you lovely ladies will just follow the hallway around and check in with my friend Peter, he'll tell you how to find Bruce." He winked at us again—adorable—and gestured toward where we were supposed to go.

"Are we not just going to sit?" I asked as we bustled down the hallway, the sounds of hundreds of voices in the main theater spilling out at intervals where exit doors flapped occasionally.

"Guess he wanted to see us before we sit." She wiggled her brows.

"You can make that face all you want, but not until we talk about Mr. Amir."

She whipped her head straight, held it high, and I took the note. We reached Peter, who smiled warmly at us.

"Right through this door, and when you find the men in suits who look like security, you've found 'em."

Both more than a little bewildered, we followed the instructions and came to a T in the back hallway. I looked left, and my breath seized in my throat.

There he was. Jack McKean. *The* Jack McKean. The star of the movie being screened tonight, standing casually in an immaculate suit, all kinds of tall and dark and unrealistically handsome and chuckling with someone.

Gram clutched my arm, clearly having seen the same

thing, but then she squeezed harder. Because the man Jack McKean was talking to turned... *How is this possible?*

It was Bruce. Bruce Camden. Bruce Camden who had abs like two rowed columns of an Excel spreadsheet and brought me donuts and was more than a little adorable, and he was standing there in a stunning tux looking every bit as much a movie star as Jack McKean.

Well, okay, no. Not *every bit* because Jack had Oscars and landed in a tax bracket that was just *fun* if you're an accountant, and Bruce was human. More than that, he'd been a soldier in some prestigious black ops organization and that made him a hero, and probably a few other things, too. Where Jack looked casual and comfortable, Bruce's bearing spoke of an awareness, an alertness, that created an interesting edge.

So there they were, a hero on screen and an actual one, chatting in their suits like they were just shooting the breeze.

But oh, boy, did the man wear the tux. He did the stripped down, sweaty, and dirty thing *real* well, don't mind if I do, but this?

This was devastating.

CHAPTER SIX

Bruce

Movement down the hallway caught my eye, but the typical drip of adrenaline didn't hit when I realized it was Rosie and Nikki.

A different drug hit my veins, something like endorphins, and sure, maybe it was adrenaline in there that made it feel like I should jog over and get a closer look at her. Luckily, I hadn't forgotten who I was or what I was doing here.

"This them?" Jack asked, nodding to the two women making their way toward us.

"Yep." I smiled at them as they came to a stop. "Glad you made it. Rosie Renwick, Nikki Hastings, this is Jack McKean."

Jack smiled his billion-dollar smile and held out a hand to Rosie. Unsurprisingly, she wasn't fazed by the uber-A-list celebrity's presence or by the prospect of shaking his hand. She grinned, batted her lashes, and shook.

"Nice to meet you, Jack. Love your work."

I stifled a laugh and studied Nikki as she accepted Jack's proffered hand next. She wore more dramatic makeup tonight, and it did nothing to calm the thrum of my heart pounding as I stood there and watched her clasp her delicate fingers around Jack's hand.

"Nice to meet you," she said, far softer though not weak or embarrassed. Her cheeks gave away her blush, and I couldn't deny I loved to see it, even if it was due to Jack McKean and not me.

Not that it should be because of me. Or that it ever would be. Or that I had a right to want that. I didn't. I wouldn't. It couldn't. *Whatever.* Point was, she looked really beautiful, and the blush just clinched it.

"Likewise, Nikki. Bruce here has been telling me that you're new in town. Did he mention I'm thinking of getting a place in Silverton?" Jack asked, then finally released her hand.

Bit of a long handshake, but I couldn't begrudge him for enjoying it, nor could I her for the same.

Nikki's lush lips opened, then shut for a moment before she spoke. "Uh, no. He hadn't mentioned it. I can't tell you much other than Bruce and this one make a nice welcome party, should you need it." She elbowed Rosie, who grinned.

Jack smiled, and I could swear his eyes sparkled. "Good to know. I have a few friends in the area, and I've wanted to spend more time here, so I pushed for Silverton for the screening."

"It's nice that you chose a place like this."

Nikki's voice hadn't wavered, and if I was reading her

right, she wasn't tongue-tied or losing her cool in any way. *Interesting.*

"I think so," he said, still all charm.

My watch buzzed and signaled the next phase. "Time to get to the entrance for photos. Take a minute and I'll be right behind you."

Jack nodded and grinned at the women. "Ladies, a pleasure."

They murmured their replies, and Jack slipped inside the green room. He'd be hopping in a town car, and they'd circle the block and arrive at the front as though he'd just come from elsewhere, all for the photos.

"So you're his security tonight?" Rosie asked, clearly completely delighted by this news.

"Thought it might be fun to meet him. He's a good guy." My eyes found Nikki's, and my stomach dropped low. *Wow*, she looked good. The teal of her dress made her eyes practically glow back at me, her hair all smooth and shiny and soft framing her face and brushing her shoulders. *What would it feel like in my hand? Against my chest?*

"He seems nice," Nikki said, eyes slipping over my tux.

"Oh, pardon me, but I promised I'd meet a friend inside and we'd sit together. I'll save you a seat, Nikki." Rosie patted my arm in her usual fashion and bustled away right as Nikki looked back up at me.

"I'll come with you, I—"

"No, stay and chat a minute. I'll see you soon." Rosie flipped her hand without a backward glance and was halfway down the hall despite her heels.

Nikki gave me a sheepish look. "Okay, then."

I wasn't about to complain. "Actually, this is perfect. I wanted to ask you about your work."

Her brow pinched down. "Work? Did Rosie say something?"

I didn't want to throw her under the bus, but honesty seemed paramount about now. "She did. But it wasn't bad, or purposeful. She just mentioned it off-hand, and I was wondering if you'd had any luck."

It'd been a whopping twenty-four hours—less—since Rosie had dropped the knowledge.

"Uh, no. Actually, it's looking a little bleak. At least for now. Keller Accountancy can hire me when tax season starts, but I'm in a hiring dead zone right now, I guess."

I nodded at her phrasing because it was exactly right. Summer tourist season had closed out with the end of August, and fall was a slow shoulder season here, at least relatively. Ski season would bring in crowds, and then obviously the new year would bring in a lot of business for the accountancy, but she wouldn't have any luck with retail, waiting tables, or anything else for at least eight weeks.

Which was why I'd brought it up. "I'm sure it's well below your capabilities and not in your interest based on what Rosie has told me about you, but we do have a position open at Saint Security. It's temporary, but it could be interesting. If you're at all inclined, I'd love to have you come in on Monday and see if it feels like a fit."

Her brows rose as I spoke, and her pretty lips parted before a smile pulled them into a quick flash of teeth and happiness. Just as quickly, she sobered and nodded. "Thanks. I guess I shouldn't automatically say no, even though I have no idea what happens at a security company like yours. Other than hanging out with A-listers, right?"

I grinned. "Exactly. It has its charms."

Another buzz at my wrist prompted me back to work.

"I've got to run and get him inside, but I'll hope to catch you after. Enjoy the movie."

I gave her one last smile, let my gaze linger on Nikki's, then turned back toward the green room. Time to do the job.

Exhaustion pawed at me, but I stayed focused on the ten-minute drive home. One blessed bonus to the event being here in town was the minimal commute. Jack was a good guy, and fortunately, no one had gotten too wild or grabby with him. Any locals wouldn't dream of behaving that way, and the hundreds of visitors here for the festival seemed to understand that even celebrities had a right to personal space.

I turned off the SUV and sat for a minute, staring blankly at the garage wall through the windshield before summoning the motivation to exit. This week shouldn't have dragged at me so much, but it had. In the past, I might've shoved that to the corner of my mind and tried to pretend it didn't matter, but I was at least attempting to acknowledge my humanity these days.

Not that I'd ever seen myself as superhuman. I wasn't that arrogant or misguided. It was more that I'd worked in an organization that put me and my peers in situations where we were both trained and enabled to do things that created a sense of invincibility and confidence.

It'd been an interesting shift these last few years—moving from active deployment cycles and executing missions to leadership and planning roles back home to stay closer to Kiley and then, last year, getting out of the Army entirely. I was still figuring it all out—*we* were.

Speaking of, I should see what Kiley thought of the movie. The afterparty had just ended not long ago. I'd seen her and her friend slip out with a wave, so they shouldn't be asleep yet.

"What'd you think?" I asked, wandering into the kitchen to toss my keys onto the counter, only to shift into high alert.

The house had that feeling—empty. I had no idea if it was training or if everyone felt this sensation, but I knew she wasn't home. After hollering up to her with no answer, I confirmed it, then shot her a text on my phone.

Her response came quickly. *"I'm at Tara's. I told you I was staying here."*

I exhaled slowly, scrambling for control and willing my pulse to slow. I had no patience for texts, not when I wanted to throw my phone across the room, so I called.

"What's up?" Her greeting was all nonchalance.

"Ki, you were supposed to come straight home. I get home and you're not here and I'm a little... concerned." Not a terrible job of keeping my crap together, I had to say.

"I told you I was coming to Tara's. We have a group project to work on this weekend, so we're doing it tomorrow." Her tone said something like, *this is so obvious and I don't get why you're even calling me.*

"We talked this morning, and you said you were going there to get ready, driving with Tara and her mom to the screening, and then her mom was bringing you back here for a sleepover. At what point did we discuss you staying there?"

I tried not to let my frustration seep through the phone,

but I'd nearly met my max, and it was hard. The end of a long day at the end of a long week and now I got to face down my need to keep her safe and her need for space as though that wasn't the very tension keeping me up so often at night.

"Bruce, I'm fine. I'll text when we're up in the morning and let you know when I'm home. I'll send you a proof of life photo in two."

I scrubbed a hand down my face, breathing through the frustration—with myself? With her? With this house for feeling suffocating after looking forward to getting home all day?

"Okay. But in the future, we need to talk about this stuff ahead of time."

"Got it. Night, Boo. Pic incoming."

She ended the call, and sure enough, less than a minute later pinged a photo of Kiley and Tara with heads bent together, sweatshirts instead of evening dresses on, faces scrubbed of the makeup they'd worn only a few hours ago. Kiley's peace sign had me rolling my eyes. I set the phone down and stared at the image.

She looked happy. Tired, maybe, and so much like our mom it hurt a little at times, but she was safe. I gave the photo a little thumbs-up and then shoved off the counter and straight out the side door.

The cool night air hit me, and I sucked in until my lungs couldn't hold any more. As I slowly released the breath, I paced to one side of the back patio, then the other. After another moment, I stopped and cupped the back of my head in my hands as I looked up at the stars.

The Big Dipper sparkled proudly overhead, and my eyes found the three stars making up Orion's Belt. The entire sky was scattered with pinprick stars, the mountains behind me deep purple shadows like slumbering beasts waiting for day.

In North Carolina, I'd sought the ocean for perspective, sometimes driving the two hours to the coast and back in a morning, just to get a glimpse. Just to be reminded of how much else there was beyond me and this moment—whatever small thing that had stunted me. Here in Silverton, miles from the ocean, I'd found the mountains and stars had the same effect. As someone who took care of people—my family, my business, my friends, etc.—I could easily get it all out of perspective.

"Everything okay?"

Nikki's smooth voice startled me, and I straightened, dropping my hands, eyes finding her lit by the glow of the moon. She still wore that stunning dress, but she'd shed the heels for slippers.

"What are you doing out here?" I asked, pure curiosity overriding much of the angst overtaking me moments ago.

She tucked her crossed arms close to her body. "I'm a night owl and I haven't really looked at the stars since I got to town. It was always one of my favorite things."

"They make a good show of it," I said, eyes flashing over the long line from her chin to the vee in her dress as she gazed up.

"That they do." She offered a small smile. "And you?"

I could say the same—something to pass off reality and put the blame on the glittering stars. It wouldn't be entirely wrong. But in this moment, maybe because of the vast sky and that exact feeling of smallness I'd thought I needed, it felt imperative to tell her the truth.

"I was out here trying to breathe. Trying to convince myself I'm not failing Kiley with every decision I make." My eyes slid to her in time to see her lips part and her body move closer.

"You know, I have no idea what it's like to take care of someone else, but based on the little I've seen, it seems like you're doing a decent job."

Something about the word choice surprised me, and a laugh tripped out. "Decent, huh? You're not going to tell me I'm an amazing guardian and Kiley could never ask for anyone better?"

I'd heard it. I appreciated when people said it, though I could never fully believe it.

Nikki's brow furrowed. "Why would I tell you that if we both know I'm not qualified to make that assessment?"

It was the oddest thing, but her honest, straight-forward response smacked against my thick skull and jarred my brain. When was the last time someone was simply honest with me?

Of course she couldn't say I was doing a good job—she had no idea. She'd seen how amazing Kiley was after staying with her the other night, but that was just Ki. And the fact that Nikki wouldn't point to the base fact that I'd become Kiley's guardian as proof I was doing right by her made me borderline wild. It made this aching tightness loosen in a way it hadn't ever. Like *finally*, someone wasn't trying to console me. My friends loved me and wanted the best for me, but I often worried that blinded them to the very real possibility that I was screwing this up.

The darkness still surrounded us, but her words were like dawn overtaking the moment, brightening the sky and widening the world into a broad, dazzling daylight.

It made me want to thank her for her honesty. And with more intensity than I'd ever felt, it made me want to slip my hand into her hair and kiss her.

In this instant, in the wake of my wildly up-and-down week, the idea of being close to this woman who wasn't afraid to tell me the truth settled over me like an answer.

This was a question I shouldn't be asking—I'd promised myself I wouldn't. And yet here she was, breaking past any defenses I had with her fearless honesty and that wrinkle in her brow hinting at curiosity and compassion.

I hadn't thought about what I wanted in a partner in years, but there it was. The honesty. The absolute lack of hypocrisy or even propriety and sticking to the politically correct. A rawness that spoke of potential and truth. The answer I'd been searching for but hadn't put my finger on, knowing I'd feel it in my gut when—*if*—it ever happened.

This kind of person.

Here she was.

CHAPTER SEVEN

Nikki

Bruce had an odd expression on his face—not upset, but kind of... stunned into stillness. Maybe not shocked outright, rather just like he hadn't expected my honesty. Not that I hadn't wanted to reassure him, only that I didn't have the ability to.

"I don't mean that to sound bad. I just... I hate when people say something to make someone feel better, but you know very well they have no ability to pay the compliment or offer the promise."

It'd been a pet peeve of mine since early on. Maybe it came from having parents who habitually lied and tried to pretend everything would be fine when they knew, or should've known, it wouldn't be. It had certainly driven me further into my love of math—it didn't lie. It didn't try to pretend everything would be fine.

He was quick to respond. "I'm not upset, just... taking it

in. But I appreciate it. You don't know me or Kiley, so how could you speak to how well it's going?"

Whatever odd demeanor had struck after my earlier comment had washed away, a wave of understanding sliding between us and clearing it.

I nodded, appreciating his understanding. "Exactly. What I can say is that she seems like a happy, secure kid who cares about you and other people. She's smart and funny, and you're certainly..." The awkwardness of any number of the things I might've said struck my tongue momentarily numb.

With a small chuckle, he prompted, "And me? What's your observation of me so far, Nikki?"

A thrill slipped through me like a sunrise, head to toe receiving the scintillating awareness that hearing my name on his lips brought. He'd said it before, but not in a quiet moment between us like this. Not something almost intimate, special.

"Uh, well..." I shifted on my feet, fleetingly wishing I'd worn my heels and not my slippers. They would've given me a few more inches in his direction, and for some reason, it felt like I needed that about now. "You seem like you've got a lot going on. Like you're the one keeping things going in a few different ways."

His lips pressed into a line—not a smile or frown, more like a signal of acceptance, and paired with his single nod, I supposed he did accept my read. Little did he know, I had a lot of other things to say already—he was thoughtful, considerate, polite, kind, and jaw-droppingly, ridiculously, perilously handsome.

But those were things I'd be keeping to myself. Except... except for that slight downward pull and a flash of something in his eyes before he looked back up at the stars. It said something I didn't catch, that I'd guess wasn't for me to see at all, and yet, I barely resisted the impulse to grab his arm and tug at him until he gave me his dark gaze so I could inspect him and find it. Mine that expression for all its worth and understand it.

I'd always been curious by nature—something more than one foster parent had been troubled by. Teachers either found it delightful or infuriating. Gram had always embraced that part of me, just like she had everything else once we'd found each other.

What it meant, though, was I couldn't stand here quietly after something like that.

"Why did it just look like I disappointed you?"

My voice came out soft in the night air, that sense of vastness in the sky conversely pairing with a feeling like everything had moved in close. Maybe Bruce and I were even standing closer, now that I thought about it. We stood only a foot apart. The evening chill had hit, and I folded my arms and pressed them close to conserve heat—no chance I'd abandon this conversation to go get a sweater.

With a heavy sigh, he looked down at me. I saw the moment he realized I was cold—his eyes skated over me, and instantly, he was shrugging out of his tux jacket.

"Here, take this."

But instead of handing it to me, he held it by the collar and slipped it over my shoulders.

The warmth of it—of *him*—enveloped me instantly, right along with the scent of fresh soap and mint and maybe cologne? Or maybe that was just the other things combining into something the Fates and Universe called "Nikki's Catnip." Because it smelled *so* good. I forbade myself from inhaling too obviously, from gulping down the scent, knowing I'd never forget it, and praying that somehow this wouldn't be the only time I experienced it.

A dangerous thought, that one, but I couldn't pretend I didn't feel it down to my toes. And I'd probably been quiet a little too long, not-so-discreetly sniffing the heavenly scent of his jacket, so I pushed out, "Thank you."

He nodded, not looking at me. We both stayed still for a moment, and I wondered if maybe he wouldn't answer my question. Then after another beat, he finally spoke.

"I wouldn't say I'm disappointed. I've just been in my head about a lot of things, and I guess it's not a surprise that that's what you see—I'm a doer. I take care of people, I fix things when they're broken, I solve problems." He stopped, eyes flicking to me and then away.

"But?" I pushed, oddly desperate for his answer.

His gaze hooked into mine, his serious expression so loaded with significance, everything in me paused.

"But I'm tired, Nikki. My default is smothering Kiley and I know that, I see it happening, but I don't know how to stop it. I just—" His exhale cut off his words.

When I was sure he wouldn't finish the thought, I spoke. "Can I ask you a question about her? Or, rather, your dynamic with her?"

"Sure."

"I know you've hinted at things between you, but I'm wondering why you're..." I loosed a breath, needing the right words and knowing I'd probably bungle this. "You seem very protective of her, but not necessarily in an older brother or even fatherly way. It's... I can't put my finger on it."

He laughed, but it wasn't a joyful sound. "We have the same mom. I left home when I was seventeen, joined the Army, and never looked back. I wrote and called on and off, but I didn't go back, and my mom wanted it that way. She didn't want me around, because my dad was violent, but miraculously, not with her. Only with me."

We swallowed that down, the reality of his life opening up into a layered, complex thing, a Diophantine equation that might've seemed simple at first glance. "I'm sorry."

He shook his head, brushing that away as if it didn't matter, before continuing. "I didn't find out about Kiley until she was nearly five. I'd stayed away that long and"—his jaw flexed, the moonlight showing the sharp slope from his face to the shadow of his neck—"I should've showed up sooner. I missed a lot. And for a while, they all seemed to be functioning really well—I'd visit between missions, whenever I could, and Ki was happy, our mom seemed stable, and Carl, Ki's dad, put on a good show."

My heart kicked, worry for whatever was coming invading my chest. He exhaled, the sound one of exhaustion and surrender, and continued.

"At Kiley's twelfth birthday party, I noticed the track marks on my mom's forearms. She'd started using something heavy. Long story short, it took another two and a half years of fighting—trying to get my mom through rehab, then watching her relapse, all while her husband was dealing. I didn't find that part out until Christmas almost two and a half years ago. Ki called me and—"

His abrupt halt forced my hand. I reached out and gripped his forearm, wanting him to know I was here—I wasn't scared away by his story. My hand met the cool skin of his wrist, and his eyes snapped to the point of contact. He swallowed, then his gaze found mine.

"Anyway, I went and got her. Right then. And luckily, I had a lawyer friend or two who worked with CPS and a bunch of other entities that got Kiley under my guardianship. Her dad's in jail, I don't know where our mom is now after we tracked her down and tried to get her into rehab last time, and Kiley's legally mine."

I had no idea what to say—how to console or encourage him. So I just said, "I'm sorry you both had to go through that."

His dark eyes held mine for another beat before he spoke again. "I am, too. And I'll never forgive myself for missing the signs things were getting worse. I will *never* forgive myself for not realizing what was happening."

His voice had turned ragged, and my heart squeezed at the vicious truth there. He blamed himself in more than one way for Kiley having to endure what she did, and something told me he hadn't said it all.

"You got her out. She needed you and you were there for her, even if it took a minute for you to figure it out. That's important."

He didn't acquiesce or accept my words, so I doubled down. "I don't know everything, but I can see you're trying. That's what she needs. Maybe you're a little over the top at times, sure, but you're out here agonizing over everything, and let me tell you, not every kid has someone like you. Her parents weren't, and even though it doesn't feel like it, you're giving her a gift in doing so. It doesn't mean you won't mess up or hurt her or make the wrong choice, even accidentally, but it does mean that your effort matters."

His brow furrowed as we stood there, our gazes locked, bodies connected only by my hand on his wrist. The chill night air clung close, colder now in the aftermath of our conversation.

"You sound like you might know something about this," he said quietly.

"I might." But even this kind of conversation felt new

and a little dangerous to the parts of me I'd held separate. I wanted to share, and I wanted to hide it all away. I admired him for sharing, but I didn't know how to reciprocate. Not yet.

The fact that I wanted to, even part of me, signaled progress. Growth. And at some point later, when I reviewed every second of this night, I'd be proud of that feeling.

The security light in Gram's driveway flickered off and drew our attention. I dropped my hand, finally breaking the connection between us, but he grabbed for my fingers and held them fast before I'd retreated completely. Despite the heaviness of the moment, the discussion, the truths we'd both just shared, my stomach somersaulted, head over heels.

His warm, calloused hand enveloping my much smaller one had my pulse scrambling and my thoughts scattering all over.

"Should come back on as soon as you get close," he said, more familiar with my own grandmother's security system than I was.

"Yeah," I said lamely, the magnetic pull between us unlike anything I'd ever felt.

We stood there for another moment, only the stars and moon lighting the world around us, our hands still clasped. The scent of him clung close with his jacket around my shoulders, and I knew if I stayed there much longer, I'd do something insane like try to kiss him.

"Thank you," he said, that voice rich and dark as the night.

I slipped his jacket off, and he took it before I dropped it. "Thank you, too."

Everything out of my mouth felt silly, too big and too small all at once. A not unfamiliar feeling, and a sure sign it was time to cease speaking before I said something rash.

And yet, I hated to think of walking back, the light flicking back on and washing away the darkness.

But it was late, and as much as I liked him, as much as I felt the incredible chemistry between us, he'd offered me an interview. I didn't know whether that would work out or what would happen, but indulging in another touch, even a kiss, would certainly make those waters murkier.

So I raised my hand in an odd wave. "Good night, Bruce."

"Night, Nikki. Sleep well."

As I tucked into my bed a while later, my thoughts zipping in all directions and circling around the conversation and everything he'd shared, I doubted I'd sleep at all. I'd wanted to tell him about the mess of my past and how I knew his worry over Kiley was more than some kids ever got from their parents.

And more than fear of that feeling, a spark of hope and curiosity had ignited. The aftermath of our conversation hadn't been dread over him asking about my past, but rather anticipation and the ever-increasing little fire in me to see if I might actually share it.

Logically, I could see he might appreciate knowing I'd been through something like his sister had. In the heart of me, though—in that quiet place that felt like Bruce Camden was trying to pry it open without even realizing it—I worried he might not be ready for the reality of me or my past.

CHAPTER EIGHT

Bruce

Tristan Donnelly waited patiently while I gathered my thoughts. This wasn't a particularly unique scenario, since I bet Tristan's default setting rested on *waiting patiently*. He was the least likely to rush a job, the steadiest hand I'd ever met.

Handy when your job is defusing bombs—or was. Tristan had retired from the same unit many of us had come from. He'd gotten out around the same time I had and was solid as a rock. When he agreed to come work for us here, Wilder and I had toasted some of the special Scotch billionaire Julian Grenier had given us the day we'd formed our partnership. Tris was that good, and that was referencing his all-around skills as a former operator, his explosive ordnance disposal experience prior to joining the unit, and his general steadiness. Oh, and his world-class close-combat skills second to exactly one person who still worked at the unit back in North Carolina.

Wilder was unflappable until it came to Sarah and his little one. The same could be said for me with Kiley, I supposed. But Tristan? I didn't think I'd ever seen him sweat.

And thank goodness, because we had Kenny and Beast to deal with, both of whom had enough opposing energies so the calmer the baseline around the office, the better.

"We've got an interview coming in a bit, and we've got to retool staffing again. Maybe hire more people or figure out how to work some freelancers when we get bigger jobs. Especially because Wilder's not going to stop having a human child who needs care and attention, and Amani and Ben are out long-term. This won't be the only show they can't stand in for."

The film fest had gone off without a hitch. Jack McKean's new movie had set the world ablaze and had won the grand prize for the festival, not to mention he'd seemed very pleased with Saint Security's work, as had the event director and everyone we'd interacted with save the possible exception of Crade. That poor excuse for a human had been less than impressed when more than once, whoever of us was guarding him had shut down his harassment of attendees. I wouldn't apologize for it. Personal security was supposed to be hands-off. If someone engaged in bad behavior, we didn't step in until it became a danger to the principal.

Sorry, but not on my watch. Or any of my people's. We simply weren't going to tolerate that, and we'd be unlikely to sign a contract to guard him again because of it.

"True enough. I hate to see you scrambling like this again. Do we have the budget to staff up?"

Tristan's question was a good one, though not one he'd normally concern himself with. And the fact that I couldn't directly answer it made me more than a little uncomfortable.

"Not sure. Sarah was managing the budget, and Wilder's had an eye on it. You know numbers aren't my strong suit." I didn't love admitting that, but I'd also found that pretending I could see the full scope of the business when I looked at whatever accounting software we'd purchased starting out only made me feel worse.

Tristan nodded, taking that in stride. "Well, if you make this hire, it should help with some of the admin load."

A sigh escaped me. "Yeah. Wouldn't mind that."

He nodded, his dark hair longer than I'd ever seen it on top. We got away with less military-looking cuts because looking like a soldier didn't exactly help efforts at being covert on a mission if we were using a cover identity, but it still tripped me up to see us all letting the hair and beards grow unchecked.

Well, not all of us. I'd had a beard for a few months last winter, and after Kiley begged me to shave it because it looked like "a dead animal had stitched itself to my face," I'd acquiesced.

"We've got a down weekend and then the next self-defense class week after next, right?" he asked, likely more for my sake than his.

"Yeah. Should be good. I think we've got a few spots left. We're about eighty-percent last I checked the online roster." One more thing I shouldn't be doing but had taken on since Sarah had been on maternity leave.

Tristan's face didn't change, but he nodded. "Good."

I felt like such a whiney jerk lately, and this wasn't how a boss should be talking with someone, even if we were more friends and coworkers than boss-employee. "How are you? Have you heard from your girl?"

That stoic face didn't let my comment flap him, of course, but he didn't ignore it. "Every few days, as usual."

"How long have you been talking like this?" I clicked out of my email and shuffled a few papers around on my desk.

"Fourteen years, on and off."

Had it been that long? I could vaguely remember hearing about her every now and then. "Really? I guess time flies."

He nodded.

"But you've still never met in person?"

"Nope."

That had always perplexed me. This girl and her family had adopted Tristan through some program where families sent soldiers messages and care packages while deployed during the height of the war in Afghanistan, and they'd kept up contact for years. She'd been pretty young when it'd all started. It never seemed romantic, but she'd been a constant for him. Knowing how not much else had been, I felt more than a little gratitude to this person who'd stood by him even if she didn't realize she had.

"Jaws, we got a Veronica Hastings here for an interview?" Kenny's head appeared in my doorway. He'd used my nickname—we all had them—but I hadn't expected to hear *Veronica Hastings* out of his mouth.

Was her first name really Veronica? Weirdly, that made my chest warm.

"Ah, good. You can bring her back, if you would. I meant to be out there, but looks like she's a few minutes early." A glance at my watch proved it—a full ten minutes early. She'd fit in well on that front, at least.

"Back in a sec," he said, then patted the doorframe.

Tristan stood, and right as he was leaving, Nikki arrived in the doorway. My stomach clenched at the sight of her, just as beautiful as she was in my memory. Today, she wore a black suit with the jacket open. The shirt underneath was a creamy color that looked both feminine and professional, and I added it to the list of things she looked great in. I suspected there wasn't anything that wouldn't make the list.

"Hi, sorry for being a few minutes early," she said, eyes tracking from Tristan to me, then back to the man who stood directly next to her, and she held out a hand. "I'm Nikki."

He took it with an even shake. "Tristan Donnelly. Nice to meet you. I'm just leaving—have a good morning." Then he tipped his head toward me. "Jaws."

"Oak, see you later."

With one last nod to Nikki, he moved down the hallway, and I waved Nikki farther inside my office. "Please, have a seat. Thanks for coming."

Thanks for talking with me the other night. Thanks for not telling me I'm doing a great job just for the sake of the platitude. Thanks for being honest with me. Thanks for standing in the moonlight and making me feel something.

I'd moved on from the reeling, falling sensation that'd hit me during our conversation after the premiere. I'd promised myself all those lightning strikes about her being exactly what I wanted were rooted in that moment of stark truthfulness paired with her in that dress and the intimacy of the dark, cool evening. The sense she was seeing me, hearing me, and not placating me.

But the thrumming in my chest at her arrival, the primal awareness as she entered my office, shot holes right through this carefully constructed web of faulty logic.

I stood and took a minute to collect my thoughts—or rather, gather up those saccharine feelings, tie a lead weight to them, and let them sink to the bottom of my mental sea— then grabbed the pre-printed packet I'd created from the top of the fancy cabinetry holding files in the corner. When I turned back, Nikki was sitting with her hands lightly in her lap, looking alert but comfortable.

"So... Veronica."

One of her brows arched, and the faintest smile hit her lips. "Yes. Exactly no one calls me that, but it is my legal name."

Maybe I shouldn't have been charmed by that, but I was. I liked it. I liked that her name was Veronica and she went by Nikki. A silly thing to enjoy, but I did. "Good to know. I'll stick with Nikki."

Her smile stretched a bit wider. "Please do."

I nodded. "So if you don't mind, today we'll talk about the job, what we do here at Saint, and then if you're still interested, run through a few questions for you to make sure it's a generally good fit. After that, we'll do a background check and the usual stuff and get you hired, again, if it seems like a good fit for both of us."

"Makes sense," she said, all business.

I launched into a basic explanation of what Saint Security did—lots of personal security work, setting up security systems, and branching into more now that we'd established our baseline work. "We're adding new capabilities all the time. You may have gathered a lot of our staff is former special operations and other agency talent, so we have a breadth of knowledge that can extend in a few different directions."

She tipped her head to one side. "Like?"

Well, I couldn't tell her too many details at this point.

To know the full ins and outs, she'd essentially need to be read-on to the Saint scope of things, and we couldn't do that just yet. "Well, one example is that Tristan and I are running self-defense classes now. We're also going to branch into other kinds of courses eventually. We can also do K and R recovery if the need arises in conjunction with someone we're hired to guard, and we sometimes advise on other things." And that'd all stay pretty vague for now.

"K and R? Kidnap and ransom?" Her eyes grew wide.

"Yes. Not a constant issue, as you'd imagine, but we do have expertise in that area."

She blinked once. "How does one develop expertise in that area, I wonder."

Not a question so much as a statement.

I could tell her that much as it was, in some circles, common knowledge. "The unit where quite a few of us worked dealt with a fair amount of recovery work. When Americans end up kidnapped, especially in certain regions of the world, in many cases, it's special operations who go in and get them. It's a lesser-known function, but obviously an important one."

She absorbed that information. "Huh. Good to know. So you're all experts, and it makes sense to do that kind of work."

Again, another statement. "Yes. And so, there are a few other capacities we're developing. Obviously, our resources here are fairly different than they were on active duty, but we do have a solid foundation growing and are working on funding streams that will assist in more complex work as needed."

A.k.a. a bunch of jargon to say we had money to keep us going, and we had Julian's deep pockets to reach into if we happened to need it, though that wasn't how we wanted to proceed. So far, we'd only needed his help once outside the initial investment to get Saint Security up and running.

"And what do you think an accounting major with zero background in this kind of thing can do for you?" she asked, tugging at each side of her suit jacket as she leaned back in her chair.

"I think you'd be a very overqualified administrative manager. Sarah, my partner's wife, has been our admin but is on maternity leave. We've handled it, and she's been doing some part time lately, but I know she doesn't want to. Your duties, should you choose to accept them, would be everything from basic admin like answering phones up to hiring your replacement when you get bored of us."

Her brows rose. "Please explain."

"From what Rosie's said, you're an actual genius who has an advanced degree in accounting. While I know we can expand your purview beyond basic admin since Sarah's duties have always been well more than that, even I know we don't have enough work to keep you busy in terms of accounting."

Her eyes narrowed. "Rosie's got a big mouth, I guess."

I chuckled, instantly enjoying that response because it wasn't what I'd expected. I didn't normally even like the unexpected, and yet, every time this woman gave it to me, I wanted more. I'd gotten so used to people being polite and adhering to conventions, and even though nothing about Nikki overtly neglected those kinds of manners, she did tend to step past them in a way that hadn't yet failed to delight me.

"You also just handed me your résumé, and a simple glance"—I made a show of eyeing the impressive spread of credentials listed on one sheet—"tells me all that, too."

She tilted her head again. "I'm pretty sure it doesn't say I'm a genius. I would remember that."

I huffed a laugh. "Fair enough. That was all your Gram's fault. But humor me and believe that this job won't be enough to keep you occupied for long. I also heard from a little bird that you will likely have a spot at Keller Accountancy come the new year, so I'm thinking you'd want to head over there then anyway. If you're interested, this could bridge the gap."

"That little bird needs to learn to keep her little mouth shut," she said, totally straight-faced.

For a second, I worried I'd overstepped, too many assumptions foisted on her and that all of it might just drive her to refuse me. *This*. Refuse this.

"I'm sorry. I didn't mean to—"

"It's fine. I shouldn't be completely surprised, but I'm trying to figure out what's in it for you if I come on for three or four months. If I really accept with no intention of staying, isn't that just setting you back when my time's up?"

That I could answer with all confidence. "No. If Sarah wants to come back, that's around the time she'd be ready. And if she decides she wants to stay home or change plans, whatever, then we start the search for someone longer term."

Her eyes narrowed again. "Feels like a better deal for me than you."

"That's because you haven't seen my spreadsheets."

She chuckled at that. "Not a big Excel guy?"

"I'll let you come to your own conclusions about that in time. I don't really want to throw myself under the bus before you even accept the position."

Her lips twitched, but she held in her smile. "Well, consider it accepted. Now what?"

"Good news. Now, we talk background checks and make sure you don't have some sordid past that can get you extorted and put our whole operation in danger." I tossed it out there, this preposterous notion, and chuckled at my joke as I straightened her resume on my desk.

Until my eye caught on the way her lips pursed, her shoulders raising a touch with tension, and she shifted in her seat. I'd interviewed enough, and studied people even more, to know this signaled a shift. Her body language made me brace for what would come, the signs all pointing to her preparing to reveal something she didn't want me to know.

She swallowed hard, and as was her usual, said something unexpected. "We should talk about that, because after we do, you may change your mind about wanting me."

CHAPTER NINE

Nikki

Bruce had no tell, at least that I could see. I wasn't exactly a poker extraordinaire or anything, but the fact that his face didn't change, his brows didn't wing up, his eyes didn't widen… it proved notable.

"Please, tell me whatever you feel you need to." He nodded just slightly, and one of his big hands gestured with a casual wave.

Honestly, I admired the calm. I tended to be a bit more reactive, and if someone I was trying to help told me they might have a sketchy past, I wouldn't be able to play it this cool. Whether this was a sign he was simply unflappable, or a signal that he'd mastered the art of deception and therefore could prove to be an excellent liar and thus not someone I wanted to be working for, time would tell. For now, I dove in.

"I had a fairly extensive record as a teen. I was in and

out of juvenile detention before someone finally contacted Rosie." Not for the first and inevitably not for the last time, I thanked God they'd finally tracked her down.

Bruce kept that same unaffected demeanor and tipped his head enough to show me he was acknowledging but not interrupting, so I continued. "Long story short, I was in foster care on and off from ten to seventeen after my parents were killed in a DUI—their fault. Gram was in her *off the grid* phase here in Utah and she's actually my great-aunt, though for all practical and relational uses she is and always will be my grandmother. My parents weren't in communication with her after they tried to swindle her out of money before I was born and she had no idea about me, so the courts or whoever worked my case way back when didn't ever get ahold of her. But one angelic case worker believed my claims that I had a relative out here—my parents had mentioned her a few times over the years—and actually drove out here to find her."

Bruce's brows rose at this.

"Exactly. I probably owe my life, or at least my relationship with Rosie and lack of adult incarceration, to Elena Diaz." We still kept in touch, even after more than a decade.

"I'm glad she was assigned to you," he said, sincerity in every word.

"Me, too."

The conversation paused, a natural settling of the moment between us as our eyes met and we both absorbed this reality. What he said next... it mattered.

After the premiere and all that honesty he'd given me, I hadn't returned it. Not right away. But in this context, I'd felt compelled to. I didn't want to be a liability for his business, nor did I want to see the disappointment on his face when he inevitably did find out about it. I'd determined to tell him everything sooner rather than later—the facts, straight up. And now, he had them. Now, he could deal with them, and me, however he saw fit.

And I'd know him better based on whatever that turned out to be. More insight into this man felt imperative, even if getting it meant laying myself bare.

When he did speak, it came without trepidation or question. "I'm assuming your adolescent record is sealed."

I nodded.

"Why tell me about it, then? You shouldn't have to disclose any of that, even if you're getting a background check."

A good question. "I figured you should know. If the concern is potential extortion and the idea that I have a sealed record that *could* be exposed would put me in danger of being bribed to keep it from being revealed, it stands to reason that my disclosing it directly removes this possibility and therefore reduces my risk one hundred percent, therefore making me a more attractive candidate."

He didn't need to know the other part—that I already wanted him to know me more than I'd wanted anyone else I'd ever met, and *this* was a tough yet necessary step in that direction. Doing it in this setting would allow me to proceed with a friendship with him and employment here in good conscience.

Right. Because all you want from Bruce Camden is friendship and a job.

He didn't smile outright, but something about him did— a slight wrinkling around his eyes, the muscles in his cheeks tightening enough to *oh so subtly* pull the corners of his mouth into a curve. "Very logical."

"It is."

"Anything else?"

I shifted in my seat, a bit more comfortable now that I'd gotten everything out in the open. "Not that I can think of. Feel free to ask me anything, should the need arise."

His eyes narrowed just a touch. "Would you tell me about what happened in California?"

I'd anticipated the question in that I'd be unlikely to have an interview after getting laid off that didn't ask about it. Even though it felt a little like someone twisting a knife in my back to tell the story again, I did.

"I worked for the accountancy for eight years. I did traditional work and tended to do it very well. You already know I'm adept with numbers, so even though the US tax code is utter nonsense, I can enjoy the work."

"Makes sense."

I liked that he stayed engaged in the conversation without needing to expound on my answers, and it certainly worked to keep me talking. "At some point, the boss's son took an interest in me—not romantically, but more as a curiosity or something. He found me one day at a happy hour event and he said a few things that sent up red flags, particularly in terms of his role in the family business. After that, with no boyfriend to distract me, no family around, and nothing else to occupy me, I did some digging, reported my concerns to his father, and, well, here I am."

My cheeks heated as the words slipped out—this was not the version of the story I'd told Mr. Keller at my other interview. I'd merely mentioned it had been time for me to make a change and my old employer and I hadn't seen eye to eye.

"He got you fired?" Bruce asked, his eyes narrowing.

I sighed before I could stop myself. "I think so. I'm pretty sure they didn't want to fire me outright for fear of how it would look."

His jaw flexed. "Do you have any interest in forensic accounting?"

I blinked, surprised this was his response. No second-guessing me or raging at the injustice like Gram had. He simply absorbed the information and ran with it. "I've looked into it, but I don't have experience."

"Noted. Any questions for me at this point? I can't tell you much until you sign our protocol of NDAs, but ask away and we can circle back to anything we need to later."

I had approximately seventy questions, but for now, I'd settle with a simple one. "They call you Jaws?"

Stunningly, Bruce's cheeks brightened, and somehow, I had a feeling he didn't normally blush at a question like that. *Odd.* Not bad odd, just... surprising. And more than a little affecting on that handsome face.

"Nickname from work. It sounds kind of hokey, I guess, but we all have them. Usually on comms—the radio—we have call signs based on our roles on a mission, so it's not like someone's saying the nickname *Jaws* over comms like you see in the movies. But they do get used day to day. Since not everyone comes from the unit, we've encouraged first names in lieu of nicknames all the time." He picked up a pencil and tapped the desk with the eraser side.

"Is it because the shark from Jaws is named Bruce?" I wondered aloud.

He grinned, and something tipped over in my belly. Goodness, the man was lethal with a smile.

"Good guess. It's actually because my buddies used to say I got a particularly shark-eyed focus when I needed information."

He swallowed, and it struck me *this* was his tell.

My head tipped to one side. "Did you interrogate people?"

"No. We had operator investigators who did that. There were occasions when my team needed information and supposedly, I got the dead-eyed black gaze of a great white while getting it." He shrugged, apparently having accepted the name.

The whole thing made a chuckle slip from my lips. "You seem far too animated for that. I can't imagine you dead-eyed. But it's certainly a... creepy image."

Half his mouth kicked up into a casual grin. "Well, we can always pretend it's because of the movie if that's better."

I laughed. "And Oak?"

He glanced at the doorway behind me like he could see Tristan where he'd stood earlier. "He's solid."

"Hmm. I like that." Maybe I shouldn't have said that aloud, but something about a man as a solid, reliable tree seemed nice.

For that matter, Bruce could probably go by Oak based on what Gram had told me and what I'd seen so far—unless that whole expert in deception thing proved to be a little too true. However, knowing his line of work—or his former work—entailed subterfuge at least to some degree, it made sense. It didn't raise the hairs on my arms or give me a bad feeling, and that meant something.

His phone rang, drawing my attention to the device set on a table just behind him within reach of his desk.

"One sec, sorry." He pulled the receiver—an actual corded phone—and answered. "Go for Saint one."

His tone had changed. His focus fell to the wall on his left, where clocks showing the time in five time zones ticked away in unison, and yet again, I found myself resisting a swoon.

This was really not like me. I didn't recall ever feeling *swoony* around a man. Maybe for fictional characters or thinking about the great minds in mathematics. But sitting across from my potential new boss as he did his job had me fluttering internally and feeling a little hot in my suit and that was just... new.

My ex-boyfriend had been a decent guy. I'd made certain I never dated any actual jerks, but the farther I got from my time in California, the clearer it became that I never dated anyone I could actually fall for. I'd always assumed I was too logical and my past too vivid—that those hard-earned lessons about only trusting Gram and maybe myself had meant I wasn't built for romance.

Every interaction with Bruce save the first one proved otherwise. Even now, in an interview, I liked him way too much. Not admired or found him intriguing. I *liked* him. I wanted to spend time with him, to know him, and for him to know me.

Distressing and... curious.

"We'll circle up and discuss. Send whatever you need on the secure networks and we'll review it before end of day. Very good." Then he hung up and turned back to me. "I apologize for taking a call during your interview. Normally, I wouldn't, but that line is reserved for certain clientele. I can explain that all after your intake."

After the NDAs, no doubt. "Sounds good. I guess I'll let you get to it and you can let me know if anything pops up that creates questions." I stood and stretched out my hand.

He took it in his, shook it, and released me, all firm, sure, and professional.

And yet. All that professionalism, the quick shake and release, the firm assurance in it—none of it could cover the flood of warmth the contact sent into my chest.

"Thanks for coming in, Nikki. I'm sure I'll see you soon."

"Yes. You, too—or, just, yeah. Thanks. And see you."

I turned and exited his space, fully aware that my mind had partially shut down after the handshake and the swirling in my belly and brain. I'd admitted to myself I'd never reacted to someone like this, and the reality was, it proved more than a little disconcerting.

Especially if he just became my boss.

CHAPTER TEN

Bruce

By the end of the week, I found myself dragging again. I had to figure this crap out or it was going to drive me insane. Why did the things that usually filled me with energy feel like such a drain lately?

Tristan, Kenny, Beast, and to my surprise, Wilder, all pulled up in rapid succession before I ever had a chance to shut the garage door. *This can't be good.* At least, Kiley was out at her math club so she wouldn't be here to witness whatever hellfire was about to rain down on me.

"You guys using my house for a boy scout meeting or something?" I asked, slinging my work bag over my shoulder.

Kenny snorted a laugh. "Nice try, Jaws. You know why we're here."

"Do I?"

None of them commented, but they followed me inside.

My eye snagged on Nikki as she hauled a trash bag into the can Rosie kept parked at the side of her garage. My fool heart flipped at the sight of her tiptoeing in her slippers, her hair in a high ponytail creating a perfect little arc at the back of her head, and her cozy-looking clothes making me wish I could wander over and wrap her in a hug.

What is wrong with me?

I didn't have these kinds of thoughts. Sure, I wanted what Wilder had, but I needed time. Kiley needed time. There'd be... time.

When she turned and saw us, she lifted a hand in a quick wave, then scuttled inside. It took me a second to let my hand fall away.

"Oh, I see," Kenny said.

My head snapped to him. "What do you see?"

He shrugged. "I have eyes."

I brushed that off, and they followed me inside. I didn't have the mental energy to guess what they would say or how I'd respond. And honestly, part of me was relieved they'd just showed up. There'd been no time to dread the conversation like I would've if we'd made plans. It was a good old-fashioned ambush, and though I should've felt annoyed, I couldn't ignore the twinge of relief that persisted through me dropping my bag onto the counter and unloading my lunch container, my coffee mug, and my water, and then pulling out beers from the fridge and distributing them to each man.

"I might have something I can dig up for dinner." I'd planned on leftovers since Kiley was eating with her club.

Beast just blinked at me, his gray eyes unimpressed or somber or... you know what? I had no idea, as usual with him, but he didn't respond. Tristan made a sound, and Wilder patted my back. "Pizza's on the way."

Wow, they'd really planned this. Kenny uncapped a beer and handed it to me, then turned and tromped into the living room. My eyes shifted to Wilder, who just raised a brow. We loved Kenny, but he was the youngest in a few ways. It wasn't just that he'd served the least time with us, as though serving in the EMU—Exceptional Missions Unit—was the only thing that garnered respect. He would've done twenty in the Army and most of that with EMU if he hadn't ended up with a medical discharge after an injury left him with only three fingers on his left hand. There were people who still served active duty with missing fingers and even limbs, and Kenny would've been the one to do it, but when he heard about Saint, we managed to woo him and his borderline toxic positivity over to us. It made his nickname —Barbie—all the more apt.

I loved the kid—I did—but sometimes, his boundless energy in the face of what had been alarming tragedy *plus* difficult injury just didn't make sense. I had my own messed-up past, and I'd done a decent job of spinning it in a positive way, but times like this, when I just wanted to mope a little and try to avoid thinking about my pretty neighbor, I wasn't so sure I appreciated his persistent cheeriness.

Slumping into a chair opposite Wilder, with Kenny and Tristan on the couch and Beast standing like that was most comfortable for him, I didn't even fully raise my hand but waved them on in a *bring it on* gesture. "Let's have it. Commence intervention, or whatever this is."

Wilder's gaze didn't waver, yet his eyes narrowed a bit in warning. Kenny chuckled, Tristan shook his head just once, and Beast made a bullish, impatient sound.

"Fine. You don't want a preamble, here we go. You're working too hard, taking on too much, and you need your own life." Kenny tipped his metaphorical cap to me despite currently wearing an actual ball cap.

"I have more of a life than any of you saps with the exception of Wilder."

I gave him a nod of acknowledgment. He had come into his own in ways I couldn't have imagined and yet had always hoped for. He'd opened himself up to loving Sarah, and man, did he do it well. I'd never seen a happier woman, even with the challenges a new baby and sleepless nights brought. He'd done that. And he'd kept boundaries with work that allowed him to maintain it.

When you spent twenty years eating, sleeping, breathing, and *living* your work like we had in the Army and especially in special operations, it didn't come easy to suddenly *stop* doing that. I'd looked forward to the change, but I could admit I hadn't exactly nailed down the balance thing.

"It's not only about family," Tristan said quietly.

Regret niggled at me for the suggestion. Who was I to say that the only way to have a life was a wife and kids? I didn't have either; maybe I never would. But I did have Kiley, and I didn't appreciate the insinuation that she didn't count.

"I know. I didn't mean to make it sound like it did. But —" I sighed. Why was I fighting this? Why not just man up and admit what'd been going on?

"Come on, Jaws. Hit us with it," Kenny urged.

Beast grunted, face unchanged, but even the small show of support did its job.

Running a hand through my hair, I sighed again. "I'm tired. Just kind of... worn out. I think maybe it's like what happens right before you retire or something, but I didn't have that because I was focused on Kiley and getting our lives figured out. I had energy from getting the business set up and recruiting and I just kept working. I never stopped—never wanted to."

They all nodded along, clearly understanding. I wondered if it felt this way for any of them, but it couldn't. Not exactly, anyway. None of them had taken over guardianship of a sibling twenty-plus years their junior.

"It's okay to be tired," Wilder said, his steady voice one I always listened to. Each man here had my respect, but Wilder and I had been through it *all* together these last two decades. It was only this last year or so when our lives had truly diverged.

"I know. I'm just not sure how to... recuperate. Get over it. Whatever."

Kenny snapped and pointed at me. "That's the point, though. You don't just get over it. You rest. You stop doing everything for everyone. You're only one person and you've got a lot on your shoulders. Like you said, none of the rest of us has any idea what it's like to be responsible for a teenager, even Wilder."

Wilder made a regretful sound. "My mother claims teenagers are exponentially more challenging than babies, and I tend to believe her, knowing what I put her through. My baby has nothing on Kiley."

"Kiley's great, though." Even if I hadn't quite cracked the code with her yet. I mean, we had a good thing going, but something about this new school year starting and maybe getting a year older made it feel like we were growing farther apart, not closer. "It's more that the things I normally enjoy doing aren't as energizing. I feel drained and I don't like that."

Wilder shook his head. "That's on me. I've been out a lot, and—"

"No, truly. You're doing what you need to. I admire it. I don't want it to change. I'm not complaining, believe me."

He let out a breathy laugh. "I do. But I know it's contributing to this burnout."

The words jabbed at me. Was I burnt out? Could I really be burnt out only a little over a year after retiring? That seemed so backward. Not like me, certainly.

"What about non-work stuff? You said things with Kiley are good—that's great. What else?" Tristan asked.

I thought through a laundry list of things I did. "I like book club. I go to the town council meetings, which are increasingly interesting, and I'm planning to brush up on my skiing skills this winter."

Or, I'd considered it. I lived near a world-class ski resort and it seemed like a good idea. Granted, it was only September. I had time.

"And the hot new neighbor?" Kenny asked, eyes widening when I tossed a pillow at him.

"Don't say she's hot," I grumped.

"Why? She's a fox." He batted his lashes.

Tristan, Wilder, and Beast all sighed.

I glared. "You can't talk about her like that. She'll be a coworker starting Monday." Something in me tightened. Or loosened. Or... reacted at saying it out loud. "Which is exactly why there's nothing else to say about her."

Kenny was aghast. "Because she's coming to work for us *temporarily*? Seriously? Wilder and Sarah hooked up when she was an employee. It's practically written in the business plan that the boss should get with the sexy secre—"

"Just stop right now." I opened my mouth to say more, then ended up momentarily annoyed into silence.

Kenny chuckled, clearly so pleased with himself, as Tristan shoved his shoulder. I had to smile at the quick action. Tristan was reserved in practically every way, yet he didn't stop himself from messing with Kenny when the kid needed it.

"She seems smart. Beautiful. The granddaughter of your favorite neighbor. Right up your alley, no?" Wilder asked.

It hung on the tip of my tongue to refute all of that, but the same sense of relief rushed in at his words. True, it fell well short of how I felt about Nikki—how I stupidly *already* felt about her—and yet, the fact that he saw it gratified the part of me that weirdly felt like we would be good together.

"She is an actual genius. She's..." A breath whooshed out. "She's gorgeous, and smart, and honest, and funny, and kind, and she's Rosie's great-niece, which doesn't hurt the cause. I like her, obviously. I was probably preprogrammed to have a crush on the woman. Someone up there ordained that I was made for her or something. But..."

A beat of silence passed before Kenny slapped his thighs. "But?"

"It's not the right time. Kiley has two years left in high school. I'm not going to start up a relationship when she needs me to be focused on her—to show up for her." Even if rehearsing the plan made regret wind tight around my chest.

"Jaws, dude. No one has ever showed up for their sister better than you have, all right? You dating someone isn't going to change that." Kenny reached for his beer and took a swig before returning it to a coaster on the coffee table.

"Agreed," Wilder said.

Beast grunted. "He's right."

Tristan studied me for a moment before he nodded, confirming.

But their opinions didn't matter. And I wasn't going to

live my life thinking of myself as some kind of hero because I took in my own sister. I'd never forget how I *wasn't* there for her for so long, and now I only had a few years to make up for it. "I appreciate the sentiment, but I don't agree. I need to be here for her. Period. And I'm not going to sacrifice my availability to her for someone I just met. I never planned on pursuing a relationship until she graduates high school, at the earliest."

Two years wasn't all that far away, anyway. Right?

Right.

Before any of them could respond, the back door leading into the kitchen closed a little louder than usual and our attention swung to the space behind me. Footsteps padded inside, and Kiley came into view.

"Hey," she said, eyes flicking to each of the men she knew well by now.

"Hey, Kiley! How was mathletes?" Kenny asked, way too enthusiastically.

She rolled her eyes, but a deep blush instantly burned her cheeks. She absolutely had a little crush on Kenny.

"It's not mathletes, it's just math club. Anyway, I'm going to head up. Lots of homework. Good to see you guys." Her gaze jumped to mine, and she gave me a smile that didn't quite meet her eyes.

If it had, I would've felt better. I would've felt certain. And yet, as she plodded up the stairs to her room, dread pooled in my gut.

"What're the odds she didn't hear all that?" I asked softly once the sound of her door clicking shut reached us.

Kenny made a face, and Tristan winced. Wilder said nothing, and even Beast's silence didn't reassure me.

I didn't want her to know I felt like I shouldn't make plans until after she graduated. She could stay here as long as she wanted, and as a kid who had been *unwanted* too much for one short lifetime already, I refused to give her any sense that I was biding my time. That wasn't what this was. This was me wanting her to know she was worth any amount of sacrifice. That she, just her, was enough, and I didn't need to go looking for anything else.

So while Kenny started gabbing about something he'd heard about Dorian, our resident recluse, I prayed she hadn't heard a word, and that loud door slamming, that thin smile, didn't mean what I feared they did.

CHAPTER ELEVEN

Nikki

Suit on, hair and makeup perfect, and stomach growling, I strolled into Diner with my bag over one shoulder and a mission: eat breakfast and hopefully see the one other person I knew in town besides Gram and Bruce.

"Hey, there you are. Good to see you!" Catherine grinned at me from across the space as she off-loaded a small carafe of coffee and a plate piled high with pancakes. She held up a now-free finger in the *one minute* sign, and I nodded.

A few booths were occupied, but most of the place was free. I could hear voices in the back behind the swinging door, likely where the other waitstaff were. Or maybe Catherine held down the fort by herself at this time of the morning, though I couldn't imagine that would always work if it got busy. The bright red booths around the perimeter were obviously the preferred locations for seating, the regular tables scattered in the middle completely empty.

A glance at the max occupancy sign and the schematics gave me a best guess at square footage. Then I mentally measured the booths, calculating the numbers from there— yep. They could install another row of booths down the center of the space and increase booth seating while maintaining a section for the free-standing chairs and improve traffic flow. Maybe I'd mention it.

Or maybe it'd be one of those things I thought of as useful that would offend or bother whoever I told. I'd had enough of those moments in my life to know I shouldn't just blurt out my thoughts.

In less than a minute, Catherine bustled over and waved me to a nearby booth.

"How are you settling in? Are you off to another interview?" She set down a water glass.

I nodded in thanks, appreciating her friendly chatting and good memory. She seemed genuinely interested, which both confused me and was exactly why I'd come. I loved Gram, and I was so grateful she'd wanted me to come help her, but it was different talking to someone your own age. Plus, more than I ever had before, I was feeling the press to take some time and make friends. If I was going to be caring for Gram and making a life here, the time had come to do that right.

"I got a job, actually." Temporary though it was, it felt good to end the joblessness I'd been moping over for the last few weeks. My little side project thanks to Kiley's inspiration had been coming along well, too, though I wouldn't be explaining that to anyone until I'd developed it even more. I hoped what'd hit as a spark of inspiration when I saw that light in her eyes would grow into a gaming app to help teens and adults develop their advanced math skills. But that just sounded too downright nerdy to open with, so basic job it would be.

"What? That's amazing. We need to celebrate." She positively beamed at me.

"We do?" I coughed, realizing how unsociable that sounded. "I mean, I'd love that."

Impossibly, her smile widened further. "Are you free Friday? We could go out. Unless you've already made friends and have your own thing going, but—"

"No, no. Other than Gram and my neighbor Bruce, I barely know anyone but you. Plus I'd like to get to know you better, if you've got room for a new friend." Somewhere in a past life, I would've rolled my eyes, but I'd come here for this, hadn't I?

Floating in and out of foster care had made this part of me hard. I felt the shield that forever threatened to raise readying, and yet, I'd psyched myself up for this all week-end. Well, this, and whatever this week of work would look like, but that was another issue.

Catherine sat in the booth opposite me and clasped her hands under her chin in the most oddly adorable move I'd ever seen. "Please be my friend."

I chuckled. "I thought I was asking you?"

She shook her head, smile all kinds of sparkly. "I realize I may not seem it, but I'm kind of ridiculously shy until I get to know people really well. I have no idea why, but I feel comfortable with you, and I have a feeling you'll like my friends, too. Can I invite a few others—just a small group, and we'll all get drinks at Craic on Friday?"

"Sure. Yeah. Just... I mean, you have to tell them I'm kind of a nerd, okay? Give them fair warning."

She rolled her eyes. "You'll be in good company, trust me. Now, what's for breakfast?"

And from there, we chatted on and off as she brought my food—a southwestern omelet and breakfast potatoes. I skipped the specialty side item, which she promised was the best thing since sliced bread but better than bread, because I knew I couldn't be too full or I'd regret it all morning.

When the time came to go, I waved at her from across the diner again as she bussed a table. She mouthed, "Friday" in lieu of shouting over the rising din of patrons and the music, and I nodded, then left.

I hoped I'd like her other friends and vice versa, but for now, I needed to focus on the most immediate obstacle—the building sitting kitty-corner from Diner itself. Maybe I shouldn't think of it as an obstacle, but that's what it'd become for me since I'd seen Bruce on Thursday afternoon and heat had flashed through me.

Because the truth was, I really, *really* liked Bruce Camden. I was drawn to him in just about every way a person could be, and now, I was stepping into his world to become his employee. I'd need to be professional in a job I was overqualified and yet not at all qualified for. I'd need to keep my rapidly expanding attraction for him under wraps. I'd need to make sure this squirrel brain didn't end up stepping on anyone's toes and create more problems for me.

So... yeah. Obstacle.

Or maybe I shouldn't think of it as an obstacle, but a conjecture needing a proof. *Yes.*

This whole situation—both work, and even life—was something I needed to look at like an advanced conjecture or problem. I needed to come up with my theorem and create the proof. And I could only do any of that by keeping an open mind and... starting. After all, Andrew Wiles never would've solved Fermat's Last Theorem if he'd never started.

Not a perfect metaphor since I didn't have my conjecture yet, but it went something like, *I can work at Saint Security without falling completely head over heels for a man I already like way too much.* Or, for the larger new reality of my life, *I can build a life in Silverton when I have utterly failed to do so at any other point prior to this second.*

Yeah. Sure. Conjecture out. Now to start on the proof...

My pulse increased at the thought, a little jet of hope injecting into my bloodstream as I breathed in the warming September-morning air and checked my watch. *Time to go.*

With one last steadying breath, I entered the little log-cabin-looking building I never would've imagined housed the stylish décor and high-tech features inside. The reception desk sat empty, as it had for my last visit. I hadn't gotten a tour of the whole building, but after leaving, I'd taken a guess at how much space they had based on the building's dimensions and what I had seen. Somehow, it made it feel less opaque if I knew the square footage, even at a guess.

They must've had a sensor for people entering the building, because in a flash after I'd stepped all the way inside, Bruce was there.

"Happy first day," he said, all kinds of ridiculously handsome in a plaid button-up and dark green utility pants.

No. Not handsome. Couldn't be thinking like that. And I'd already crawled around in my own head long enough that I blurted, "And to you. But, uh, happy three hundred fiftieth day."

Half that definitely-not-gorgeous mouth quirked up into a grin while his brows flashed a furrow. "Three hundred fiftieth?"

I shrugged one shoulder. "I recalled you saying you

arrived mid-June. It was a rough guess on the days you've worked here assuming you took most weekends but no extended time off. I'm probably way off."

Another half-smile. "I think you know very well you're not *way* off. The only variable is the fact that I have no idea what the real number is, but I'm going to take your word for it."

He gestured for me to follow him with a tip of his head. I assumed he'd stop at the desk where I'd eventually be sitting, but instead, he continued all the way down the hallway to his office, where I'd had my interview. It had just enough character to make it comfortable, but not so much that you could learn much about the man. I knew without asking that had been strategic.

He rounded his desk and sat, so I took the seat across from him.

"We'll take a beat here, and then we're going to head into the all-hands."

A tilt of my head asked the question for me.

"Every other Monday, we do an all-hands-on-deck-style meeting where we round up, debrief, and deal with assignments. The one at the first of the month is always our bigger group, and then the one later in the month is usually locals-only. It's perfect timing for you to dive right in since these will be your coworkers, but I can't have you join us until you've signed the NDAs."

I pulled a folder from my bag and handed it over to him.

He nodded and flicked it open, then sifted through the pages to check signatures as he spoke. "Thank you. Do you have any questions now?"

I waited for him to look from the contents of the file before speaking. "I'll wait until after the all-hands, if that works for you."

He tipped his eyes toward his watch, then nodded. "Works perfectly. Why don't we head in and we can meet people as they arrive. Typical start time is nine thirty."

He stood, and I took note and did the same, then waited for him to lead the way back toward the conference room.

"We're lucky that we only ever have a handful who can come in person, or we'd be SOL for space. We're already working on expanding to a larger building."

I entered the conference room to find three people sitting and chatting—two men, one woman. They all turned to size me up when I entered—and that's exactly what it felt like. A sizing up. Gone were the friendly smiles of Kenny or the shy politeness of Tristan. Here was a steely-eyed blond woman, a stone-faced giant, and a man who looked like his second job was masquerading as a mountain man.

"Veronica Hastings, meet Eddie James-Williamson a.k.a. Ed, Jude Rawlins a.k.a. Beast, and Dorian Forrester, a.k.a. Stone. Veronica is our new admin and may also be helping me out with some accounting projects. She's newly local and well vetted." He turned to me and held out a hand to the woman. "Eddie's one of our newer members, with just four months on hand, but she's also Wilder's sister-in-law, so we'll forgive her for not leaving her life as a spy to join the fun here sooner."

Surprise flashed through me at his words, but Eddie seemed unperturbed. She stood and extended a hand. "Nice to meet you, Veronica."

"Nikki, please." I wondered why Bruce would introduce me as Veronica anyway, but maybe he felt like he needed to use my legal name or something.

Eddie nodded. "We're glad to have you, and I know Sarah will enjoy maternity leave a lot more now with you on board."

I smiled, hoping that would be the case.

"Beast's a personal security expert and a man of few words, but he's also got secret smarts, so don't count him out based on the nickname." He grinned when Beast grunted and gave me a sharp nod.

"Nice to meet you."

Bruce grinned at me, then notched his chin in Dorian's direction. "And we have no idea why he's here because he's technically not an employee, and yet he's been showing up to monthly all-hands since he moved to town over a year ago."

The man sat blank-faced without any reaction other than the most minuscule nod of all time in my direction. Already, I had questions.

"Are we doing introductions and I missed them? Shame on you, Jaws." Kenny waltzed in and opened his arms wide. "You already know me, nickname Barbie, the man, the myth, the legend."

"The idiot," Beast said on a cough behind his hand.

Kenny feigned a lunge and Beast didn't even flinch. Another ridiculously handsome man walked in with a folder under one arm, studiously focused on his phone, followed by a woman with olive skin and brown hair whose eyes darted around the room in a quick sweep.

"That's Adam Carter, a.k.a. Doc, and Jess Korbel, a.k.a. Pop," Bruce said, right as the man in question raised his head and speared me with stunning blue eyes, and *wow*. And Jess's were this mesmerizing green I could see from across the room, plus she looked like she could be a fitness model. Had they just collected all the best-looking people? Did applications for this place usually require headshots?

"Welcome aboard," he said, and Jess tipped her head to me, right as Kenny was whispering something presumably insulting at Beast while Beast seemed to be glaring in the newcomers' direction. *Interesting*.

Tristan arrived and set a hand on Kenny's shoulder. "That's enough now," he said in that quiet, steady way he had.

My eyes met Tristan's, and he nodded. Such a calming energy, especially in contrast to Kenny's showboat approach. Tristan had this feeling surrounding him I would describe as chill—not cold, but simply calm, cool, not about to be ruffled. Bruce possessed something similar, except every time I made eye contact with him, I felt like my insides had discovered nuclear fission and the atoms were splitting and exploding, moving from heavy to light and rendering me mildly radioactive for the next million years or so.

Okay so maybe my bedtime reading last night on the latest advancements in clean energy, one of which was the recent progress in nuclear fusion, had caught up with me. But my insides didn't combine—they divided, devolved, practically fell apart in little internal atomic booms of attraction like now, when Bruce's hand brushed across my lower back and urged me into a seat at the table.

Wilder strolled in a moment later, a baby cradled in his left arm, and everyone in the room visibly responded. I didn't bother noticing anything other than Bruce.

Bruce, my neighbor and boss and impossibly good guy in a gorgeous body with a perfect smile and a local business and what I was gathering was a really attractive brain... he reached out right as Wilder said, "Hold this for a minute."

And Bruce took the baby with the biggest grin I'd ever seen.

And I died.

CHAPTER TWELVE

Bruce

Wilder liked to pretend this baby didn't have him wrapped around his tiny months-old finger, but it was all lies. We all knew it.

We all felt it, too, and he wasn't even our blood. But in the same way that none of us were technically related, this place had become a family. I used to say brotherhood, but we were missing parts to it, and now with Eddie as our slightly grumpy little sister and Jess on board, it just felt right. Add to that the Washingtons, as our resident married couple, and we were one big extended family, especially when we factored in the patron Saint, Jane, as the resident mother hen to our larger familial tree.

Which had to be why I took genuine joy in holding my best friend's baby. I'd never been a baby guy, but little James Saint had to be one of the cutest of all time, and he'd barely nailed down holding his head up and smiling.

"All right, let's get into it," Wilder said when he slipped into the chair at the head of the table and passed me a bottle. I took it and the proffered burp rag and went to work, ever-mindful of Nikki's presence next to me.

As though I could forget. I'd known the instant she'd entered the building—not just because we had state-of-the-art security systems but also because I could swear the air had changed. Like something in me had become primed, ready to light some kind of flame and start an explosion the second I saw her.

Maybe it all sounded a bit dramatic. It *was*, in truth. And it felt entirely too accurate.

Nikki Hastings had a hold on me, and I honestly didn't know how it'd happened.

Forcing my mind back to the moment and not letting it get lost on the rabbit trail that was the mess of my way-too-intense response to my new employee, I focused on the meeting and the squishy little babe in my arms.

"Boots, Cookie, and Hijack are running late, so let's give 'em a minute," I said, aware our guys dialing in would be slow to tune in this morning. "The Washingtons should be popping on any second."

I'd felt Nikki's eyes on me as I'd taken James, but I hadn't *seen* them. Did she like babies? Did she want kids?

Do you need a slap upside the head to stop thinking about this woman like that?

I smiled down at this little beefcake in my lap and watched as he destroyed the bottle. I'd learned the hard way I had to stop him midfeast and burp him, so I did that now, leaning him up and steadying him with my right hand while I patted his back with my left.

"You're getting stronger, my man. Good work," I whispered.

A sharp exhale drew my eyes to Nikki, who was indeed watching me—or at the moment, looking at James's ridiculous little drool face. I quirked a brow to ask her what was up to avoid drawing attention to myself or risk Kenny making an obnoxious comment.

She shook her head slowly, a dazed quality to her expression. "Cute baby."

I grinned, then dropped a kiss to James's head. "The cutest. He's the official Saint mascot baby, so naturally he'd be adorable."

Her lashes fluttered like I'd done something to her. *Interesting.* It wasn't that I worried she was immune to me. I knew well enough to know she found me attractive, yet something told me Nikki didn't value physical attraction or chemistry as the main thing in a person she might end up dating.

Not that we were going to end up dating. She was my employee, and I had obligations. But. You know. For the sake of discussion.

"The people who are running late—they're coming in person?" she asked, pulling me back to the larger moment of our meeting.

"They'll do it by VTC—video teleconference. It's basically a secure Zoom." If she didn't swoon at the sight of me with a baby, surely my riveting conversational skills would wow her and her actual genius brain. I consoled myself by watching James polish off the rest of his bottle in record time.

"Are they... abroad? I guess I hadn't realized you all have people overseas." Her gaze slid around the room, noting the various flat screens affixed high on the walls and finally the camera mounted at the far end of the room.

"Two are out of state, one is overseas. The Washingtons

are on long-term assignment with a client who is spending six months in Singapore. Typically, we don't have five out at once. Two are on personal security details and one is assisting with a K and R."

Her brows jumped. "Wow. That's... impressive."

I nodded, hiding the smile that wanted to beam out at her like an idiot and instead kept a handle on the little zip of pleasure that shot up my spine at her words. "We're finding it hard to keep people local. Not everyone is willing to travel, so that makes our ability to staff jobs that require it tricky, but that's all part of building these first few years. We're figuring it out, and with your help, I hope."

She nodded, accepting that calling easily enough. I didn't have a great sense of whether she was at all excited about the job, or merely accepting it as a stopgap. I could live with either, though selfishly, I wanted her to like it here. I had no illusions she'd choose to stay, but I didn't want her to think my whole life's work and the thing I'd chosen to prioritize so much I lost sleep over it sometimes got boring.

Tristan caught my eye and nodded to James. I chuckled, then stood and passed him the little chunk and the burp rag. Wilder got as close as he ever got to smiling at us, clearly only thanks to our devotion to his son.

Boots and Cookie popped up in one frame, and Hijack's screen flickered to life on the other. Instantly, Wilder started the meeting.

I appreciated him taking the lead today. It had to be related to the intervention he and Kenny, Tristan, and Beast had staged a few days ago. Wilder's word, like any of these people's, was solid. If he said he was going to show up more, he would. Problem was, I didn't feel great about him picking up the slack. There was a reason I'd taken it on myself. I was part owner in this business, and I didn't have a baby.

"Right, Jaws?"

My attention snapped to the screen, where Boots waited patiently for me to respond. "Uh, right. Yep. We want the COAs for managing a crowd surge for sure. We may be able to employ them for other clients depending on where we end up."

Next to me, Wilder nodded like he agreed, and Boots piped up. "Ms. Halter is handling it all really well. It's just..." His brow furrowed, and he glanced at Cookie. "I don't know. None of this feels healthy."

Goose bumps prickled my skin. Boots was a seasoned operator, and while he was relatively new to personal security in a civilian situation, if he was saying something wasn't *healthy*, that was cause for alarm.

"You want to pull her?" Wilder asked, clearly having the same instantaneous elevation of concern.

Boots shook his dark head. "No. I'm just saying it out loud, for the record, and the second it gets any worse, I'm pulling her."

His jaw flexed, and I could see the frustration.

Jenna Halter had recently shot from hilarious comedic actress to superstardom when she'd thrown herself into the role of an Elfin queen in the latest high fantasy supernova of a film series. It'd been an oddly slow build for the series from what I could tell, or at least, for *her*, but now, she needed a personal detail. Since she was best friends with Wilder's sister-in-law Callaway Rice, she'd come to us.

Delightful, but it presented problems. First, she was on a press tour for the film that was running her ragged, even with her short stop in Silverton for the premiere. Second, her management team and the producers had expectations that verged on unreasonable. And finally, she hadn't been herself.

At least, that's what Boots and Cookie had said. And while they weren't longtime friends of hers, I believed they could sense a shift in her these last few months. We couldn't technically "pull her" from anything, but we could put up a good fight. The fact that she'd gone with us and finagled contracting our guys for her security instead of the production company's had already made waves, but I was happy to say Saint Security had come highly recommended by several voices the execs couldn't ignore—particularly Jack McKean.

Anyway, none of us liked this situation, but we really had no say. The guys were on it, though, and so we'd watch and wait and see how the situation developed.

"Team Washington? How goes it there?"

Malik spoke first. "All good. Smooth sailing."

Amani nodded in agreement. "Yep. Cake walk."

I smiled internally, appreciating their brevity as much as I did the absolute certainty that they had everything in hand there. Malik and Amani Washington had both been operators at EMU. They met there, married there, but their opposing deployment schedules had stressed them, and when Wilder and I approached about joining Saint, their only requirement had been that they work together. It hadn't come as a huge surprise, and so far, we were finding it to be a dream setup. Once we agreed, they'd submitted their retirement packets and hadn't looked back.

After a few more minutes, we wrapped. These meetings only worked if we were truly checking in, and none of us delved into real details of our given responsibilities. It wasn't the time for a deep summary or airing issues. It was a check-in.

"See you all in a few weeks, and on Friday if you're

around," I said, watching the VTC screens go dark and everyone disperse.

"Friday?" Nikki asked quietly.

That familiar thrill shot through me, and I nearly smirked at myself. I'd managed to keep my mind on the business a good eighty percent of the meeting. I'd managed not to try catching her subtle clean scent or think about how much I liked the way her lips naturally curved up at the corners.

Victory!

"We do a little happy hour on Fridays for anyone who's free. It's just a morale thing. You're welcome to join us," I explained as we waited for Eddie and Beast to exit. I then turned to Wilder, who was retrieving James from Tristan. "We putting him on the payroll?"

Wilder pulled him in and got this look on his face that made my heart squeeze. My God, it was good to see the man so happy, so full of genuine love and joy. He'd been broody and solemn most of the years I'd known him, but that was nothing special. A lot of men in our line of work were introverts and tended to be extremely smart and capable. While that might seem like something that left us ready to make friends, it could isolate. Hence why the team element of being in special operations was so key.

What'd pulled me in about Wilder had been the man underneath that quiet, somber air. He was a lover, soft in a way that might surprise people—he had this huge heart and he wanted to share it. And now, he did—with Sarah, and this one. He'd made even more room for his mom and brothers, their wives and kids, and even his stepdad and stepsister. Then for Eddie, his new sister-in-law. And me. I'd been the lucky recipient of his friendship, his brotherhood, for years, and I would never take that for granted.

"I think we'll let him coast on his good looks a while longer and be the mascot, as long as he's not bothering anyone." He raised a brow like he was really asking the question.

"Of course not," I replied, right as Tristan said, "Don't deprive me of baby snuggles, Saint."

Wilder's full-blast grin had me chuckling, and when I turned to glance at Nikki, the sucker punch of her charmed smile reinforced the odd beauty of the moment.

"You know, not that I ever thought about it before right this moment, but I never imagined a bunch of former special ops guys at a security company would be so... baby friendly." Nikki's grin faded once she stopped speaking, and then as though she realized she'd misstepped, she rushed to add, "I mean, not that men don't like babies, or that it's wrong to have a baby here, I just... sorry. Sorry. That was inappropriate."

I tipped my head to the side to study the flags of red high on her cheeks, embarrassment painted clear as day on that skin where nothing could hide. But Wilder spoke first.

"It's an understandable assumption, Nikki. I'm glad I happen to be the owner and have the first baby among employees because it lets us set the tone. I'm doing a terrible job with boundaries, but we want people to live their lives."

I nodded. "We've lived the version of the story where everything gets swallowed up in favor of the job. We don't want that for anyone here. And having lost enough along the way to know what actually matters, we want it all for every person who walks in the door. We want full, whole lives."

The words hit me. Was I living a full, whole life? Could I say that? Wasn't that what the guys were trying to get me to see a few days ago over a beer and pizza?

She swallowed, like something I'd said had affected her, and I watched that slim line of her neck, her throat working, before I wrenched my eyes away to focus on Tristan, who'd started speaking.

"They offer amazing parental leave, sick days, PTO… it's a good place to work. Might not be able to take our word for it yet, but you'll see." Then, he performed the usual subtle dip of his head in farewell, and Tristan was gone. After Wilder got James all packed off to his office, Nikki and I returned to sit across from each other at my desk.

"Sorry if we put the pressure on about the job, but we're all happy to be working for ourselves." That was the least of it. Well, maybe not the *least*, but it wasn't the main thing.

"I can see that. And while I don't mind the hard sell, I should say I have already accepted the job and I'm eager to start. So, boss, please walk me through how I can help." She leaned forward, bellying up to the opposite side of my desk, and rested her elbows on the surface like she was ready.

Internally, I sighed. I liked this woman too much. I liked how forthright she was, how she didn't play games, and HR forgive me, I liked the way the creamy skin of her collarbones looked soft against the dark black of her suit jacket.

But I couldn't be thinking that, so I nodded, a casual smile there to cover the jolt of *boss* coming from her lips while I lightly fantasized about tracing the dip at the hollow of her throat with my thumb, and we got to work.

CHAPTER THIRTEEN

Nikki

Gram's expression seemed far too cagey as she held out the trash bag for me.

I narrowed my eyes. "Please tell me why you have that look."

Her brows arched high. "Me? Look? This is just my face, Nikki. I can't help my face."

With another assessing glance, I waited for her to give herself up, but no. Instead, she flared those brows yet again and waited for me to take the handles.

"Fine. I'll take it. But I'll be ready in like ten minutes—I can't just go then?" I'd gotten wrapped up in working on my game development until I'd noticed the time, then rapidly fixed my hair and makeup, and thankfully already wore jeans and a blouse I'd changed into after work. I needed just another minute to leave myself a few notes about the next steps before I took off and shifted my brain into social mode.

She shrugged. "If you want to leave me here holding this garbage for another ten—"

I snatched the barely full bag and stomped dramatically toward the door, but she only snickered as she bustled into the kitchen behind me to wash out some of her paintbrushes. The screen door shut when I exited, and I plunked the bag down in the can, then let the lid drop.

"You two seem to go through a great deal of trash."

Bruce's voice had my attention snapping to the right and finding him sauntering to the edge of his driveway.

Busted, Gram. That sneak had wanted me to run into Bruce as though I didn't work at his office every day. Not that I'd seen him all that much after Monday morning. The man had meetings stacked up the *entire* day Tuesday and had been out at least half of Wednesday. He'd had something else Thursday, which I later found out was a dental appointment he'd taken Kiley to, and then today... well, he'd likely just gotten home. He and Wilder had made me leave at three this afternoon with reassurances I'd be paid for the whole day, but they clearly didn't take their own leeway, as it was after six thirty.

"I think it's less the trash and more Gram shoving me into your orbit," I said, unwilling to play the oblivious neighbor. He was an incredibly smart man—no way he didn't see my beloved Gram throwing me at him every chance she got. She'd probably been doing it for ages now, but it'd had no teeth until I'd waltzed right into her trap.

He gave me that half-smile I liked a little too much and toed into the grass between our yards. He'd demur, no doubt. Say something charming and obfuscate the matchmaking efforts of his neighbor while leaving me with as little embarrassment as possible. It was his way. He constantly worked to put people at ease, and if you weren't watching for it, you'd hardly notice it happening.

But I noticed everything Bruce did, so when he stopped less than a foot from where I stood on Gram's back patio and dipped his head a bit, I couldn't believe what he said.

"I'm not complaining."

I laughed gamely. "Guess not since you hired me."

His jaw flexed. No idea how I noticed that except I was studying him closely, our eyes locked.

"That I did. And you accepted the job, which means you must not mind being in *my* orbit."

"I probably shouldn't have said it like that," I said, disliking the way it made this sound.

This, like there was something between us. Like *this* was something with a name.

He leaned closer, maybe, or I did. Somehow, we were only inches apart. I was looking up at him—not straining or anything because yes, he was tall, but I liked that. No—I *loved* that about him. He was all masculine and gorgeousness physically with this capable, tuned-in air that made every other man I'd ever dated look like primordial ooze in comparison.

Not that we were dating.

"Can't say I mind the idea, but I think it's probably the other way around, Nik."

I swallowed, the nickname sending a shiver up my spine for some odd reason. Why would I like that?

Oh, I don't know. Just this beautiful man talking to you like he knows you, or wants to...

"How so?" I somehow responded.

His smile crept in, a slow, sly thing. "Pretty sure I'm in *your* orbit."

I huffed a laugh. "Maybe this planetary metaphor has run its course."

That smile widened. "Fine. I defer to your genius."

My eyes rolled before I could think to stop them. Why did Rosie have to tell him that? And was he making fun of me because of it? I didn't think so—Bruce just didn't seem the type, but that old bruise felt newly tender as I adjusted to a new place.

"Hey, sorry. Should I not mention it?" he asked, ever perceptive.

"No, it's fine. I'm not sad about it. But there have been times when that fact about me has become a punchline. And I don't like that."

Look at me, sharing my feelings.

His hand brushed my wrist before he held me there, and his dark eyes captivated mine with an intensity I hadn't anticipated.

"I'm sorry. I would never want to make you feel like I was anything but lightly enamored by your intelligence."

My mouth dropped open, and warmth spread through me, hot water into a tub that'd gone lukewarm. "Oh. Well, yeah. Smarts are hot."

He laughed, and a grin lit his entire face and washed away the somber mood that'd struck. "Smarts are indeed hot." Then his eyes took on this hooded quality, and he glanced at my mouth, swaying toward me. "There you go again."

"There I go again doing what?" I asked, my words almost a whisper. Something about him looking at me, standing so close, touching me... it'd certainly dimmed my ability to follow his thought process.

"Being gravity, I guess." With a blink, he dropped his hand from my wrist and stepped back. "And there I go on the whole space, planets thing. Anyway, you're off, and I've got to go get ready, so... great job this week. Have a good night."

And then, he turned on his heel and walked back toward his house. More than a little stunned by... everything, I sent a feeble "Have a good night!" after him, and then scurried back inside to get my shoes.

I was quiet for the next few minutes as I slipped on my heels and grabbed my purse, completely abandoning the notes I needed to make on the game. My mind buzzed a little, like I'd already had a cocktail on an empty stomach, and I didn't even bother giving Gram a look as she smirked at me and winked before I left.

Being gravity, I guess. Wow.

By the time I pulled into the parking lot down the street from Craic, I'd miraculously straightened myself out with logic.

As I walked, I tallied up the truth. I liked Bruce. A lot. And nothing I'd seen this week at work had helped that situation, other than continually reminding myself he was my boss.

But truth? He'd only be my boss for a few months. And history had a habit of setting the tone, so the fact that Wilder, the other owner of Saint Security, had married the last person who held my position? Well... it didn't do much to tamp down the *hot for my boss* feelings.

Because yeah. I was. And *he* wasn't helping one bit. The whole thoughtful, concerned thing? The charm? The smile? The rough hands on the skin of my wrist? *The words!?*

Right now, I needed to fold those piles of feelings into a little cube in my head and leave it there while I went to meet my new friends—or so I hoped. I'd reminded myself dozens of times this week that I could do things differently here. I wasn't changing who I was, just opening doors that were right in front of me.

It'd felt like every door in my past life had closed, and on this side of things, sliding out of my car in the cool of a mid-September evening in Silverton, I wondered if I'd had more of a hand in closing them than I'd realized.

I'd certainly played a part in the breakup with my boyfriend. I'd only been loosely interested in him as things stood—a pattern I recognized in myself. Probably why the reality of my instant attraction to Bruce paired with my near-immediate like of him as a person had shaken me so much.

And continued to do so.

But what I couldn't shake was the suspicion that maybe I'd stood by and watched everything else implode—losing touch with friends, pushing a little too much at work, refusing to play the games my boss and his son seemed to expect. Things I'd done on a larger scale as a teen and in my early twenties—cue the adult version. Subtler and without a stint in juvie, I'd kept everything and everyone at arm's length so effectively that when I lost it all, the only part of me that really *hurt* over it was my pride.

"But I don't want that." I said it aloud as I clicked the lock on my keys and pulled my purse higher on my shoulder. I didn't want to play games, and I sure as heck didn't want to work so hard for a life I was only just barely interested in.

So... here I was, walking into a bar I'd never been to with plans to meet a woman I'd talked to exactly twice and some of *her* friends, with whom I may or may not actually get along. *If loner angry teen Nikki could see me now...*

"Hi. Hello. Hey, um, are you by any chance Nikki?"

A petite blond woman waved at me to get my attention, as though her saying my name wouldn't do the trick. "Uh, yes. Are you one of Catherine's friends?"

She beamed. "Yes! I am. I'm Dove. Catherine's running two minutes late, and I think Jo and Elise should be here any second."

"Nice to meet you, and thanks for flagging me down. Should we go ahead and get a table?" I glanced inside, and from what I could see, the place looked bustling.

"Oh, Kieran has one saved for us, but sure. Let's go ahead in and get settled." She tipped her head toward the door, then turned.

I followed, taking in the dark wood exterior and the large glass doors that were open and allowed tables to spill onto the sidewalk. More bistro tables were situated behind a small wrought-iron fence to create the designated space. Inside, a gorgeous, polished wood bar sat in front of a mirrored back wall and shelves of all manner of bottles ranging from simple to wildly ornate and expensive-looking decorated the setup. A dark-haired, dark-eyed man looked up between bodies seated at the bar and lifted his chin to Dove and winked. She grinned, winked back, and moved toward a section of the bar with enough purpose, I figured she knew where she was going.

"So how are you settling in?" Dove asked, bright blue eyes startling me a bit now that I had them in full focus.

"Decently well, I think. Job's good, and I'm meeting people." I tipped my head to her, and she grinned. "I came to help my great aunt, who's like my grandmother, but other than taking out the trash and grabbing groceries after work, I don't feel like I've done much for her."

The clamor of other revelers clanged around us for a beat, and before we could sit, Catherine arrived.

"Hey! So glad you two found each other. Elise and Jo are almost here." Catherine's genuinely pleased smile greeted us.

Dove jumped in after giving Catherine a full-body hug. "Nikki was just telling me she can hardly tell Rosie needs any help."

Catherine's voice was filled with fondness. "Oh, Rosie's so independent, though. From what I understand, a lot of folks end up needing help after an event like hers, but she's done so well." Her encouraging smile didn't waver.

In fact, it looked downright full of admiration. So did Dove's.

But my mind snagged on the loaded term *event*, and it had no chance of moving past that turn of phrase without more information. "She's had an event?"

Their brows wrinkled as they studied me. Catherine spoke first. "Dove is a nurse..." Her tone was stuffed with uncertainty, like she could tell I was confused but wasn't quite clicking with *why*.

Dove quirked a brow at Catherine, but filled in more. "Yep, I'm a nurse. I mostly work at the clinic, but I do rotations at Silverton Springs sometimes, so I see a lot of our county's older population as well. I've thought about specializing in palliative care—it's so needed, you know? But I feel like I haven't quite learned everything I need to know before I transition."

"Ladies? Order?" A waiter gave us a toothy grin he must've thought looked appealing and held up his paper pad and a pen.

I spiraled internally, unable to speak. What event? *What event!?*

"I'll have a lemon drop," Dove said.

"I'll just have a beer, thanks." Catherine's words came

out softer, and I noticed she only flicked her eyes up to the man for a minute before focusing on her fingers.

"And you, miss?" the guy said.

"Uh, a pint of something local. Thanks." And maybe because I couldn't let it go even if it did seem a little rude, I pinned Dove with a look. "Can you clarify what you meant by *event*?"

Catherine's brows rose high on her pretty face. "The stroke?"

I swallowed hard, rocks and bits of metal shredding their way down my windpipe as her word echoed in my ears. "Stroke?"

"Oh, no. You didn't... she didn't tell you? How could she not tell you?" Catherine took my hand in hers and squeezed.

I turned to the two of them, Dove's face utterly stricken and Catherine's aglow with sympathy. "Tell me everything."

CHAPTER FOURTEEN

Nikki

Catherine shook her head, lips pinched, before jumping in. "I shouldn't have said anything. I definitely shouldn't have phrased it that way. She *did* have a stroke, but it happened before we saw her. She had an incident..."

Her eyes shifted to mine, and I registered the panic clawing at me. Logically, this made no sense. I'd seen Gram not an hour ago and she was fine. Whatever they were referring to had happened before I'd arrived, and Gram had obviously recovered.

Yet, she'd asked me to come. And I'd been so mired in my own self-pity over losing my job and feeling like my life was falling apart, it hadn't even registered that this was akin to the Earth halting its spin or changing the angle it spun on its axis. Such change meant major things, even one degree of change. The fallout would be monumental, and the cause would have to be... catastrophic.

Catherine continued even as Dove had crossed her arms and clammed up. "She'd lost consciousness and fell. When she woke, she'd hit her head, lost some blood, and was understandably very concerned."

Terror ripped through me at the thought of her falling alone in her house with no help. No one would've known if she'd needed help. A list of to-dos began compiling itself in my mind as Dove pressed on.

"Testing revealed she'd had a minor stroke. It'd come and gone, fortunately with minimal injury, and—" Catherine grimaced when Dove reached for her and grabbed her wrist. Not forcefully, but enough to halt her words.

Dove spoke then. "I'm sorry. I don't think we should say anymore if she hasn't told you. I know that's awful, but this may have already violated HIPAA—"

"No, Dove. You didn't say anything. It was me." Catherine clasped her hands together in front of her and sort of clutched them to herself. "I'm so sorry, Nikki. I didn't think—"

"Say no more. Truly. I'll talk with her. I just... I can't believe she didn't tell me."

Yet as soon as the words left my mouth, the lie made my stomach twist. It felt like I shouldn't be able to believe she didn't tell me, but that was her way. Rosie was warm and loving, but also eminently private about her own issues, and she would never want to worry me.

It was part of the reason I'd so easily accepted when she'd invited me to come live with her and help out. But a not-small piece of my mind had suspected it'd been her way of getting me here without me feeling guilty or like more of a failure. She'd give me the permission of helping her, and then when she didn't really need my help, she'd give me one of those mischievous grins and I'd be too settled here to do anything but accept her coup.

Reality sank like stones into the pit of my stomach. She hadn't been altruistically calling for my help. She'd actually needed it.

"I'm so sorry. I never meant to break this news. I—I truly don't know what to say other than I am so sorry." Catherine worried her lip, and the twinge in her voice made me wonder if she might cry.

Her genuine emotional response gave me all the information I needed. She was an honest person, and it hadn't been gossip—that first comment about Rosie doing so well had been meant as an encouragement. I wished I could take it as such, but now, all I wanted was to get home and check on her.

"I know you're worried, but she's doing really well. I see her every Thursday at the Springs with friends. I talk to her often. If you want to go, we won't fault you. But if you're up for staying..." Dove waited, her pause saying everything.

If I could get past the shock, they wanted me to stay. I exhaled, cleared my throat, and nodded once. "Let me just go call her. I realize it happened... whenever it happened and I've seen her every day for well over a week now, but I can't shake it. She's..." I exhaled again as my throat tightened. "She's all I have."

Now, more than ever before, I recognized that truth. She was all I'd ever *let* myself have, and even then, I'd made sure to keep miles between us until just recently—to be sure she couldn't leave me since I'd left her. What did that say about me? What did that say about my ability to be here for her now?

"Of course, take as long as you need," Catherine said.

"If you need to go, we'll do this another time," Dove added.

I exited quickly, practically stumbling out of the pub as I waited for Gram to answer.

"Nikki? Aren't you out with your friends?"

"You had a stroke?"

Silence greeted me on the other end, a stark contrast to the stream of chatter humming from the pub.

"I planned to tell you once you were settled."

My teeth clenched, and I flexed every internal muscle of control I had to not lash out. It wasn't my place, in the end, and I didn't want to guilt her. I only... *what?* I wanted to chastise her for not telling me the truth from the very beginning—for not calling me the minute she got to the hospital.

"I understand you're upset, and I hope you'll allow me to explain my reasoning to you. But I hope that you'll stay there with your friends and let yourself have a good time knowing I'm safe and sound, tucked in with my tea and cookies and a movie, and I'm not up to the conversation tonight anyway."

While her response heartened me, it also made me want to tear my hair out. She had to be the most stubborn person on the planet, and her saying she didn't want to talk about it tonight meant she absolutely wouldn't. If I left and went home, there'd be no chance of getting to the bottom of what'd happened, why she didn't tell me, and whatever the prognosis actually was.

That all-too-familiar fear and dread snaked through me again.

"I hear it, Nikki. Don't go there. I really am fine, and I know I need to explain things to you but please trust me that I'm okay. I will see you when you get in later, and we'll talk tomorrow, but only if you promise me to stay and get to know those girls. Catherine's a sweetheart, and I know her friends are good people."

A sigh escaped me loudly enough she could hear it, no doubt, but I followed it with my acquiescence. "Tomorrow. No excuses."

I could imagine her nodding before she confirmed. "Tomorrow. Now go have a beer and some fun."

She ended the call. I blinked down at the screen, my mind a traitorous blank. I couldn't tell what I felt or what I wanted to do now. On one hand, I wanted to race home and yell at her for keeping this from me. On the other, I recognized she didn't owe me that. She didn't owe me anything.

It was me who owed her *everything*. She'd done nothing short of bringing me back to life years ago when I was lost and broken and so angry, I could hardly walk down a sidewalk without lashing out at the flowers I passed.

She'd tell me tomorrow. The fact that she had kept this from me might've sent me running to my room and locking myself away from everyone even a few years ago, but now, I saw clear as day that Rosie couldn't be my only support. Yes, she was my Gram and I loved her completely, but she was her own person with her own life I knew next to nothing about. I hoped she'd let me in a bit, but she was right to push me to stay here.

I needed friends, and though they'd dropped a bit of a bomb on me, they hadn't meant to. In some ways, it made me like them even more than I'd already been predisposed to—they'd been supportive. Understanding. No pressure to stay or go or anything.

"Who do I need to disappear?"

Bruce's voice sent a flash of surprise and heat into the

mess of emotions already suffocating me. I turned to see him, and sure enough, he looked as beautiful as always. Though now, he was frowning down at me like he'd meant his question.

"Disappear?" Since I had no context for his question, I wondered if I'd been thinking so hard, I'd missed something.

"Well, I might've said kill, but I'm trying to keep my word choice less violent for Kiley's sake."

His chagrined smile made a small laugh escape me. "Why are you killing people?"

He notched his chin toward my phone. "You look distressed."

I glanced at the phone, then tucked it into my purse. "It's Gram. We just..." I searched for the right words. "Need to have a conversation."

He nodded. "Okay. So no one needs to be unalived because they hurt you?"

I laughed despite myself at his ridiculous words. "Correct. And I sincerely hope that's not what Saint Security actually does, because I would be very disturbed to discover that about my new place of employment."

One side of his mouth curved up and made his cheek crease in a stupidly charming way. "Absolutely not."

"Good."

"Are you going back in?" His eyes slipped past me to Craic's door a few feet away, then back to mine.

Moment of truth, though I'd already decided. "Yes. Yes, I am."

He grinned. "I worry that you sound like that's a punishment and not a pleasure."

Some odd impulse made me want to tell him. He knew Rosie, and at this point, he'd had to have encountered her stubborn streak. But if she hadn't told me, I doubted she'd told him. And maybe part of me worried she had told him and finding that out would spoil any chance I had of going in there and trying to get to know Dove and Catherine.

With yet another sigh, I shook my head. "No. I'm just getting my head on straight. I need to do this."

He nodded once. "All right, then. Shall we?"

I dipped my chin to acknowledge his words and moved ahead. Craic's door was propped open, so I walked all the way in, then slowed when I reached the small crowd clogging the entrance.

Then, a warm hand settled on my lower back. I glanced over my shoulder to see Bruce eyeing the space from one side to the next, then spotting my friends. He guided me toward the table with his warm palm practically burning a hole through my shirt, and stopped only when we'd reached Dove, Catherine, and two women I hadn't met yet.

"Ladies. I think Nikki's joining you?" His voice was all charm and ease.

Nothing like what I felt. My awareness had shrunk to the point of contact on my back. And when he said, "I'll leave you to it" after each of the women at the table had greeted him, his hand disappeared, and I looked up in time to see him wink and step away.

"Okay, I'm sorry, but that man is..." One of the women I hadn't met yet fanned herself with the laminated drink menu.

The other stranger smashed her eyes closed and looked something close to miserable. "He really just is."

Catherine sighed. "He really is. Are you two dating, Nikki?"

My eyes widened, and her question snapped me back into consciousness. Everyone's attention arced to me.

"No. No. He's my neighbor and Rosie's. And now, he's

my boss." A fact I desperately needed to cling to when the nerve endings in my body were trying to figure out some form of bribery to make his hand come back and touch me again.

The new woman with caramel hair snickered. "Yeah? Pretty sure my boss doesn't look at me like that."

The other one sighed. "He doesn't look at anyone like that. Trust me."

"Nikki, this is Elise Cordero." Dove pointed to the woman with dark eyes and what seemed to be a perpetual smirk. "And this is Jo Malcom." She gestured to the woman with a pained expression and gorgeous, long brown hair. "Elise, Jo, this is Nikki."

Dove smiled at us as Elise eyed me for a moment before speaking.

"Nice to meet you, Nikki, and welcome to Silverton. How about I buy you a drink and you tell us all about how you ended up with Bruce Camden wrapped around your finger when no one else has managed to get him to give them a second look?"

CHAPTER FIFTEEN

Bruce

I shouldn't have touched her.

We'd touched before—handshake, hand on wrist, things like that. But my hand had found her lower back like it was meant to be there, and that wasn't something a boss did. It wasn't something a man who was trying not to get tangled up in a woman he liked way too much, because he needed to stay focused on supporting his sister did.

Did I want to touch her? Yes. Very much. Just one fleeting press to the silky fabric of her shirt and the curve of her spine? Absolutely not enough.

The walk to the other side of the pub, where Tristan had slipped in while I escorted Nikki, felt long and uncomfortable, like I shouldn't be moving away from the woman, but closer to her. The call of her on my mind and body like gravity yet again. Clearly, I couldn't be trusted.

Dorian had refused the invitation, Kenny would run

late since that was his MO, and we'd have a few more trickle in. I always showed up on time because that was me, plus it let me leave on the early side. Tristan tended to head out when I did, and I usually found myself impressed he came at all considering crowds of strangers weren't exactly his thing. To be fair, that could be said of most of us.

"You okay?" Tristan's question came as he set down a full pint, then notched his chin toward the other beer on the table—mine, evidently.

After a swig of the golden ale, I swallowed hard. "Yeah. I'm good." With a glance over my shoulder back toward Nikki, I mentally slapped myself. *Get a grip, man.* "Just making sure Nik got to her girls."

The answering silence made me turn to Tristan in time to see his brow pop up. "Nik?"

Clearing my throat, I ignored the question. What would I say? Nicknames were part of the way we did things. They became signals and monikers that held reputation. But simply shortening her name wasn't a *nickname*, it was a sign of affection. And I wasn't about to attempt protesting against the fact that I felt affection for Nikki Hastings, because I did.

"Is he pretending he doesn't want to sit in my spot?" Kenny asked as he slid onto a stool between me and Tristan.

"Why would I want your spot?" I asked, finally facing him.

He snickered. "Because you can't keep your eyes off the table at your six, and if you were sitting here, it'd be a lot easier to stare."

I ignored him but narrowed my eyes at Tristan, who tucked his grin into his pint glass. "You can both shut it. She's my neighbor, and we're becoming friends."

"You and the new admin?" Jess asked as she slipped

onto the stool opposite Kenny right as Adam brought a tray with a pitcher and a bunch of pint glasses. "Oo, thanks Doc."

With an exaggerated sigh, I gave her a look she had to recognize. As one of the best female operators and now one of our best Saint Security employees, she had to know this one well.

"We're friends."

The chorus of "*Sure*" and "Uh-huh" and Tristan's traitorous silence had me sliding off the stool. "You know what? Time for another round. I'll go get it."

No one said anything, the conspicuous presence of Adam and that full pitcher pointing a flashing red arrow at my nonsense claim, but I wasn't going to acknowledge that.

Grumbling under my breath, I made my way to the bar and forbade myself to glance toward Nikki's table. I didn't need to tempt myself with another look at her—that auburn hair and her casual, appealing outfit. No reason for it to call to me, but it did because *she* wore it.

As Kieran pulled our beers and Gem shook a Boston shaker for her patrons down the line, I marveled at my response to the newest Silverton resident.

I'd never been like this with anyone else. The only thing that held my attention—with a constant buzz in my mind, as though it held my hand and always lingered on the tip of my tongue—was work. My active-duty time had consumed me, and I'd let it, welcoming the enveloping stress and demand of a job that instantly became my whole life.

Not until I'd realized how bad the situation was with Mom and Kiley did I begin to come down from the perpetual high of being the best, the literal answer to some of our nation's more complex scenarios. And once I did, the guilt set in—the reality that I'd been so consumed with work, I hadn't noticed my own mother's decline, my sister's father becoming more erratic, and my sister struggling in her own ways.

I'd never had more clarity than the moment when Kiley looked at me and said, "Boo, I'm scared." And I'd never felt more violence course through me, which was saying something for a man who'd spent much of his life ridding the world of terrorists.

By the time Kieran had filled a tray of drinks, I'd grown restless, the pull toward Nikki almost unbearable. It'd taken every bit of willpower to give her space to learn her job and not constantly check on her and take her lunch and show up on Rosie's doorstep to ask how she was feeling about things at the end of each day.

At least, I recognized this wouldn't be the right move. Smothering her wouldn't endear me to her. Perhaps the worst part of all this was that I shouldn't want it, and yet, I did to a bone-deep degree. I wanted her to like me, to need to be around me the way I seemed to require proximity to her, and I wanted her to *want* me.

I'd been wanted before. I'd had women make that clear.

I had never been so desperate to have one particular woman want me, nor had I felt this unbearable desire for one person—body, yes, but mind, too. Maybe it was her genius—maybe I was one of those idiots who found big brains irresistible. Perhaps it centered on her honesty, that stark willingness to tell me the truth even if it made the moment uncomfortable. She wouldn't compromise her opinion or the truth just to make someone feel better, and I found that eminently appealing. I couldn't fault myself because she had everything I wanted and never realized could be packaged together in a way that didn't just appeal to me, it *demanded* of me.

It demanded my attention, my time, my concern, my care.

Goodness, I was tired of the way it all chased around me, never letting me rest from thoughts of her.

And yet.

As much as I protested, I kind of relished it, too. Because even though I didn't know why I'd decided to latch onto this woman at a time so patently bad, it felt like... something.

"You get waylaid by the pirates?" Kenny asked as he snatched a beer from the tray I set down.

"The pirates?" Jess asked.

Tristan tipped his chin toward the bar, where Kieran and Gem were serving up drinks at a rapid clip, each hand busy with its given task.

"Oh—wow. Yeah. I see it."

And if I hadn't become familiar with the typical female responses to Kieran, I would've laughed at the way her gaze hung on him and her mouth stayed open, like it'd lost its way home.

"Yeah. Kieran's the most piratey, but Gem..." Kenny's voice faded out as his own gaze snagged on the female bartender. Kieran had a dark-haired, dark-eyed look that made him appear a little rough. His lighter skin and Gem's dark arms were both tattooed intricately... really, Gem's standing next to Kieran gave her the pirate vibe, but Kenny had nicknamed them after hearing my friend Dahlia Wallace mention that Kieran's romance hero trope was pirate.

"It's busy tonight. I wasn't trying to rush them. I was gone for, what, five minutes total?" I said, pushing back against Kenny's attempt to make it seem like I was lingering.

"Whatever, Jaws. I know where your head's at."

Kenny's ensuing wide-mouthed smile and wink had me this close to shoving him off his stool.

But as the evening wore on, I did nothing to dissuade them from their suspicions that I had my mind on Nikki. I couldn't, because there she was, front and center. So when she, Catherine, Dove, Jo, and Elise wandered over, all giggly, every atom of my existence stood on alert.

"Well, hello, ladies," Kenny said, because of course he did.

Catherine smiled and blushed instantly, and the other three giggled. But Nikki sidled right up to the table and stood next to me, the curve of her hip against my side. This effectively lit me on fire internally, not unlike how it feels to dump quick-clot powder into a wound. The burn, the heat... and yet none of it wrong or painful like the battlefield medical tool. No warning signs or flashing awareness of how this would hamper my efforts to complete a mission.

Nothing but a pure kind of pleasure-pain that made me grit my teeth to keep from tracing the belt around the edge of her jeans and tucking my thumb into the waist at the other side, close and proprietary.

I wouldn't do that, because she wasn't mine to touch, even if that flare of wanting made it feel like she should be. Even if her nearness made it feel like she wanted to be.

Then her eyes were on me, those long lashes blinking in at a lazy clip that unlocked the riddle—her inhibitions were lowered. Maybe not all that much, but more than they'd been an hour ago when we'd talked. Enough that she didn't mind leaning into me, or staring into my eyes without break-ing, a little longer than she ever had before.

"Hi," she said, so quietly no one else heard it over Kenny's questions for the others.

"Hey. You feeling okay?" My arm did what I'd wanted

to for a while now and made contact, my hand sliding to her lower back. I'd touched her there before, so it seemed okay. It wasn't possessive—not exactly. And everyone at the table already knew I liked her.

Her teeth caught her lower lip, eyes still on mine, and flames licked through me. The intensity in her gaze, the lazy calculations happening inside that mind, captivated me.

One corner of her mouth pulled up into a little grin I'd never seen before.

"I'm good. You?"

"Very good. How are you getting home?"

Her brow furrowed a touch. "I'd planned to drive, but then I had two beers on an empty stomach, so, probably not."

"I'll take you."

"No, you don't have to do that. I can—I'll call a rideshare." Her gaze shifted around, and her cheeks flagged with a blush.

The look I gave her spoke for me, and she huffed silently as I stood. Without breaking eye contact, I asked, "Ready?"

Her lips parted, but Kenny interjected before she could speak. "You leaving, Nikki? You and your girls don't want to pull up a chair?"

My gaze shifted to him, and I'll admit, I glared at him. Because the instant I'd offered, the desire to be the one to take her home clutched at me, and there was no going back. To have her in my car, in my space, and to deliver her safely had become a mission I'd assigned myself and would certainly not fail.

"These two have to get up early, and Bruce offered to give me a ride, so I'm at his mercy." She glanced at me, then smiled at the table.

"Have a good night, then. Drive safe, Jaws." The taunting lilt in his voice would've made me roll my eyes if he hadn't followed up with more. "And ladies? Always a pleasure."

I could've sworn his eyes lingered on Elise, but then he winked at me just to piss me off, and I urged Nikki to follow after her friends.

"Be good!" he yelled as I exited, my own cheeks heating as I held the door for them.

Normally, I wouldn't be affected by their razzing, but they'd touched a nerve. Not by harassing me—they were idiots, though they were also supporting me in their own weird way. It wasn't their commentary that bothered me.

It was the brutally vivid imagination I had and one that revealed that, when alone with Nikki, I had absolutely no desire to *be good*.

CHAPTER SIXTEEN

Nikki

Bruce had good hands.

Big. A little rough, like he used them, but not pure callouses or anything insane. Warm. Steady. Strong.

Really? Two beers and I was rhapsodizing about the man's hands? I'd enjoyed the pretzel bites and chips and guac we'd ordered, but my appetite had flagged considerably after the news of Rosie's stroke, even as my desire to guzzle about ten beers had grown. Granted, I didn't *actually* want to do that, nor would I—a key difference between Nikki at thirty-three and Nikki at twenty.

But two beers had been enough to drown out the peevish little voice in my head that told me I shouldn't be close enough to touch Bruce. It was *just* enough to let me relax and enjoy that he held my hand on the way to his car, and apparently enough to send me into paroxysms of admiration over his hands. Granted, were I a poet rather than an accountant, I could've written sonnets about his forearms and odes to his biceps. I'd jot down haikus for his jaw and scribble an elegy for the loss of my reason thanks to the knowledge of his cut chest and abs my very first view of him had given me.

I must've made a sound, because Bruce glanced at me. "You good? Going to be sick?"

"Gosh, no. I'm not drunk. You really think I pounded through enough alcohol to be that inebriated? I would've had to make drinking my job over the last hour." He couldn't see my mildly irritated expression, but I caught the flick of a smile over his face.

He chuckled low. "You've clearly never been in charge of a bunch of soldiers before. They often do drink like it's their job."

I grinned at that. "Best not to disappoint Uncle Sam."

"Indeed. Just so long as I'm not on cleanup crew." He shook his head like the memories had taken ahold of him. "I do not miss those days."

"You got out last year, right?" I asked, though Gram had mentioned it.

"A little over eighteen months now, actually. But my days babysitting soldiers came to an end quite a few years ago. In the unit where many of us served out our more recent years, there aren't many lower enlisted soldiers. Of course, there are idiots everywhere, even when we specifically test and assess to avoid them, but it's nothing like a bunch of homesick eighteen-year-olds who suddenly have steady paychecks and can't wait to buy a fifty-thousand-dollar brand new pickup and blow the rest on video games and Rockstar energy drinks until they're old enough to get beer." He shuddered.

I laughed. "Should I be concerned I reminded you of all of that?"

He pulled onto his and Rosie's street and grinned, full-out. My stomach flipped.

"No. You don't remind me of that at all. But sometimes, Kenny does, and sometimes bars do, and sometimes the memories just hit, you know? Funny how that happens."

He eased into his driveway and parked, then slipped out of his seat, and before I realized what he was doing, he opened my door.

I unbuckled and turned to get out, yet he stood there, brown eyes set to stun.

"Uh, hi," I said, because it'd been so brilliant when I'd said it earlier. Nerves shimmered through me, and my heart pattered.

"I should let you get out," he said, eyes tracing over my face one feature at a time. *Eyebrows. Eyes.*

"You could," I said.

Nose.

"I could."

Right cheek. Left.

I nodded.

"Or," he said in that low, rich voice that made smoke curl in my belly.

Chin.

"Or." It was all breath out of my mouth. Pure anticipation.

Lips.

But he didn't lean in yet. His head notched to the side like he was disappointed in himself. "Or I could kiss you."

That smoldering gaze found mine, and I pulled in a breath, trying to steady the riot inside me at his close attention, the way he'd stepped between my legs.

"That is a thing you could do." I couldn't have repeated whatever weird sentence I'd cobbled together to save my life.

"It'll change things, Nik. I'm not a man who's going to pretend I don't want you after this, especially if I taste you now."

I sucked in a breath, everything in me fluttering and so very, very interested in everything he'd just said. "Okay. That's okay."

Even if part of me attempted to shout that this was a terrible idea and falling for my next-door neighbor slash boss who was ten thousand galaxies out of my universe was not smart, I tipped my chin up in welcome.

And Bruce, as he'd proven every time since I'd first spotted him, didn't disappoint. One of those big, warm hands rose and slid along my neck, his thumb gliding over my throat and his fingers curling against the side before his whole hand slipped around back and drew me into him. Complete control.

Complete and utter bliss as he bent and his lips touched mine. A light press, then a break. A pause to look in my eyes, and then Bruce Camden broke my brain. He made every synapse pause on its journey except those registering pleasure and joy and need and heat and something foreign, something almost terrifying that I'd never felt.

Something told me this kiss *would* change everything. Just like he'd said. Spaces on a crossword in my mind quickly filled, clues and answers dancing, and it almost felt like he'd known just how much this kiss would mean. How utterly consequential these seconds, now minutes, would be.

When he pulled back—and make no mistake, it was his self-control and not mine that ended the kiss—his gaze held something I'd never seen or imagined. Clear, no regret to read, but such an intense expression, I sucked in a breath and forgot where to go with it.

I expected him to say something, but instead, he just stared. Like I was the answer, the missing piece, and I had absolutely no idea what to do with myself now. Not when his fingers gently tucked a few strands of hair behind my ear, then he leaned forward and pressed a kiss to my cheek and stepped back.

My palm slid against his as I held onto him and stepped down from the truck, then plodded behind him on wooden legs. If he hadn't worked his ridiculous magic on me that halted all logical thought, I would've had questions. But I couldn't think of anything except *Bruce Camden just kissed me* and *He's right. This changes everything.*

"I'll talk to you tomorrow. Sleep well, Nik."

I slid my key into the lock and stepped inside, then let my eyes linger on him as I closed the door before I sank against it. My thoughts a jumble as usual, a smile crept over my face and I touched the pad of my index finger to the bow of my upper lip.

Yes, that changed things.

CHAPTER SEVENTEEN

Bruce

Cliché though it might've been, I walked home on clouds.

Kissing her had been... it'd been—

"Are you and Nikki dating?"

Kiley's voice startled me enough that I fumbled my keys, and after juggling them between my hands, finally caught them and dropped them onto the counter. A juvenile impulse made me want to pretend I had no idea what she was talking about and skulk to my room, but the adult, the guardian in me, spoke louder, even in the wake of recent events.

"You okay? I thought you were sleeping over at Janie's?" I eyed her slouchy sweatpants and baggy shirt, her face scrubbed of makeup and her hair pulled away from her face. None of this was particularly unusual, and yet her being here sort of did send up an alarm.

If she needed me and I hadn't been here because I was out at the pub with friends or even taking Nikki home, I'd make it up to her.

"I'm good. I just wasn't feeling great, so I came home."

Alarm spiked again, and I crossed the kitchen in three easy strides, then squinted at her. She might be a little pale, though her cheeks were red now, and maybe increasingly so. She hugged herself around the waist and had a little hunch in her back like she hurt. Without thinking, I put a hand on her forehead to feel for a fever, but she shoved it away.

"I'm not sick, Boo."

"Then why do you—" *Ah*.

"Yeah. Period. Super fun. Did you want any more details?" She cocked her hip and crossed her arms and gave me so much teen attitude, I might've laughed if I couldn't see the strain around her eyes.

"Not particularly, but do you have everything you need? I can run to the store. Tampons? Ice cream? Heating pad?" I catalogued what else she might need, turning to check the freezer for her favorite flavor.

She whipped around and padded away from me, her fuzzy slippers skating across the floor toward the cabinet where we kept the over-the-counter meds. "No, I'm good. Seriously, I just need some pain reliever and then I'm going to read in bed."

We still had her ice cream. I'd make sure she had a good breakfast tomorrow, too. She'd only grabbed a banana before school today, and even though I normally harassed her about that anyway, she needed more to fuel her body. I should've been emphasizing that. I should be making her eggs or whole grain protein waffles—something to give her body what it needs to function properly and grow.

How many years had she lived off the bare minimum, scraping by with whatever scraps she found in our mom's house? How had I—

"I'm fine, Boo."

Shutting the freezer, I looked over at her. "I'm sorry you don't feel good."

Her lips thinned, then pulled down in a frown. "You know what would make me feel better?"

"Donuts?"

Her smile flashed. "Maybe. But also, for you to go out with Nikki."

I shifted on my feet. "How is that related to anything?"

She gave me a glare I recognized all too well. "Because I don't want you to put your life on hold because of me. I appreciate what you're doing here—giving me a home and a life. I know it's a sacrifice. It's a really good thing you've done. But I don't want you to suffer for it."

About ten things happened inside me at once, but the overriding need was to make one thing very clear. I paced to her and took her by the shoulders.

"Ki, I need you to understand one thing before this conversation goes any further. I am not suffering. You living with me is not a sacrifice, it is a *joy*. There is not one ounce of me that regrets becoming your guardian. The only thing I regret is not doing it sooner."

Her chin wobbled, but this kid had been through a lot and rarely let me see her break down, even now. She pressed her lips into a line to recover, then nodded. "Okay."

The response came too quickly, but I accepted it for now. "I don't want you to think I'm giving anything up. I'm only gaining—time with you, getting to watch you grow up... it's good."

Her lashes fluttered, and I could see her debating with herself over something.

"Just say whatever you need to say. You can tell me anything." I hoped she knew that—believed it. I hoped she felt safe to say whatever she needed to, even if it was that she hated me for taking her away from her life in North Carolina or that she missed our crappy mom or that she wanted to hang out with her trash pile of a dad. I wouldn't *like* any of those things, but she could say them. She had a right to any feelings.

I let my hands drop and watched her swallow hard.

"I heard what you said to Wilder and the guys. Last week."

The words pierced my gut, a deep ache hitting immediately. "What did you hear?"

She huffed. "That you put your life on hold. That you need to take care of me and not do anything else. But I call BS on that, okay? I'm not that hard to handle, and you can date someone and still keep me from imploding or whatever it is you're worried about."

Ah, great. This was bad in about ten different directions, but that was life with another human. "I don't think you're going to implode. I think you need stability and someone who's tuned into you. I work a lot already, and I don't want something else to take my attention from you, okay? I want you to know you're loved and supported, and you have someone who has your back, always."

She rolled her eyes and appealed to the ceiling. "I know that. Obviously."

The words sounded right, but that defensive posture, the edge in her voice, told me we hadn't resolved this. "I love that you want me to have a life, but I *do* have a life."

And yes, maybe I'd decided to put part of that on hold, though I honestly couldn't say whether this decision was still in place after tonight.

"Yeah. You work, you come home, you grocery shop, you make me dinner and take me to dentist appointments. It's the stuff of dreams, huh?" Her hazel eyes skewered me.

A chuckle tumbled out, her dry delivery so perfect, I had to appreciate it. "I can see how it doesn't seem like all that much to aspire to, but it's a good life."

She sighed, a long-suffering sound that might've earned her an Oscar if she had played it across from Jack McKean on film. "Okay, it's good. Let's say I accept that. I then raise you the suggestion that next door is a woman I happen to know you have a thing for, and based on that dopey look on your face when you walked in earlier, you're not even trying to deny it. So why not take her out? I have my own life and I have, like, a million things going on. You can go on a few dates and not neglect me."

I sobered at this—at how she'd so clearly seen my interest in Nikki. "I didn't realize I was that obvious."

"No? Well, then I'm gonna have to call into question all your special unicorn training or whatever you did in the Army because you are *not* stealth."

I cracked up at that. "Yeah? Maybe they should take away my retirement or something?"

She shrugged a shoulder, then grabbed a spoon from the utensil drawer. "Definitely disavow you or whatever. It's an embarrassment, frankly."

Good grief, this kid. "Well, thanks for your kind words."

She pulled open the freezer, grabbed a pint of her favorite ice cream, and nudged it shut with a hip.

"Anytime, Boo, anytime." She raised her spoon in salute but paused when she reached the stairs. "And seriously, ask

Nikki out. Think of it as a favor to me. Anytime you go out with her, I can stay out with Marcus or have a friend over, right?" She turned and winked.

"That's not—we'll talk about that," I said as she disappeared up the stairs. She'd played me like a fiddle, the mini con artist, and I couldn't do anything but appreciate it.

I reheated some leftovers and ate them in a kind of daze, my mind replaying the conversation and teasing through every piece of information she'd let slip through her quips, and more so, those things she'd taken time to think about before saying.

She had this soft heart she didn't want me to know about, like revealing it would make me love her less. Like if I knew she wanted me to be happy, it might bother me, or if she explained why it bothered her that I'd wait to date, I'd be mad. It had to stem from the way she'd grown up—feeling like a burden, and then ultimately, becoming one, or so she thought.

Having her here wasn't a sacrifice, though what stuck between my ribs was the realization that I'd been thinking of it like that. Shame twisted around my heart and squeezed, a ratchet strap drawing tighter and tighter at that truth. I'd been thinking about waiting to start my own life, at least the part of it geared toward finding a partner and making a family beyond me and Ki, as a sacrifice.

I didn't think I'd actually consciously thought of it like that, but there it was—the ugly truth. Kiley had seen it and called me on it, and though I hated that she had a reason to, she'd given me a gift tonight.

She'd made me see myself without spin, and she'd given me permission to do something I didn't realize I'd needed her go-ahead for until she'd given it.

Her blessing.

And she'd given it, even if it'd come in a joking way, and even if it'd ended with a spin that made it seem like all she was after was more time *without* me.

Finally, my thoughts shifted back to Nikki. It'd been an effort not to let my mind and body sink back into the memory of her warm body, her lips, the way her breath caught, and how good she felt in every way. I'd held it off as long as I could, but as I sank onto the side of my bed and flopped back onto the soft comforter, I cut the leash.

Her hands on my shoulders, the back of my neck, in my hair. Her mouth responding to mine, opening for me when I demanded and answering every press with one of her own. She'd wanted the contact, wanted me close, as much as I'd wanted her.

But had she felt it?

Had she been thunder-struck by the realization like I had?

I'd only heard of things like this happening. It'd become a fable of sorts, a kind of lore passed down in dark times to give us hope.

Someone had whispered of it on a mission in the black of night while we waited without comms to infiltrate an enemy compound. We'd arrived at dusk and had to sit for hours until the dead of night, and he'd told our team about the legend of the operator's love match. I'd been annoyed, had only half-listened as he spouted some story about how the operators who were pure of heart always found their soul mate. It'd been a throwaway in my mind at the time.

I hadn't believed it until I'd seen Wilder and Sarah, though even then, they'd already had a history, a story that needed an ending, and I'd assumed it was that.

But when my lips touched Nikki's, something cosmic shifted into place. I'd never thought about stars aligning or fates at work, but this felt so unbelievably *orchestrated*, so completely full of magic and purpose and rightness, I believed.

I'd found my soul mate, and now, I just needed her to recognize it.

CHAPTER EIGHTEEN

Nikki

Gram sat nestled into her favorite chair in the living room by the time I dragged myself out of bed the next morning. I'd lain awake for hours turning over every minute of my time here, and especially the time just before I'd gotten in bed. Any hope of using those late-night hours to make progress on the game had fallen by the wayside after that kiss.

"You look like you've been on a journey." Her brows arched high as she sipped her coffee.

I plodded into the kitchen, legs leaden, and poured myself some of that very necessary caffeine. "I think I traveled a thousand miles in my head last night."

Her gaze tracked me as I moved to the couch and got situated, alternately clutching the almost too-hot mug to me and taking sips. All the thinking I'd done last night had turned my mind to mush.

Or maybe that had been Bruce Camden busting the basic algorithm of my being. Yeah, either way.

"Did you make new friends? Those girls are lovely."

For some reason, this irked me. "How do you even know them?"

"I see Dove at the clinic, and she and Catherine both have grandmothers about my age and we're friends. But you forget that I've lived here nearly all my life, and I know most everyone who was here before the boom."

"Boom?"

She grinned. "A few years back, we had a boom. It's continued to this day. There were a few factors. First, the state opened a road they'd previously closed, thereby making the commute from Salt Lake City Airport about half of what it was. Second, Jonas Bauer moved in and took the reins on the resort and ended up expanding it, though it was a bit of a battle. And third, Julian Grenier partnered with the little Morrison boy to start the neighborhood where all the celebrities live now."

A guffaw tripped out. I couldn't recall ever making that sound, but the way she'd said *the little Morrison boy* as though Jamie Morris was an eight-year-old playing in the front yard instead of the grown world-renowned rock star deserved the response.

"Don't be so shocked. I knew him before he ever picked up a guitar. I remember when this town was nothing but Odds and the first-generation Diner and Will Morrison set up his lodge." She looked a little wistful as she took a sip.

"I didn't think about it like that, but I guess you would." She'd lived here almost all her life save a stint in California. She'd come back before I was born—when things got bad with my parents.

"Point is, I know them. They're all good girls, just like you."

My turn to raise a brow, which she swatted away like a pesky gnat in the air. "Don't tell me you think your sealed juvenile record precludes you from having nice friends?"

The warm mug tethered me to the moment, keeping me from flying off to distant times when I'd been so angry and wounded and lost. "I think it might've, for a long time. But coming here—I talked myself into getting a fresh start. I told myself I needed to *try* and not let my past, both the distant past and the more recent—shade everything."

She nodded approvingly. "Good. That's just the thing."

Frustration spilled over, and I couldn't dance around it anymore. "You asked me to come help you and I'm glad to, but you never told me about the stroke. How could you leave that out?"

She took a small breath, studying the bright blue-and-red rug on the floor in front of her before speaking. "I know it's not enough, but here's the truth."

I straightened, bracing.

"Getting old isn't for the faint of heart. The stroke was... kind of miraculous. Everyone said so, your new friend Dove included. And while I was very happy to be the recipient of a miracle, it took me to a hard place. One I'm not sure I can explain very well, except to say that I didn't want to face it."

Logically, I understood her reluctance to some degree. That had clicked on some level, especially as someone who preferred keeping things close. But the tender insides that seemed to be closer to the surface merely by stepping into Silverton, the great-niece in me... that part still ached at the thought of her keeping something so important from me. "I'm sorry. I'm sure it was a shock. I guess I just don't understand why you wouldn't have at least called once it was over. I don't want you to think I can't handle things."

Her regretful smile looked so sad, it felt like a slap. "I am truly sorry you found out the way you did, Nikki. I love you and it's true that I didn't want to upset you, but I know you can handle a lot—more than I think anyone should have to, really."

We sat with that truth between us for a moment before I answered. "And then, you did ask me to come. You asked me to help you, but you didn't tell me why."

Saying it out loud, part of me wondered why it even mattered. Did it? When I liked it here and I'd been so relieved to have a purpose, to have a place to go and a reason to go there?

"I wanted it to be your choice. I didn't want you to come out of obligation."

Why that made my chest tighten, I couldn't have said.

"I do have an obligation to you, but it's not a bad thing. I don't—" I cleared my throat. "I *want* to have people I'm obligated to. When you grow up like I did, it's a burden *not* to have anyone expect anything from you, either because they underestimate you due to your past or because they don't know you well enough to think they have a right to. I *love* that you took me in and cared for me when you did, and—"

"I wish I could've spared you all the rest. I wish I'd found you sooner."

Her voice shook, and I had to grit my teeth to keep the emotion brimming at the edges of all my frayed parts from rushing over.

"You came when you found out. And you dealt with me at what was my absolute worst. I have you to thank for any normalcy and semblance of a life I've had, and I was honestly relieved to have you mention coming back here." There, the whole truth of it.

I'd spent just shy of two years here, finishing up high school online a year later than I should've graduated, then doing odd jobs in the town and for her, keeping my head down and doing my best not to get close with anyone while I knocked out a handful of virtual community college classes. I'd loved her then, but I'd still been so angry with my parents for dying, and then with her for being unreachable for so many years that I spent in foster care. By the time I left for in-person college back in California, I'd had a twinge of regret. I'd wondered what it would've been like to just stay here with her and make a life near family and be... happy.

But the thought of failing at that had driven me away. Maybe more so, the fear of her failing me had gripped me, so I'd only made sporadic trips to her and she came as often as I allowed. Yet, we'd grown close on those visits and during phone calls and texts over the years, and I'd started therapy on campus, then continued it after. My growth, her steady presence even from afar, and the connection we had by blood and bravery meant she was the dearest person in the world to me.

Losing everything in California, I realized more and more, had been a kind of a choice. Losing Gram now? I couldn't handle it. And that, more than her not telling me, was what scared me so much. The thought that she wouldn't have asked if my life hadn't been falling apart had me shuddering inside, and yet, here we were. Facing the hard things head-on.

"I'd hoped maybe that would be the case. I didn't want the stroke to confuse things for you and honestly, though my chances of another one are increased now, I'm no worse for the wear. Psychologically, it has taken a toll, but I think I've moved from feeling sorry for myself into a determination to live my life to the fullest. To stop pretending I have all the time in the world." Something flashed in her expression, then she tucked it away.

I hated that thought, but having lost my parents at a young age, I'd never escaped the reality that we didn't know how much time we had. I'd coped with it first with anger and acting out, then with working myself into a version of life that'd ultimately meant very little to me. Amazing that I'd only realized this now, years down the line, once it was all stripped away.

"So you don't really need my help? I've been wondering what it is I'm supposed to do with you," I joked, hoping it would lighten the heaviness in my heart.

She shook her head. "I mostly need you to tell me about my strapping young neighbor and whether he's a good kisser or if it's all just a pretty face." She winked.

My mouth dropped open, and my cheeks flamed in an instant. "Were you spying on us?"

Her cat-that-ate-the-canary smile made my eyes grow wide, then she chuckled and waved me off. "I'm not *that* bad, child. I heard his truck pull in and saw you get out. Tempted though I was, I gave you your privacy. But I did note a certain passage of time that told me you must've had a riveting conversation or..."

Could a person expire from embarrassment? I was solidly in my thirties, and yet the thought of Gram knowing I'd been kissing Bruce was... well, for some reason, it made me feel about fifteen.

"You're a busybody," I said, scowling at her.

"That isn't in dispute."

The way this woman wasn't fazed by me.

"I'm not sure I can live here if you're going to be... whatever this is." I nodded to her and tucked further into myself, cradling the barely warm mug to my body like it'd save me from my nosy grandma.

But her expression made me pause. I could've sworn it was something like regret etched on her face, the lines bracketing a mouth that'd always smiled wide deepening.

"You don't have to stay, Nikki. If you'd rather—"

"Please. Please believe that I want to be here. I know I was desperate when I called, but I did have options. I *want* to be here. I want to take care of you, if there's any way to actually do that—if you need anything. And I'm... oddly hopeful about everything." The blush softened, though I could still feel the heat there. *Everything* now encompassed a lot more than simply figuring out a semblance of a life.

Everything was Gram. Work. New friends. The mountains.

Bruce.

"Well, I think he's a good thing to be hopeful about."

My head snapped to her. "What?"

"You said 'Bruce' all dreamily, which I'll take as my evidence that he can deliver more than just a delightful show when wielding an ax." She winked again.

I died. I'd always known my tendency to be direct had come from her even if it hadn't been through blood, but clearly, it'd diluted through the generations in comparison. "Gram! You can't talk like that."

She pressed a hand to her chest. "Can I not? Who says?"

I laughed and ducked my head to hide my now even more brightly burning blush from her.

She pushed out of her chair and steadied herself on the arm of it for just a second before she said, "Speaking of

Bruce, it's been on my schedule to spend time with Kiley tonight. Will you come?"

Tonight?

Weirdly, I'd sort of been planning on seeing Bruce. But if Gram was scheduled to hang out with her, then he must have plans. A date? *Did* he date?

We'd kissed—like, *really* kissed—last night, but as I'd reminded myself a thousand times since the blessed event and *thank you so much for the reminder, brain* again now, I had no idea what it meant. Maybe he was just a man who liked to kiss women. Just... willy-nilly.

"Nikki? Are you free?"

I snapped out of my nonsensical spiral. "Sure. Of course. I'll be there."

And I would *not* succumb to the tug of disappointment in my belly or the sense of loss not seeing Bruce had caused. A lot of good had come out of this conversation, and there was no reason to feel like anything was wrong.

CHAPTER NINETEEN

Bruce

If I chopped wood every day this fall, I'd still likely have more to chop, and we'd still have to buy a cord of wood this winter. I'd chopped as much as I could earlier in the summer, so at least that would be properly seasoned come winter. None of this lot would be ready to burn until late in the season, but it helped with the restless energy, so I'd take that happy byproduct.

I'd spent all morning refusing to call Nikki. Not that I didn't plan to, but since I woke at six and had a feeling she'd sleep a bit longer, I needed to wait. No man called a woman he'd kissed for the first time less than twelve hours after. Or maybe people did that—I had no idea. I hadn't been in a relationship in years and certainly not one in these circumstances.

Certainly not one my gut told me was *it*.

"You realize that chopping wood is, like, super loud and annoying and you probably woke Nikki and Rosie?" Kiley stood with her back to the banister of the deck stairs, right at the bottom on the stone pavers I'd laid last summer.

"Did I wake you?" *Chop.*

Her dead-eyed glare, not unlike one I had to give bad guys and idiots, answered for her.

I let the head of the ax drop into the stump and stick, then brushed my hands together to soothe the raw feeling I always got after wielding the tool for very long. "Sorry. Didn't mean to disrupt your beauty sleep."

Her eyes narrowed. "You saying something?"

I chuckled, relieved her hackles were only put-on and not actually that reactive. One never knew, these days. "Obviously, that's not a comment indicating you require beauty sleep to be beautiful, Ki. It's merely an observation that beautiful people sleep. In my world, we call that beauty sleep."

She smirked. "In your world?"

I nodded, taking a swig of water from the bottle I'd left on the little bench by our bee and butterfly garden. That'd been Kiley's idea and the first sign she wanted to have her own stamp on things. It was still my favorite part of the back yard.

"Yes. In my world. It's serious business, sleep, so you can trust that I am an authority on the matter." I was talking a bunch of nonsense, but it'd been a while since we'd just blown smoke.

"Yeah? Is that why you're so bad at it, then?" She crossed her arms and kicked one leg over the other in a pose so relaxed, it would've made me smile but for the insult.

"Bad at something? You couldn't possibly be talking

about me." I chuckled when that garnered me the biggest eye roll in history. "Careful. They'll get stuck like that."

She scoffed, then laughed. "That's how I know you're not just my brother—that right there."

And even though she'd said it light and jokingly, I felt it. Dang, but did I feel the reality that I was more than her brother. I was her guardian, and that title held weight. It was both duty and honor, privilege and responsibility, and one I'd gladly bear. It was a gift to watch her grow into whoever she'd be, especially considering how little I saw of her when she was younger.

I hated that my being her guardian meant our mom hadn't been able to be a parent to her. But I'd never been more appreciative of my idiot self for getting into the Army at seventeen and doing whatever I could to save up and build the things I'd never been certain of as a kid. I hadn't built a family, but I had the makings of one already—me, Kiley, and this place.

"Seriously though, I think Nikki likes to sleep in, so you might want to adjust your quiet hours or something." She turned and trudged up the stairs to the deck, then leaned on the railing and spoke down to me. "And you should probably throw on a shirt and think about showering before you try to flirt with her, because you're all sweaty and gross and it's not cute." She made a face and her eyes flicked up toward the neighboring house, then she swirled on her feet and padded inside.

I turned just in time to see Nikki step out onto her porch. Her hair was slung back in a ponytail, face makeup free, a fluffy mint green robe hugging her upper body and—I swallowed. Her legs and feet were bare, and a flash of heat sent my heart beating faster, my own feet moving toward her like they ran this show.

Her robe ended just above her midthigh, and nothing stood between the end of that soft-looking material and her painted toes, and I wondered if I'd ever wanted to touch something so much. Not the robe—the miles of skin revealed below it.

"Hey. You're out early." She smiled when she noticed me, then her eyes flared.

I should've put on a shirt. I could've popped inside and showered and knocked on her door now that I knew she was awake. But I'd had no thought in my head other than the compelling need to be closer to her, to be near her *now*.

"I was a little restless this morning. Thought I'd get some energy out."

She bit her lip, and a handful of other ways I would like to *get some energy out* battered my mind.

"That's, uh, yeah. That's good." Her gaze slipped down my torso, snagged on the tattoos shadowing my pecs and over my shoulders, and then hit my face again.

I grinned when her blush darkened. How I loved the pale complexion that gave her away. Otherwise, she had a stellar poker face—at least sometimes she did. Right now, her expression said something, and it wasn't that she found me *gross and not cute*. On this, Kiley was apparently wrong.

"Hope I didn't wake you up. Kiley said I need to observe quiet hours until at least ten for the sake of the neighbors who might want to sleep in." I glanced at my watch—nine fifty-eight.

She shook her head, an amused smile gracing those beautiful lips. "I appreciate the sentiment, but I don't sleep in that late and Gram's up at eight or earlier most days. I think maybe she was pleading for her own sake."

"Could be," I said, finally reaching the step of her deck. I set a hand on the post marking the end of the railing, just next to where she stood. Even having my hand within a foot of her made me feel hotter.

"So... what gave you all that energy so early?" she asked, eyes boring into mine.

"Just... thinking." Over the years, I'd earned a reputation for being charming. Glad to see my ability to finesse and flirt had failed me so completely right when I wanted it.

Still, one side of her mouth slid up into that reluctantly amused smile she did sometimes, and I didn't mind so much.

"Sounds profound."

I nodded. "It sure was, right until Kiley came to tell me to pipe down and that I was all sweaty and gross and not cute and I couldn't talk to you until I'd showered and put on a shirt."

Her lashes fluttered. "Well, she's a smart kid, but nobody's perfect."

A laugh tripped out, her comment so dry and unexpected, I grinned full-out at her. She smiled back at me while my stomach did somersaults. God, she was pretty and funny and smart, and I did wish I wasn't all gross, because I couldn't invade her space like this even though it was all I wanted.

"True, true. No one cares about sleep."

She rolled her eyes as though exasperated. "You know very well that's not the part she's wrong about."

I played dumb because *obviously*. "Really? Well then, what part is she wrong about?"

Her eyes narrowed on me. "You know you're gorgeous, Bruce."

I had no lack of confidence, true, but I didn't know *she* thought that. She was honest enough I didn't doubt she'd tell me the truth if I asked, though who wanted that? Granted, I was fishing like a pro right now. Thankfully, she seemed to be enjoying it.

"So you don't mind me all sweaty and gross and not cute?" I tilted my head toward her. We were only about a foot apart, but I stood on the ground and she on the slightly raised deck. She set her coffee onto the wide railing and got closer, leaning in another six inches.

"That's where she's wrong, and you know it."

"I'm not sweaty?" I was pushing this.

I was an idiot.

I'd accepted my plight.

She shook her head slowly, biting her lip in a way I *knew* she meant to get to me, and *mission accomplished.*

"You are that," she said, her voice low and a little raspy, textured with the morning and little conversation.

"I don't need a shower?"

Her grin flashed before she tucked it away. "I'm sure you could benefit from one, though I'm not complaining."

Pressing my lips together, I hid my answering smile. "Then what's she wrong about?"

She held my gaze, steady and mesmerizing with her light brown irises practically hypnotizing me. "She said you aren't cute."

I waited, ready for whatever she was going to tell me. Ready to slide my hand into her hair and hold her by her ponytail, steer her mouth to mine, and devour her.

Then she closed the distance and pressed the quickest kiss known to man to my lips, just enough to send fire racing through me to chase after her, but she'd already pulled back.

"You're not just cute, Bruce. You're adorable."

And then, she tapped my nose like I was a toddler, gave

me a huge smile as she grabbed her coffee mug, and sauntered inside. I could've sworn she'd been swaying her hips
with more emphasis than usual, and though I didn't mind
the view, she'd stunned me with her quick exit.

And I felt even more like a goner than I had before.

CHAPTER TWENTY

Nikki

I'd escaped with my life this morning, but just barely.

What I'd really wanted to do was touch the taut skin stretched over rippling muscles, never mind the sweat and dirt. Who cared about such things when he was all sparkly-eyed and charming and even just a touch embarrassed.

I'd also completely forgotten to ask about hanging out with Kiley, or what his plans were for the day, or if he'd like to make plans to kiss me like the world was ending again sometime soon.

You know, just casual topics of conversation. I'd thought about the kiss, yes, but I'd given him a little peck just to make clear I was still very much interested. Not that he seemed insecure about that considering the way he'd sauntered up in his jeans and boots and no shirt and all that chest.

Maybe I could petition the town—something about sightseeing and the betterment of the tourist experience in Silverton if Bruce was required to spend at least a few hours a day shirtless outside his home?

I didn't *love* the idea of other women ogling him, but I sure did enjoy the prospect for myself. Plus, I couldn't blame anyone for wanting the view. It was just so... unreal. I'd dated attractive men here and there, yes, but no one had looked like someone had painstakingly carved each muscle from granite.

Okay, you have to stop thinking about this man while you're helping his sister with her homework. Because, yeah. I was sitting here at the table in Bruce's kitchen chatting with Kiley and helping her with her math club work, and I did *not* need to be remembering just how much self-control it'd taken to keep from sweeping a hand across her brother's glorious abs.

"I think I kind of hate calculus." She stared at the page in front of her, then slumped down and her forehead *thunked* on the table.

"Ah, I see where we are." I slumped along with her, resting my head on the table facing her so that when she blinked open those pretty hazel eyes, they found mine instantly.

"Yeah? Where are we? Is hating calculus a thing all super geniuses experience or is it just for us mortals?"

The snark was strong with this one, and apparently, Rosie or Bruce had told her something about me, but that was entirely beside the point. "It's less calc and more the shocking lack of brain food."

She made a face. "Is this where you tell me it's time for some carrots and hummus or a protein shake or something?"

I reared back. "No."

She laughed despite herself, then lifted her head. "Really? You're not going to try to stuff me with natural peanut butter and apples for the fiber or offer me cheese sticks and edamame and—"

"I had no idea it was this bad." My hands on her shoulders now, I gave her as serious a gaze as I could muster. "I'm going for supplies. I'll be back in five minutes. Your mission, should you choose to accept it, is to preheat the oven, wash your hands, and get out a large bowl and some measuring cups and spoons."

Her amused grin bolstered me, but her excited "Okay!" sent me jogging to Rosie's. I threw a smattering of ingredients into a bag and ran back, all under five minutes.

When I burst through the door, she had prepped the space and was washing her hands. I set the ingredients down and joined her, and we got to work. Thankfully, Rosie had bought the ingredients, planning to make cookies tonight, so the butter and eggs had been sitting out and had already come to room temperature.

"So who is the monster who suggests you eat those horrible things?" I nudged the eggs her way, along with a measuring cup for her to crack them into as I tipped the last half cup of flour into a bowl.

She chuckled. "I think you can guess. It's Superman himself, obviously."

"Superman?"

She gave me a look that said something like, *as though you hadn't noticed.* "Yeah, you've seen him. I know he went and talked to you earlier before he took my very wise suggestion to clean up first."

Okay, bold. I hadn't expected her to be so direct, but I certainly appreciated it. "He did."

"And you kissed him."

The baby blush I'd been sporting deepened, but I focused on packing brown sugar. "You were spying?"

She shrugged. "I need him to get a life, and you are the first person he's seemed interested in since I've lived with him."

A small sigh escaped her and drew my attention. Her expression had dimmed.

"Does it bother you? I think, so far, it's all just friendly and flirty. It's nothing serious. I don't want you to think I—"

"That's the problem, though. He's bound and determined not to have anything interfere with his ability to take care of me or whatever, like I'm this huge project he has to stay so focused on. And I get that he feels bad for how things were for me, but I feel like he's missing out. I know for a fact he would never say it out loud, but it's the truth."

She crossed her arms, staring at the bowl in front of her as I gathered my thoughts. *Wow.* I hadn't seen that level of honesty coming and recognized it for the rarity it was. And I wondered if maybe it was time she knew a bit more about me.

"Did you know I was in foster care for a while?" I asked, watching the fine grains of sugar slither into the large glass mixing bowl.

She jolted. "No. Why? When?"

"Here, unwrap these and put them in here." I handed her two sticks of butter as I stirred the two sugars to combine them. "My parents died when I was eleven. Rosie was here in Utah and wasn't in contact with them or really anyone at the time, so they couldn't find her. Had no way to notify her. So I went into the system until I turned seventeen."

Her mouth opened slowly, like the words wouldn't come. "I'm sorry. I didn't know."

"I didn't tell you that to make you feel bad or sorry for me. I wanted to share it because it had a big impact on me. I went through some rough years after that, even after I found Rosie and had someone to love me unconditionally. It was still... hard to accept." She didn't need all the details that came before foster care, all the mistakes after. At least not yet.

She ducked her head, nodding a bit. "I get that."

My heart squeezed. "Bruce didn't tell me much about why he's your guardian."

Her eyes found mine and she studied me. "I'll tell you, if you want. It's not a great story."

"You can tell me whatever you want, whenever you want. I'm a listening ear and as someone who had some hard times with the whole parent/nuclear family situation, I might understand more than most. But what I want to say is that I know for a fact your brother loves you and is glad you're here."

Her brows knit together, and a pained look lanced across her face. "I know. I don't want to seem ungrateful. I— I appreciate him. Even the carrots and protein and all of it."

I nodded. "It has never once occurred to me that you were ungrateful. Encouraging him to live his life isn't a lack of gratitude. I think it comes from how much you love him."

She sniffed and dipped her chin. "He's done so much for me, and I know he's glad to. He says that all the time like I might forget. But he's a single man. He just got out of the Army and can finally do whatever he wants, and now he's, what? Offering to buy me tampons and taking me to the mall?"

I plugged in the hand mixer she'd gotten out—shiny and new and very likely never before used, if I had to guess— and set it down. "Yes. He is. Because like you said, your brother is a *man*. And I'm sure there are things he might add to that list if he wasn't trying to stay focused, but he's also establishing a business and a new sense of home living here. And yes, he's doing that for you, but I think he's doing it for him, too."

She swallowed, digesting that. "I guess."

I smiled. "I don't know him all that well, but I'm pretty confident about that."

She just eyed me, more than a little bit of that teen reluctance shining through.

"Now, how about we finish up these cookies, and then I'll eat the dough but tell you that you can't, and then we'll do a few more problems before they come out of the oven?"

She scowled. "I can't have the dough?"

I shrugged. "I'm just trying to give you the authentic experience here. As an adult, I know getting salmonella from raw cookie dough with eggs is definitely a thing that can happen, though I'll need to review the statistics on that. *Ooo*, we should do some statistical analysis on the likelihood—"

She groaned. "I maybe hate stats more than calc."

I grinned. "You know, for a kid who hates math so much, you sure seem bound and determined to figure it out."

She might complain, but she didn't give up. Being innately good at math was helpful, yes; still, being doggedly stubborn and determined was one of the more important qualities—in math *and* life.

"Anyway, I'll tell you it's not safe to eat, because I genuinely don't want you to get sick, but I will eat quite a bit of it because raw cookie dough is amazing. I'm just prepping you so you know what to expect."

She gave me this perplexed look and blinked. "You know, you're a very strange person."

I laughed loudly at that. "I'm going to take that as a compliment."

She shrugged again like it was all the same to her, yet I could see a little tug of a smile at her mouth. "You can, I guess. I wouldn't tell Bruce to try to date anyone else, that's for sure."

Then she picked up the hand mixer and stuck it into the bowl, the beaters whirling and making enough noise I could only watch and smile and revel in the good feelings of the moment.

I had no idea what Bruce wanted with me, but I hoped knowing Kiley was at least verbally on board with... something... would ease his mind. I hoped it would free him up to do whatever he *wanted* to do with me—and I really hoped he had some of the same things on his list as I did.

Standing there in that pristine kitchen, the clatter of metal beaters on the glass bowl and whirring small appliance engine cushioning the moment, I soaked in the reality of those thoughts.

I wasn't shielding myself from Bruce—physically, emotionally, or anything else. I was standing here hoping he'd come home and talk to me, ask me out, and take things between us further. Having just waded through memories of my past and some of what had made me difficult to be around for so long, of what had kept me from wanting anything from anyone, I marveled at it.

It seemed far too soon, so completely illogically premature to even think, and yet there it was: I not only wanted something from Bruce... I might actually want *everything*. The question was, if he wanted the same thing, would he let himself have it? And would I be able to follow through with all these open, good feelings? Or would that past I'd done my best to make peace with come calling?

CHAPTER TWENTY-ONE

Bruce

The buttery-sweet scent of cookies met me at the door and slowed my movement to a dead stop at the sight before me.

My mind raced through a thousand thoughts in the face of that scent and the sight of Nikki sitting on my couch with her head dipped low over a laptop.

There's this thing that happens in special operations—particularly in the unit I was assigned to and others like it. Some people cave to it and others manage to withstand it, but in the end, everyone has moments when they think they're *special*.

And yes, having grown up on a steady diet of Mr. Roger's Neighborhood as my babysitter, I know we are all special and that's all wonderful and good. But I mean special as in *exceptional* and therefore deserving of exception. This translates to all manner of things.

First, it's an important ethos because in many ways, it's simply true. The amount of resources and training poured into top-tier operators across the US's black ops community is gargantuan, and coming out of that system means you are actually one of the best in the world. Period.

This can go to a person's head, though. Especially when many of the support systems in place at whatever military base or compound are made to prop up the confidence, skill, health, and welfare of the warriors. Nutritionists, trainers, special training ops that doubled as borderline luxury vacations... it sounds ridiculous on one hand, but in another way, it makes sense. And when you're the guy training to infiltrate some far-off reach and kill bad guys or rescue American hostages and literally take a bullet for the president or some other head of state—it's not just for the Secret Service, folks—you start to believe it's because *you* are necessary and chosen and at times, invincible.

I'd reflected on that mindset more than once in the last year or so since I'd left active duty. I'd inched away from the action the last two years of my career, but for a solid ten years prior to that, I'd been EMU, and I'd been the best. An elite soldier in one of the most illustrious fighting forces ever to have existed.

And yet.

And yet, since leaving, I'd come face-to-face with my humanity, my mortality, and my struggle to do simple things more than I liked to admit. The transition hadn't been easy, but all things considered, I had no regrets about how I'd handled going from demigod status to regular-guy land.

There are always small moments where I think about this odd shift—going from escorting the President through a war zone one day to tripping over the cobblestone on my front walk the next. The glare of that change could burn a little sometimes, but I hadn't felt it like that in a while now.

No, lately, I'd felt this welling sense of gratitude for the shift. The systematic deflating of my ego, of my sense of self-importance waning, had only brought me closer to reality—or at least, my new reality. I didn't need to feel superhuman anymore. The mission set ahead of me wasn't one that required a sense of exceptionalism that would keep me sharp, focused, and steeped in the belief that I could accomplish whatever task my government had asked of me.

What I needed now more than ever was the ability to get down into the realities of life with Ki, and I hoped soon, with Nikki.

Having a brilliant, beautiful woman I couldn't stop thinking about sitting in my living room when I got home amounted to no small thing. It hit me in the gut, stealing my breath and causing an ache in my heart. The scent of cookies greeting me, an occurrence I wasn't sure I'd ever experienced, made me oddly homesick.

It couldn't have been for my childhood. My mom hadn't struggled as much when I was younger, but she'd never been the cookie baking type. Or, maybe she would've been, but she'd always had to work.

Setting my keys down, I took in the evidence of a used kitchen—a large mixing bowl drying in the rack by the sink, a wooden spoon and metal beaters next to it. A tray of cookies on the stove, about half of them gone. Everything else had been tucked away save a small grocery bag of what I guessed were ingredients sitting at the end of the counter closest to the door.

My heart thudded a slow, heavy beat like this all meant something. The scent-memory effect had addled my brain, apparently, because the fact that Nikki had made cookies with or for Kiley felt like something oddly close to heart-breaking, but in a curiously good way.

What is this?

"Oh, hey, I didn't hear you come in."

Nikki's soft smile only heightened the effect of the moment, as did her quick rise from the couch and movement toward me like she was glad I was here. Like she'd been waiting for me to come through that door—looking forward to it.

"Didn't mean to startle you," I said, my voice a low rasp.

She blinked, startled by my tone, maybe. "How was your afternoon?"

Gazing at her as she approached, I could hardly remember anything before the moment I walked in. My mind had slowed and stuttered to a stop when I'd come through the door, a sense of rightness and *home* hitting me so completely, I was making a fool of myself now.

"Good. Fine."

She tilted her head and reached for my hand, the contact with her fingers sending delight shivering through me. "You sure?"

Now that she'd made contact, I took the liberty to tug at her hand and pull her closer, into a hug. A breathy chuckle slipped out against my neck as though I needed one more thing to solidify the visceral overwhelm of the moment, and her arms wrapped around my torso.

"Seriously, Bruce, are you okay?"

The slight edge of alarm confirmed just how oddly I'd been acting, but I couldn't pull away from her just yet. I didn't want to break the closeness between us to talk or try to explain my thoughts. So I tucked my face into her auburn hair and let my lips graze against her neck as I said, "I'm fantastic."

Her body moved with her chuckle, then deflated with relief. "I thought something was wrong." She held me tighter, evidently not immune to the moment.

Slowly, so slowly, I brushed my nose and lips along her skin, the tender place behind her ear, savoring the soft huff when I pressed a kiss just above her shoulder. One more second of this, and then I'd pull back and we'd move on to the talking.

Her hands slid into my hair and she leaned to the side, the beautiful sweep of her collarbone and shoulder more exposed now. And instead of moving away, I set out on the trail she'd laid before me, one press of lips to skin, one flick of my tongue, a failure to resist letting my teeth edge into her just a bit before soothing over it with another kiss.

My hands were steady at her waist, but the small gasp she made, the way she urged me closer with those fingers in my hair, had all my usual logic oozing into the floor, trampled by the bonfire of need that'd risen up in me since I'd crossed the threshold into this house.

So I moved, sliding my hands over the curves of her to her hamstrings and lifting right as she read the action and hopped. A feral sound loosed in my chest, approval for her response and maybe an unleashing of something, too. She sat on the edge of the counter and I stepped between her legs, meeting her eyes for long enough to send fire into my veins before I nipped at her mouth, barely brushing the beautiful arches of her top lip with my own.

"The only thing that's wrong is that I can't stop thinking about you." My voice was low and gruff, and my body hummed with barely leashed desire.

Her nails scraped along my scalp, and her mouth tipped up into a smile. "I'm not sure that's a problem—only if you say it is."

I chuckled low and it sounded a bit sinister. Still, something in me felt this moment was weighty—with all the wanting, yes, but with a gravity that meant things I couldn't decipher right now with her scent mingling with the sweetness of the cookies and her hands urging me closer.

"Fair point, but I'd also submit that it is if *you* say it is." I reluctantly leaned back enough to see her face right as her hands slipped down over my shoulders and clutched at the fabric of my shirt.

Her gorgeous eyes looked nearly drugged, and my hands flexed where they rested atop her thighs to keep from hauling her closer. But then, she hooked her legs around me and urged me into her space, bodies flush, and she kissed me.

The contact was all I needed to push me from the man who'd inspected every action in the last few seconds, the one trying to keep his head, into a man given over to the current. Her hands at my neck now, mine sliding up, up, up her jeans and around her hips to press her closer, one remaining there while the other mapped the ridges of her spine before cradling her neck, the back of her head.

Every place she touched sent heat sizzling through my veins, and every press of her lips or touch of her tongue sent my heart pounding harder. I couldn't get close enough, touch her enough, taste her enough.

There were far too many things between us—clothes, for starters. And—

A loud *thump* sliced through the passion and stopped me. Nikki froze, too, then pulled back and held her hands aloft like touching me was akin to getting caught red-handed in a jewel heist.

"Kiley," she said, and the word did its work.

It sobered me enough to realize I'd been thinking

about wanting Nikki so much I'd forgotten my sister—the child I was bound by duty, honor, and love to protect—could've walked in on us. And no, I wouldn't have stripped Nikki down and had my way with her right here on the counter, but it wouldn't have been ideal to have her trot down the stairs to find us in the throes of each other.

Though maybe someday when we have the house to ourselves...

"Kiley," I said, too, my breath still coming fast as I worked to calm myself. And I *did* need to calm myself. Nikki's legs had dropped away, but our bodies still pressed close. Her scent in my nose, her kiss on my lips, there was simply nothing I wanted more than to start right where we'd stopped. But my sister could walk in at any moment, and that just wouldn't work.

A smile cracked her startled face open, and then she laughed. She slapped a hand over her mouth and kept at it, and I couldn't help but laugh along with her, this interruption shifting from sobering to a bubbly, fizzing feeling unlike anything I'd felt.

"Guess we should probably..." Ever so reluctantly, I stepped back, promising myself it wouldn't be the last time we got close like that.

Her cheeks had stained red with a flush so delicious, I had to swallow down the longing the sight of her beautiful face caused in me. But she wasn't upset or even embarrassed... this was from us. From kissing and being kissed and getting close. For some reason, the swirl of red on her cheeks and crawling up her neck made my heart clutch.

Her laughter tapered off, and she hopped down from the counter once I stepped away enough to give her room. She wasn't all that much shorter than me, but the counter had provided a nice boost, and having her feet on the ground made me wish I could hug her.

Wait. I *could* hug her. I needed that closeness after the... well, after the closeness. The intimacy of kissing and the harsh interruption of my beloved teenaged sister banging around upstairs—though admittedly, I did see why that was ultimately not a bad thing.

With a predictable, slow pace so she could refuse me if she needed—not that she seemed inclined to—my fingers coasted along the dip of her waist and around to her back.

"What—" She inhaled, not exactly sharply, but enough to cut off her words.

My other arm looped around, and with hands pressed firmly but gently between her shoulder blades and over the curve of her spine a few inches lower, I pulled her into me. After a short beat, her arms encircled me, returning the light pressure on my back.

We stood like that for a few seconds, just breathing together in this moment. My heart's clattering from earlier had calmed, and the utter peace that descended on me now would've shaken me if it hadn't soothed me.

When was the last time I'd felt so utterly comfortable and settled and *good*?

Eventually, we broke apart. She rounded the kitchen island, and I gripped the edge of the countertop because if I didn't, my hands would've tried to find their home with her.

She gathered up a purse and slung the bag of ingredients over a shoulder.

"Tell her I had a great time." She flicked her eyes to the stairs, where we'd both expected Kiley to come loping down any minute.

"I'm sure she'll say the same," I said, wondering if she

knew just how true that was. "I doubt she's gotten to bake much."

She only nodded.

"I should do that more, I guess." I glanced at the sheet of cooled cookies on the oven. I didn't really bake, but who else would teach her? My mom certainly hadn't. I didn't think Rosie was big into sweets, either. But the fact that Nikki had...

"Listen, I—" She swallowed and glanced down at her hands.

Alarm rose like smoke in my chest. Would she call this all a mistake? What was *this all* anyway? A quick encounter in the kitchen because I'd showed up all antsy and ready to see her, only to find her happy to see me and I'd lost my mind?

I braced for the words, the bad news, praying whatever she was trying to find would come quickly and put me out of my misery.

When she glanced up, she had the most angelic look on her face. Something warm and vulnerable and more than a little apprehensive. "I'm in. For whatever this is. I don't know if you've figured it out yet or not, but... I'm in."

I laughed out a breath of relief. "Me, too."

"Good."

I crossed to her, unwilling to let her go without more contact. I enveloped her in another quick hug since her arms were out of commission, then kissed her temple, her cheek. "Let's get dinner tomorrow night."

Her smile soft, she seemed almost relieved as she nodded. "See you then."

CHAPTER TWENTY-TWO

Nikki

On the way out the door to meet Catherine, Gram stopped my progress as she grabbed her keys.

"Where are you heading?" I asked, gathering my sunglasses and purse.

"Off to meet a friend for brunch. You?" Her brows arched high, and her makeup looked perfect. She didn't wear much day-to-day, but it looked like maybe she'd taken extra care, likely because she was going out. She had a definite social butterfly pace to her life. I'd always known she had friends, but again, that whole *her needing help* thing had made it feel like maybe she'd slowed down.

She definitely hadn't.

"I'm meeting Catherine and Dove at the new coffee shop. I guess they've been in once and it was super cute, so they wanted to go again."

She smiled. "That was nice of them to include you. I'm so glad you're getting along."

I chuckled but nodded. Not as though we were teenagers fighting, yet a fair enough statement considering there'd been a time when *getting along* wasn't in my repertoire. In fact, the last time I'd lived in Silverton over a decade ago, I'd had no friends. I'd held myself aloof from the small-town effect here, sneering at the close-knit community rather than becoming a part of it. Doing my course work online had only aided me in staying apart from anyone who could've been a friend.

How different my life might've been if I'd allowed myself to get sewn into this little tapestry, another thread in the bustling local life. *Alas.* Something about both parents dying, toxic foster situations, feeling alone in the world at one of the most volatile times developmentally... I'd forgiven myself for the missed opportunity for the most part.

"It is. I'm grateful."

Her gaze sharpened, and she turned to me. "Don't be grateful, Nikki. Just stick."

I swallowed. How many times had I heard that, a phrase that'd become a kind of catch-all, even when I'd left. I had definitely *not* stuck before, and part of me ached with the memory of it even after all this time. Still, I got it, and I nodded in agreement. "I'm going to. I am, Gram."

The shudder of self-doubt that arced through me got elbowed into a corner. I hadn't ever *stuck* before, but I'd never had a reason to. Or, when I had, I hadn't been in a place where I could. Now I had reason, and I wanted desperately to believe I had the ability, too.

Gram had proven she'd stick. I'd pushed and pushed when I first moved here. I'd tested her in a hundred ways, but she hadn't wavered. And even after I'd left—another way of trying that faithfulness, that love of hers—she'd stuck. She hadn't guilted me or condemned me. She had supported me, loved me, visited me.

She had stuck and had shown me the beauty in it.

Needing her to understand that I wasn't going to abandon her and go back to California, that I would be here if something happened again, or even if it didn't, I took her hands in mine. "You stuck with me, even when I moved. And I'm sticking with you. I'll be here, *right here*, and nothing's going to change that."

Her brows pinched for a moment, and her smile looked a little wobbly, then she pulled it up into a grin and clucked. "I'm not worried. But I *am* about to be late, and I bet you are, too. Let's go be fabulous women about town, and I'll see you for dinner?"

My stomach flipped. "Actually, I'm having dinner with Bruce."

The smile this time was all genuine and pleased as mimosa punch. "Of course you are. You can stick with him, too, if I have my say."

I huffed, but the grin pinching my cheeks gave me away. She waved as she backed out of the garage and I followed, doing my best not to look too many times at Bruce's house. I'd slept decently well considering the earth-shattering kiss and then the agreement we'd made.

Maybe it hadn't actually been an agreement, but it'd felt like we both knew this—whatever was going on between us was something important.

With a slow exhale, I silently prayed for that to be true, and more so, that I wouldn't mess it up. I'd never felt so much for a person so quickly, and that in itself should've been terrifying. Except whenever I did feel that fear edging in, he'd do something like simply hug me. Not push for more physically or even emotionally. He'd just... connect. And that touch settled the wild thing in me that hadn't ever had something like this with anyone but Gram, though of course with Bruce it was different.

By the time I pulled into a lot at the end of Snow Street and found Cat and Dove sitting at a small table inside Joe, I'd mostly quelled the nerves over my date with Bruce tonight and shifted into anticipation for seeing friends.

"Hey, girl! Oh my gosh, I love that top."

I was learning Dove was the kind of person who led with compliments and enthusiasm. In a world full of criticism and envy and comparison, it proved kind of startling because there was nothing false in it. I hadn't known her even a week, yet I knew she meant it.

"Thank you. I love your dress." She had on a marigold short-sleeved dress with little cream flowers all over it. She'd worn a dress on Friday, too, something equally sweet and pretty. I'd gone for jeans and a teal blouse that looked great with my hair but was honestly nothing special.

"I wear dresses when I can because when you spend your work life in scrubs, there's something wonderful about feeling a little more composed." She tucked a golden flyaway hair behind her ear.

"That makes sense," I said, knowing that if I didn't wear some version of a suit to work, I might feel the same.

Catherine sighed. "I wish I felt that way. I'm mostly just tired, and even though I smell like fried chicken and pie when I leave work in my uniform, I rarely feel like pulling on anything other than sweats and a T-shirt when I get home."

Dove grinned. "You look adorable in your sweatpants, so it's great. Plus, who cares what you wear? You're amazing."

If I wasn't looking at the sincerity on her face, I would've rolled my eyes. It was the most saccharine statement ever, something another person would simply throw away, but this woman meant every word.

Catherine blushed deeply, though her soft smile seemed genuinely pleased as she turned to me. "Did you get to talk to Rosie?"

"I did, thank you for asking. We got it worked out for the most part, I think." I hoped. I felt better after I understood her perspective—not wanting to upset me and all that. Didn't mean I agreed with her, but I got it more so now. And I hoped my being here would help her feel better about letting me see when things weren't quite right. I wasn't going anywhere.

"I'm glad. She's so great and I hated the thought I'd messed something up."

Dove's worried face plucked a heartstring I hadn't realized existed.

I patted her hand. "Don't worry at all. I'm glad you said something so I knew and we could talk it out." She returned my smile with a heartened one of her own, and then I noticed the growing crowd in the shop. "All right, we better order some coffee, or the owners are never going to let us come back."

"Not true." A masculine voice had all of our heads finding it and my heart rate quadrupling.

Because there he was. The man I couldn't get out of my head.

"Oh, hi, Bruce. What are you doing here?" Dove asked, a coy little look at me in the least subtle move of all time following her question.

A flash of his perfect white teeth had me swallowing hard.

"Kiley and I decided to get coffees and new books this morning. We needed a pick-me-up."

Nothing in his expression tipped me off, but I searched his face for answers. He winked, then turned to look at Kiley, who was waiting in line at the register. Somehow, I hadn't even noticed her walk in.

"Better get our orders in before she ditches me for someone cooler," he said, an adorable expression that made me want to kiss him sketching across his face.

"Are you—is everything okay?" I asked as quietly as I could.

His gaze captured mine. "Now?" He reached down and took my hand, then pressed a kiss to the back of it without breaking eye contact. "Yes. Everything's great."

Heat warmed my cheeks, and I failed to hide my grin. Then he released my hand and moved to Kiley, chatting with the man behind the counter and nudging his sister with his elbow.

"Oh... okay. Yeah. I know we're just getting to know each other but can we please hear a little more about that?" Dove's voice was dreamy as she blinked after Bruce.

When I turned my attention to them, Catherine was nodding, wide-eyed and eager.

"Let's order and then I'll catch you up."

My gaze flicked to Bruce's back. *Ugh.* He looked great from behind, too. If I didn't know him, I'd see his tall form and wide shoulders, that narrow waist and the dark hair, and I'd be curious. I couldn't imagine encountering the man in the wild, just out of nowhere and without warning.

Granted, I'd seen him shirtless and sweaty as he chopped a half cord of wood when I'd arrived, and I wasn't sure that view was a particularly good place to start since, when I saw him later, I already knew what freakishly ridiculous muscles he was hiding.

"Your order?" A cute guy with a beard waited patiently as I blinked him into focus.

Apparently, I'd been daydreaming of Bruce as my friends had ordered. *Get ahold of yourself.* With a chagrined chuckle, I placed my order and stepped to the end of the counter, where the girls waited. More than embarrassed by my mental wanderings, I was disappointed that I'd missed saying goodbye to Bruce. A quick glance around the coffee shop showed that plainly.

"Okay. Spill."

Dove got her coffee, then Catherine, and then mine came up. We returned to our table and snuggled into the little alcove that would provide some privacy. Not that I expected anyone to be listening, and I didn't recognize any of the other patrons, but the shop was filling up and I didn't love the idea of becoming the topic of small-town gossip.

"We all have coffee, and I saw him glance back through the window twice before he and his sister walked away, so I need to know before I explode."

Dove's anxious excitement had me grinning.

"Well, I'd hate to be responsible for that after only knowing you for a few days. It's really just..." My insides followed the hill and valley trail of a cosine, and I shook my head. "Actually, honestly, it's not *just* anything. We're going out tonight, but it feels... significant."

Was that an odd thing to say?

Maybe. But it was true.

I couldn't deny that every interaction I'd had with the man felt more significant than the last.

Dove squealed and clapped as Catherine beamed. Their genuine excitement for me, a person they barely knew, had one of those hopeful rays of light shining all through my heart. Was this what it felt like to dig in? To let people in and have them do the same? Why had I hidden from it for so long?

"Oh my gosh, I love it. I *love* it. Plus Nikki Camden has a nice ring to it."

I burst out laughing, more of a cackle than anything more dignified, and both of them joined me. "I think that might be getting a little ahead of things. We've both got a lot going on, and technically, he's my boss."

Dove waved that away while Catherine shook her head. "I realize it's different, but Wilder and Sarah Saint got together *while* she was working for Saint Security. So, you know, there's a precedent if anything."

"I'm not actually worried about that, thank goodness. He's my boss, technically, but so far, he doesn't seem to be the person I report to or interact with most. And I'm not planning to be there for long." Though even saying that felt a little wrong somehow.

But that had to be the work I'd done over the years to *stick*. Like Gram said. I'd wanted to be someone who could be trusted and relied upon. I'd wanted real relationships and a community. Or so I'd said.

So I'd *stuck* in my job, in my relationship, in my apartment, for years and years and years until it all imploded. Had I really stayed and engaged? No. The last few months had painted that in red all over the pages of my life, and there was no escaping it. Which was why it made me both antsy and hopeful to think of staying here but not staying *static* here.

Ultimately, I'd confused *sticking* and *changing*. Or at least, that's how I'd been explaining it to myself.

All of this in Silverton—the friends, having family here,

getting close to Kiley and especially Bruce... all of it felt so much different, so much better, than it ever had when I'd conflated sticking with just being stuck.

"Well, I'm excited. And I hope you'll decide you like us enough to tell us what kissing Bruce Camden is like because...." Dove loosed a dreamy sigh.

Catherine's eyes narrowed on me, or maybe the rosy tinge overtaking my face. "Wait, have you kissed him?"

I stared back.

A gasp from Dove and another grin from Catherine, and though I wasn't particularly shy, I covered my face with my hands. Dove pulled my hands away, eyes wide.

"You have. *You have.* And it was good. It was... *so good* if I'm reading your beet-red blush right." She bit her lip, and I could've sworn her eyes went all sparkly like a cartoon full of hope.

I laughed, a weirdly relieved and elated sound, but finally confirmed. "Ten out of ten, would kiss again."

More shrieking, the other patrons all turning to look, and me ducking low to avoid the spectacle even though I sort of reveled in it. When was the last time I'd had someone so excited *for* me? Had I ever?

Truth was, I didn't think so. I'd only just met these two, and yet, they were proving to be more engaged friends than I'd had in California for a decade. They were making me even more excited to be here, to stretch down deep with my roots and *stick.*

CHAPTER TWENTY-THREE

Bruce

I stared at Kiley's cellphone screen and the message bubble there, racking my brain for what response would be best.

The internal conflict waffled between rage, fear, and a small voice of reason in what felt very much like a void shouting *this is not necessarily a bad thing.*

"Boo? What do you think?"

Her worried eyes pleaded with me to tell her what to do.

And this was the part of parenting that was so relentlessly hard. Because how could I tell her what to do here? What guidance could I give her that wasn't potentially wrong?

Contact from her father had apparently been getting more frequent. He'd called her from prison last summer and she'd answered. It'd been a two-minute conversation, and it'd taken her a week to shake it off. As far as I knew, he'd called twice since. I'd convinced myself he'd get lost if she just didn't answer him, and I'd be able to kick the can of dealing with this particular headache. Granted, that willfully ignored that she had answered him, though minimally. Basically, I'd been living in a fantasyland that Carl would shrivel up and crawl back into the hole he came from.

We'd had a great day. Coffee and books. A few seconds with Nikki, obviously a benefit only to me since Ki didn't get to talk to her, but still. We'd sat on the patio and read, even chatted a little. We'd played our nonsense game of giving awful names to fake new shops downtown—the winner being *Yeasty* for a new bakery. She'd done some homework, and I'd done some yardwork and then, well, this.

"This is my new phone I'd like to call u and talk."

But I couldn't throw a hissy fit like I wanted. I couldn't stomp my foot and say that it wasn't fair and that I didn't want to have to deal with her idiot father because that wouldn't be helpful or instructive or anything other than self-serving. So, instead of doing any one of those or a hundred other things like I wanted, I steadied myself with all the professional skill at controlling my emotions and facial expressions I'd honed over the years and asked her, "What do *you* think?"

Her lips thinned. "I don't know. That's why I'm asking you."

"I get that, but this is your call, Ki. If you want to talk to him, you can. If you don't, you don't have to." And I shouldn't admit how much I wanted it to be the latter, but I did. This man had abandoned her *and* our mom, and there was no love lost between us. I'd communicated with him via my lawyer only long enough to have him sign his parental rights away, which he'd been more than happy to do.

He'd just gotten out of jail, after all, and wanted his fresh start. I didn't understand why he wanted back into her life or what he'd say, and every protective instinct in me roared on high alert.

She exhaled an aggrieved breath and scrubbed her face. "I don't know. I can't tell if it'd be good or bad."

Heart aching for her, I put a hand on her shoulder and squeezed. "I'm sorry. I don't know the right answer here, and I wish I did. But I don't think there's a playbook for this. I think you go with your gut, and whatever it says is fine. But I think if you do call him or let him call you, I'd like to be there for it."

Her brows raised like she was surprised and something else, then she nodded. "Okay. Can I think about it for a while? If I do, I want to just get it over with. I want to decide so the decision isn't hanging over me."

"Makes sense. Just let me know. I'll be here."

She snagged her phone and with a mumbled "Thanks, Boo," she disappeared up the stairs.

Once she was out of sight, I ran a hand through my hair and loosed my own sigh. I had no sense of what she'd choose, but I prayed whatever she landed on would be the right thing. And I prayed Carl Caruthers wouldn't be a bigger idiot than I already knew him to be if she decided to hear him out.

After that moment to collect myself, I pulled out my own phone. My plans for the evening had just changed, and I hoped Nikki would understand.

The evening air was cooling, and in a few weeks, it'd be downright cold. I relished that after spending so many years in North Carolina, where fall didn't truly set in until well into November most years. The bourbon I sipped was smooth and oak-barrel-aged, and it'd done nothing to take the edge of disappointment and frustration off the day.

Kiley had tucked herself away under the guise of needing to do homework. I didn't blame her for retreating into herself—she needed time to think. More than a small part of me had hoped she'd emerge for dinner and decide she didn't want to talk to him, and we'd button that up with a response and be done with it.

But life wasn't that simple. Feelings about our parents, especially messed-up ones like Carl, weren't easy to identify much less act on, especially when he'd been all but nonexistent since before we'd left North Carolina.

Another sip of bourbon, the smooth smokey burn slipping over my tongue before I swallowed. The stars were glittering tonight, high enough in the darkened sky I should've gone inside. It'd grown cold, the clouds from the day drifting off and leaving the air crisp and tinged with fall. Despite the view, I stared into the liquid in my glass.

"How are you?"

My gaze lifted to see Nikki standing at the edge of the patio, arms tucked tight around her. The moon peeked over her shoulder and cast her in silhouette—still, she had the usual effect, something in me pulling taut and another something easing at the same time.

Words had failed me all day today, and they did so again now. I held out a hand to her.

She answered by approaching, accepting my weak offering, her warm, smooth palm connecting with my startlingly cool one. The fall air had soaked into my skin, and her warmth was like nestling next to a fire in the dead of winter.

"I'm sorry," she said just above a whisper.

In North Carolina, there might still be crickets chirping and frogs talking outside. There'd still be humidity and enough buggy attention for anyone daring to be out of doors that I wouldn't have sat on my porch there. Such a small thing, but sitting out here in the cool air, only the distant sounds of wildlife in the trees and the low hum of the house's central heater clicking on and off occasionally, was its own kind of pay raise.

I'd called her earlier, after Kiley had showed me the text and more importantly, her hand. She'd kept her cards close about this until today—I'd seen underneath the shell she coated herself in. I'd seen the fissures racing along the surface and I'd known. I couldn't leave her.

Even if she didn't want me tonight, even if she had no intention of calling her dad in front of me, I had to be here, and I couldn't be distracted. Nikki had understood, even without quite so much explanation, that this had to come before our much-anticipated date.

"I don't know why it's hitting me so hard." My fingers wrapped around hers tight, and I bent to press my forehead into her hand. The spark between us, the feeling of elation and anticipation every time I saw her, had morphed into something like need and respite at once.

I needed her closer, but this was different.

"You love her. You're worried for her."

Her words were soft and low. Intimate. She released my hand and let my head lean against her stomach, then sifted her fingers into my hair, nails scraping lightly along my scalp.

We stayed like that for a few minutes, me resting against

her, literally leaning on her as the ache in my chest dulled by degrees, her hands sifting through the strands of my hair until I pulled back and tilted my chin up. She held me there, supporting the back of my head and looking down at me like she cared.

Maybe I should've been embarrassed by how wordless I'd been tonight. I wasn't introverted, and this was a woman I wanted to spend time with, get to know more every minute, and yet I couldn't apologize for this. *This*, evidently, was who I was now.

"I am worried. I don't want her to hurt any more than she already has."

She moved to cup my face, her palms gentle at my jaw. "You can't keep her from pain indefinitely. It's part of the human experience. But it's wonderful you want to try—that you're working on ways to minimize it for her."

She traced one of my eyebrows with the pad of her index finger, then moved to the other. I could hardly parse out enough of my thoughts to speak, but I managed it after a moment.

"Will you sit with me a while?" That, at least, came through clearly.

Her face softened and she nodded, then bent to press a soft kiss onto my lips. It was so unlike every other time—no heat or intention, no destination or promise. This kiss simply pressed her to me, reminding me she was here with me. It let me know she'd be here, unequivocally, my gut said, and it made me recall another encounter in this very yard between us, when my world had tilted on its axis thanks to her refreshing honesty.

"Of course."

I leaned back and welcomed her, inching back on the

chaise lounge as she found her place next to me. She nestled into my side, and I curled my arm around her. "This okay?"

She gave me a small smile in the dim light and pressed another kiss to my cheek. "Of course."

Her being here didn't solve any problems. It did nothing to change the situation with Carl or to help Kiley decide what she wanted. It didn't take away the potential pain this would cause Kiley or give me clarity on what, exactly, my role was here.

But it settled the wild thing in me that'd been thrashing around for half the day, ramming into reason and logic and the perpetual fixer in me that wanted to just end the *feelings* with action.

It let that beast sit down and rest, lulled to a calm by knowing I wasn't alone in this. And for as much support and love as I had from Wilder and Tristan and even the book club friends, I'd felt lonely to the point of desolation more than once in the last year. I'd felt it into the marrow of my bones.

Yet, here she was. Not prescribing answers or making suggestions. Not telling me how I should feel. Not trying to talk it through.

She simply sat with me, sharing her warmth and touch. Fingers woven with mine, head resting back against the chair next to mine. She was just here with me, for me.

And what I'd known for an improbably long time in my gut spoke undeniably in this darkness. There was no mistaking this moment for what it was—a challenge in my life as guardian over my sister, yes. But also the moment when I knew, irrevocably and completely, that my heart belonged to Nikki Hastings.

CHAPTER TWENTY-FOUR

Nikki

I hardly saw Bruce at work the next week.

At some point after one in the morning on Sunday night, I'd gotten up and pulled him to his feet. I'd kissed his temple and told him to get some sleep, sending him and his empty glass to bed. I'd hoped he would sleep.

Bruce was a talkative guy, smooth on his feet and quick with words. The dearth of conversation had told me just how heavily this situation weighed on him. I'd known it was something serious when he'd asked to postpone our date. I'd had no worries he might be backing out or ditching me—we were adults. We were friends. There would be no games like that if he'd changed his mind.

Seeing him so upset had been oddly good. Not that I wanted him to struggle, and I certainly didn't want that for Kiley, but something about Bruce felt too good to be true. In a weird way, his being overwhelmed by what to do in an admittedly impossible situation brought him back down to earth for me.

That said, the next five days were a small form of torture. I'd see him in the morning, then not again the rest of the day sometimes. He had meetings and phone calls with international companies and check-ins with the guys overseas and off-campus meetings and so. much. going. on.

I was lucky to catch a glimpse of him during working hours, and at least two days this week, his truck hadn't pulled in until well after eight. Not that I'd been spying. I hadn't. *I'm not.*

But he'd texted on and off. Not during the workday, and somehow, I knew that was thanks to his wanting to respect the boss-employee relationship. Well, and because he likely had no time to even breathe let alone tap out texts to a woman he was thinking about dating.

He'd send something simple around nine every night. Just, "*Hope you had a good day. See you tomorrow,*" or "*Two days until our date and I can't wait.*" Little things to let me know he was thinking about me even a fraction as much as I was him.

And then came the call.

Thursday night, not too long after he'd sent the message about two days, he'd called. Thankfully, I knew he wasn't a psychopath and answered, praying this call wasn't coming for a similar reason as our only other one, which had come last weekend when he'd needed to cancel.

"Everything okay?" I asked, trying to sound less nervous and more breezy. *Mission failed.*

"Yes. I just..." A tired-sounding exhale came out. "I just haven't seen you."

I chuckled. "That's true. You've had a thing or two to deal with this week."

With a huff, he responded. "It's been crazy. Not all bad, but top it off with Ki's math club and her track tryouts and I'm toast."

"Did she make the team?"

"She did."

My heart flipped at the response because I could hear his smile. The big brother pride practically beamed at me through my phone.

"Good for her."

"Yeah. It'll be great for her to have that team dynamic. But listen, we're still on for Saturday, right?"

The urgency in his voice had me sitting up. "Yes. Unless you need to reschedule, I—"

"No. I don't. *I won't.*"

I grinned, for some reason holding my phone tighter like it might bring us closer. "Good."

"I was just thinking dinner. There's a new place which, now that I say that, I realize wouldn't matter so much to you since you just got here, but I thought we could try it."

Pacing my room now, I nodded even though he couldn't see me. "I'm good with whatever. I can imagine the same old options get a little tired."

"They can, though I don't get out all that much, as you might've noticed."

"Drinks on Friday nights at Craic with the team and maybe a coffee on Sundays. That's all I've noticed so far."

A loud gasp came through the line. "That's rather specific, Nikki. Are you tailing me?"

"Oh, no. Not tailing you. Just sifting through your garbage before you get home on your later nights. Totally normal stuff," I joked.

His laugh set butterflies winging in my chest.

"Oh, good. I was afraid you might be stalking me, but that sounds just fine," he said, that bright smile audible.

"Yep. All above board." My face hurt from grinning.

"Okay then, Nik. I'll see you soon. Sleep well."

The fact that I'd slept at all after that had been miraculous. Or maybe it had come thanks to the stimulating work. I hadn't anticipated being interested in the details of what Saint Security did beyond a kind of topical curiosity about what exactly they did and the natural inquisitive response I had to most new things. But the more I worked, the more I learned, and the more I learned, the more I wanted to know.

I liked the team Bruce and Wilder had put together. Kenny chatted with me, Adam was polite and solicitous, always offering to grab me something when he went out. Jess was competent and professional, though she'd been out of the office a lot, as had Beast. Tristan had this very comforting presence even though he was surprisingly quiet, and Eddie was just plain badass. It wafted off her. The fact that she was married to a pop star cracked me up until the day I saw Bri Williamson come through the door to pick her up for lunch and I nearly had a heart attack.

The man was stunning in person and so unassumingly nice. I would've expected a lot more attitude and a lot less genuine kindness and determination to learn my name and the basics of my history. When Bri had seen me sitting at the desk, he'd introduced himself, asked about where I'd come from, and mentioned he recalled Eddie saying I had a background in accounting. What kind of celebrity was this guy?

I wouldn't have put the charming singer with the gorgeous former secret agent in a million years until I witnessed him seeing her. We were talking and I knew the instant she walked into the room because his attention snapped to her and his face did this hot-sweet-relieved thing like everything he cared about had just entered his orbit.

And *Euler's formula,* it was adorable. But when Eddie walked straight to him and rose on her toes to kiss his jaw, then his lips, wrapping him in her arms as he did her, it did something to me. I was still sorting it out. I'd looked away, tried to busy myself with my computer and files and *things I needed to do besides watch Eddie and Bri make out,* because they'd sort of gotten into it.

Thankfully, they hadn't forgotten I existed entirely. Eddie had pulled away and given a vaguely apologetic look and said, "He just got home."

If I hadn't liked him already, the light flush on Bri's cheeks and the grin he'd made no effort to hide would've charmed me completely. The man was besotted with his wife, and I did not use that term lightly.

I'd waved them off, internally delighted to learn of this sweet pairing, and when they'd left hand in hand, I'd stared after them for quite a while.

What would it be like to feel like that? Not just happy to see someone, not just attracted and eager, but... ignited? Like someone had turned up the volume, turned off the dimmer, connected the meaningful threads into a cohesive design?

Like a problem with a proof.

Like you were made for someone, and they were made for you.

It wasn't that these two amazing people weren't already whole. I hated the thought that anyone would believe they needed another person, a husband or wife, to be *complete.* I didn't buy that ideology, and maybe it was something that'd kept me at odds with past boyfriends. I'd never needed them. Between my history with family being unreliable and my desire to depend only on myself, it didn't take a psychologist to tell me what'd been at play.

But lately, I wondered whether *needing* someone was the same thing as not being whole. I'd begun to interrogate the concept, to tease out the notion that a person is not complete if they decide to need another.

Was I incomplete because I'd needed Gram years ago? Was she incomplete for needing me now? I'd never believe that.

So why wouldn't it all apply to a partnership, a romance? Why wouldn't it be just as heroic to recognize one's own independence and ability to survive and wholeness, but then to *choose* to need someone? To submit oneself to the possibility of love, of vulnerability, and to embrace it? Why couldn't I recognize that, for example, Bruce was more than I could ever dream, and something inside me practically screamed he was made for me, to be mine?

He was his own person, and I didn't take that lightly. But he felt like... well, more and more he felt like mine. Like a choice I was destined to make, that I desperately wanted to make.

It was these thoughts that carried me through girls' night at Craic. They clutched at me as I eyed Bruce from across the room yet again, my stomach performing Olympic-level gymnastics at being so close and yet so far from him.

And it was the idea that maybe very soon, it wouldn't be a choice for me anymore even though it still seemed insanely soon to think such a thing that kept me tossing and turning that night. When I roused for breakfast late on Saturday morning, Rosie was packing up her purse and a small basket.

"I didn't know you had plans today. I would've gotten

up earlier." With my new job and her active social life, I'd only seen her for a few minutes here or there this week.

She snatched a baguette from the counter and stuffed it into the bag, then patted my cheek where I stood pouring coffee into a bright magenta and yellow mug.

"Don't worry. I do have some news I want to chat with you about, but I'm off for the day. I'm not sure when I'll be back, so if I don't see you, make sure to take advantage of Bruce."

The coffee I'd started to sip blazed down my throat, and I nearly choked. "Gram, seriously, you can't say stuff like that."

She shrugged. "I don't mean it in a nasty way. I mean take advantage of the fact that the man has it *bad* for you. Which really means you aren't likely to take anything he wouldn't very readily give." She waggled her brows, then twirled before she could see my stunned expression.

Or maybe she'd done it expressly to ignore my response. Either way, I watched her go, curious about whatever she had going on, a little jealous of the way she was wearing seven different shades of orange and somehow looking great in it, and secretly hoping she was right about Bruce.

CHAPTER TWENTY-FIVE

Bruce

I hadn't expected Nikki to answer the door so quickly, but when she did, the rapid beat of my heart gunned it through the floorboard.

"You're gorgeous."

She laughed, her smile radiant. "Aren't you supposed to say something like, 'Nice to see you'?"

With a hand on the doorframe, I leaned in. "That'd be a pretty severe understatement."

A pretty blush swept into her cheeks. "You are..." She shook her head.

"Very glad to see you." I reached for her, slipping a hand to her waist and bending to press a kiss to her soft cheek.

Before I could pull away, her hand found my jaw to stay my retreat and she ever-so-slowly placed a kiss at the corner of my mouth. Heat flashed through me, this little game of greeting and affection so much less than what I wanted from her. And yet, I appreciated her willingness to play.

"Would you like to come in for a minute?" she asked, minty breath ghosting my lips from just a few inches away.

"Is Rosie here?" I asked, not sure whether I wanted her to say yes or no to that question. Yes, because I loved Rosie, and also no, because I wanted to be alone with Nikki. Badly.

"Yes, I'm here, Bruce! Come in here and see me."

The voice came seconds after my question and made clear that Rosie had been privy to the entire interaction between us, though if she were sitting in her chair in the living room, she wouldn't have seen it, thankfully.

Nikki stepped out of the way and waved me in. I gave her a wink, hoping it'd reassure her that I didn't mind this but was pleased to see she only had an affectionate smile on her face. She wasn't embarrassed by Rosie's nosiness. Rather, she embraced it and even seemed to enjoy it on some level, if the amused grin on her face was anything to go by.

A few steps down the hallway and we entered the colorful living room of the house, Rosie's bright red easy chair extended so her feet were up, a cocktail next to her on a side table and remote in her hand. She looked a little less composed than I was used to. Rosie wasn't a formal woman at all, but she always seemed coordinated and together. Tonight, she looked dressed down, and frankly, a little tired. For a woman with boundless energy whom I'd only seen show signs of flagging for a few weeks after her stroke, it gave me a moment of pause.

"You look very handsome, Bruce. Well done." Rosie twirled her finger in the air and I followed suit, rotating with my arms held out so she could inspect the three-sixty view. "Yes, very good. And my Nikki? What do you think?"

I glanced at Nikki where she stood at the edge of the colorful living room rug, still grinning, face softened as she watched me twirl for her gram's inspection. And she was, as I'd said earlier, completely beautiful.

Her beauty and my attraction to it wasn't a secret. I'd made no effort to hide it, nor would I, because what would be the point? She was absolute magic, and I saw no benefit in shying away from that.

"I think she's the most beautiful woman I've ever seen," I said plainly.

Rosie's brows arched high, but a satisfied smirk settled into her features. "Well, I suppose that's an acceptable answer."

"Okay, that's enough. We're off, Gram. See you in a few hours." Nikki looped her arm through mine and led me away.

"No rush on my account." The amusement and more than that, the insinuation in Rosie's voice had me chuckling under my breath.

"She's relentless," Nikki said quietly.

I took her hand and knit our fingers together, the contact notching my pulse a little higher. We exited the house, and I held the passenger door for her. Rosie embodied relentless in a few ways, but I wanted Nikki to know one thing, so before I shut her door, I caught her eye. "If her determination is aimed at pushing us together, I have to tell you I have no intention of fighting it."

The exposed brick of the Silver Ridge Brewery's restaurant build-out maintained the charm of the original mill building where their brewery and pub room were located, but they'd found a perfect expansion at the far end of Snow Street, and now they had two locations, one of which was a full-fledged restaurant and bar.

"That's a good beer," Nikki said, tongue flicking over her upper lip to wipe away the lingering foam of her drink and effectively slaying any other thoughts in my head like toy soldiers cut down by an unseen explosion.

After a beat, during which my mind said really smart things like *I want her* and *more please* and *if I take a drink will you lick me, too?*, her brow furrowed and she waved her hand in front of my face to break the trance that'd overtaken me.

"You in there? Everything okay?"

I blinked reality back into place and chuckled. "I'm great. And yes, their beer really is good. Utah has a lot of great craft brews, but so far, Silver Ridge is my favorite. Plus the owners are great."

"Do you feel like you know everyone in town by now? Is a year and a half long enough to be that enmeshed?" She studied my face like she relished the view.

Likewise, Nik.

"I made it a point to get to know people. I wanted to be sure Kiley felt like she belonged here. It's not like it's a foreign country, but there's some culture shock—moving away from a military community, far away from where she grew up... it's a big change. I figured the best way for her to feel at home here was to *make* it home."

Her grin creased her cheek. "That's a great plan. I know I've only known you guys for a few months, but I think you've done that. She seems at home here."

I shifted in my seat, sipping my beer before setting it carefully on an SRB coaster.

"I hope. All this crap with her dad..." I let out a breath. "I don't want to keep him from her if she wants to know him, but I have a bad feeling about this. I don't know what he stands to gain. It just feels like he's after something, and the cynic in me, or maybe the realist, just doesn't think it's for the sake of a relationship with her."

She set her hand over mine where it rested on the table. "I'm guessing your instincts are pretty well honed."

I nodded. "They are. But not necessarily for *this*—for my sister. My family. It's always been for work, and I don't know if I can trust this feeling when I might have ulterior motives."

"What motives are those?" she asked, retreating a little to take her drink in hand again.

There was no judgment or skepticism, just pure curiosity. Just asking the question and giving me room to answer it.

I bit down on the desire to justify myself or even to soften the real thoughts. "I don't want to deal with it. I feel like we're just getting into a really good place. She's still on eggshells sometimes, still forgetting she's safe and loved no matter what, and I don't want this to set her back. Selfishly, I want him to disappear. And"—I swallowed the impulse to shy away from this most insidious truth—"I don't want to lose her."

It was ugly, maybe, that her talking with her dad made me anxious. That the thought of her getting taken away from me would send my pulse skittering through my veins like a nervous cat, and yet, there it was.

"You realize none of that is bad, right?"

My gaze snapped to hers, the bald statement surprising

me. I'd expected softening, gentle words to soothe me, maybe, and for her to tell me I was a good brother, sure, but not such a plain agreement. "Keeping her from her parents for my own sake?"

She shook her head forcefully. "That's not what you're doing. Granted, I don't know all the details, but I know enough that I can tell it wouldn't be just for *your* sake. I know we're early on here, Bruce, but I can tell you're not doing this for *you*. Maybe you aren't doing it solely for her, but she is the main factor here. You're naturally protective of her and it's not out of nowhere. It's because of a history of neglect or abuse or whatever brought you to this place, thousands of miles from her old home and as her *legal guardian*. That wouldn't be the case if there wasn't a reason, and I am not about to believe that you wanting to shield her from a person who didn't step up when he needed to is all bad."

With a hard swallow, she returned her gaze to meet mine. "I can't tell you what it means to someone who's been shuffled around to have a person choose them, be a little selfish over them. I don't want you to stop doing that for her."

The fire in her eyes made me move. I stood and tugged her from her seat. She was a little stiff, almost resistant, until I slipped my arms around her and pressed my face into her neck. Her hands clutched my shirt for a breath, holding me to her, then she backed away.

As we sat, I caught her eye again. "Thank you for telling me that."

She nodded, tucking her napkin back into her lap and breathing deeply, settling herself after the upheaval of the past few minutes. "Thank you for being the kind of person who will fight for your sister. She needs that. Don't stop."

I could've thanked her again for being vulnerable with

me—for sharing a bit of herself she likely didn't plan on. But the waiter came and served our salads and the moment was swept away.

I didn't need anything else to know she was it. This strong, tender, thoughtful, forthright woman was all I wanted, and I just needed to wait for her to catch up.

CHAPTER TWENTY-SIX

Nikki

Bruce Camden would be the death of me.

Maybe not the actual death of me, but of my circumspection? Yes. My calm? Yes. My lifelong knowledge that one doesn't fling oneself at a man within weeks of meeting him and definitely not on one's first date with said man? *Also maybe yes.*

We'd finished a delicious dinner with locally sourced everything and amazing flavors, yet most of my mind had been filled with Bruce. He'd stretched his long legs under the table at one point and apologized when he bumped into me.

And because he'd wormed his way so far into my heart and brain and everywhere else, I'd pressed back against his leg and left mine there, a connection point that felt oddly illicit considering my lower calf had pressed against the side of his shin.

Honestly, if I weren't me but I could read the internal thoughts pinging in every direction, I'd laugh at myself. But every topic of conversation that came up, every new discovery about Bruce, felt vital. Essential to *me*, not just to creating a vivid picture of him.

"Can I ask you something potentially sensitive?" he asked, leaning into the table now that our plates had been cleared.

"Ask away."

I doubted there was much I wouldn't share with him at this point. He'd been almost shockingly vulnerable with me about things with Kiley, and I wanted to meet him there. For the first time in my life, I didn't feel like I was clutching my cards close to my chest in a death grip. I kind of wanted to lay them down and let him make of them what he would.

"Rosie seemed tired. Is she doing okay?"

The gentleness of his words caught me by surprise, as did the clutch of fear that hit. "I'm not sure. I only just found out about the stroke, and I do worry she's not telling me things."

"You didn't know?"

I shook my head, lips pressed into a regretful line. "I found out because Dove slipped up and mentioned it as though I did. That was the first night I went out with them."

Understanding dawned in his eyes. He'd seen me then... he'd made it much better. But I'd had to shove down the roiling disappointment and hurt. Of course, Gram had the right to keep her information, yet it still stung. And now, especially with his observation matching hers from earlier, worry wriggled in my chest.

"I'm sorry. It didn't occur to me she hadn't called you, although for all she'd said about you, I had wondered why you didn't come to help her recover."

Guilt and shame joined the party, a veritable conga line of uncomfortable feelings step-touching through me. "Yeah. I'm sure you thought I was a pretty terrible relative. I've certainly felt like I've failed her, even though logically I know there was no way I could've known."

I'd run through every interaction we'd had during the time of her recovery, and she'd never once hinted at something being off, let alone so very, very wrong. And I'd been so selfishly wrapped up in my world burning down around me that even if she had dropped breadcrumbs, I likely wouldn't have recognized them for what they were.

Bruce's warm large hand covered mine. "I wouldn't think that, Nik. And for what it's worth, Ki and I did what we could. She has a good community here—lots of friends, good healthcare support... She was okay."

I turned my palm up, heart skipping at his tenderness. "I'm not sure I would've believed that before coming here, but I get it. I believe it and I'm here now."

Something must've showed on my face, because he squeezed where he held me. "But?"

"But like you said, she looks tired. And earlier, she mentioned she had something to tell me. When I pressed her to go ahead and tell me, she refused. I don't—" My voice caught, all sound disappearing.

Bruce remained steady across from me, not filling the space with words, not trying to erase the sudden appearance of emotions.

He really was such a good man.

Clearing my throat, I banished the verging tears. "I don't want to lose her. She's all I have." And I'd never felt that more clearly than these last few months.

"At the risk of sounding self-absorbed, I have to take issue with that," he said in a low, soothing voice.

I raised my brows in question.

One side of that handsome mouth tugged up. "I know we're new, but this is different for me than—well, it's just different. And I need you to know you've got me, too."

I bit down hard to stem the tide of what would undoubtedly be tears. I would *not* cry on my first date with this man. He could handle it, but I couldn't. I didn't want to.

And yet, what a beautiful, terrifying notion. Did I have him?

Could I have him, really?

There was nothing so heady as sitting across from the most attractive man I'd ever actually interacted with—Jack McKean and Bri Williamson might technically rival him for traditional beauty, but Bruce was word-stealing. And I'd come to know him enough that I recognized what an absolute gem he was. No way around it. He was the best of men, I already knew, and there he sat telling me I had him.

Me. A woman who'd never really had anyone other than my great-aunt, and she was technically obligated to be mine.

I could've laughed. I refused to cry.

"Does that seem crazy? I don't want to freak you out, Nik, but I want you to know that. Even if what we have doesn't... go where I'd like it to, you can count on me. And I'm pretty sure after those cookies, you can count on Kiley, too."

Overwhelmed but wanting to make sure he knew he wasn't upsetting me, I rushed in. "It doesn't freak me out as much as... stun me. Not surprise, because we've acknowledged that whatever this is means something. I know that, and I'm so glad you feel it, too. But just... I can count on one hand the people who've been there for me, and only one of them is still around. It's a big deal."

He nodded, gaze steady on mine. "I know. I want it to be. It is to me, too."

And though I didn't know all of his past, sometimes I forgot that it was his military family, not his blood relations, who'd provided such stability for him. It could be *me*, too. I could be there for him like he wanted to be for me.

"Sometimes I forget you have your own messy past, because you're so put together. You really need to let more things crash and burn so we can all get a glimpse of your humanity." I gave him a wobbly smile.

He grinned—bright and true and so gorgeous, it made my chest ache.

"I think we both know I'm barely handling more than one thing." His expression softened, and he leaned forward. "What's your favorite thing, Nikki?"

I sat back, surprised by the change of subject, but welcoming it. "Math. That sounds so silly, but I love it. It just makes sense. Accounting isn't my dream job, but it lets me deal with math and has an element of problem-solving I like."

"What *is* your dream job?"

A wistful sound escaped before I could stop it. "Teaching math. Probably at the college level because you get to dip toes into theory and such."

Something settled behind his eyes, but I wasn't sure what. It was like a decision.

"Is there a favorite thing? Some, uh, *kind* of math you like best? Or a proof or problem or—I don't even know. The stuff Matt Damon solves in *Good Will Hunting*?"

I made no attempt to stifle the beaming smile. He was just so adorable. "Oh, I have all of those. But let's see... I think one of my favorite things is Euler's Formula. It's kind of... perfect. It illuminates a lot of other concepts, and it's... well, this might sound kind of weird, but it's kind of romantic."

His smile flashed. "Romantic? Math is romantic? I really *don't* know what I'm talking about then."

I laughed, loving his willingness to engage on the subject. "Oh, it is very romantic." I dropped my voice so it emerged low and sensual. "Just think about it. All that addition and multiplication..."

His eyes flared. "More on the formula, please."

I bit my lip, admiring the glint in his eye that, if I wasn't absolutely insane, hinted at this all actually doing something for him. "Euler's formula is the equation that explains the relationship between trigonometric functions and exponential functions."

He blinked. "I am sure that means something important, but I think we both know I have no idea what."

Maybe it should've been a turn off, but I didn't need him to know everything I did. I certainly didn't know all the things he did. His willingness to admit he didn't know was more attractive than any attempt to bluster through and pretend.

"It *is* important. And maybe that's the thing. It's this small set of numbers and can mean nothing, but if someone knows the significance, it unlocks everything. It's like a message waiting on the right person to unlock it. I love that."

Any admission of something like this in the past would've ended conversations, ended dates, ended interest.

He grinned, evidently charmed by my love for the formula and not put off by it. *One more way Bruce is better than the rest.*

"I want to come back to that when you can show me on paper—maybe I'll wrap my brain around it. But for now, let's get our dessert and then go make out in my truck before I have to return you to Rosie, yeah?"

We chuckled together, the tension and fullness in my chest easing at the shared laugh and his graceful handling of the subject change. We'd end up circling back to this, and more importantly, to his vulnerabilities at some point, but I deeply appreciated that he was ready to move on, so I rolled with it.

"We better not rush too much or she'll be deeply disappointed in me," I said, winking at him with a cheesy flash of my brows.

He grinned wide, wide, wide and it was so dang charming, my heart squeezed.

"Honestly? I think if I take you home at all, she's going to be disappointed in *me*."

My mouth dropped open with a muted guffaw, then I laughed outright because he was absolutely correct. "I should be shocked, but I have to admit I think you're right."

He chuckled lightly, obviously enjoying the moment just like I was. "You know..." He leaned both elbows onto the table and ducked his head conspiratorially.

I edged forward in my seat, drawn to him—practically compelled to move closer to that handsome face. After a beat, he continued.

"I think we'll get there."

Those eyes reeled me in like nothing I'd ever felt, and heat broke open in my chest. *There* was him not taking me home to Rosie at all. I bit my lip, absolutely floored he'd just say that.. and yet, this was us. So far, every interaction had been honest, upfront. Kind of alarmingly so.

This?

This was not alarming. This was something I certainly hoped did happen. So I told him so.

I leaned in another inch and held his gaze, a small smile tugging at my lips, and agreed. "I think we will, too."

CHAPTER TWENTY-SEVEN

Bruce

Fingers knit, we walked to her front door. More than a little bit of me recognized how different this was from most dates I'd had with women I liked this much.

Scratch that. I'd never liked anyone this much. So that'd be women I'd liked *half* as much, or even less. I hadn't dated since becoming Kiley's guardian, and even before then, I'd never been a frivolous person, nor was I into one and done. That said, I hadn't maintained many long-term serious relationships because the nature of my job had always seemed a little at odds with that unless you were going to marry the person. I'd never had any clarity on that—on what I'd need to know before I asked a woman to be mine.

Until now.

This was what I'd been waiting for—this consuming reality. I knew Nikki was it for me. Call it crazy, call it an old wives' tale, whatever. The unit lore held true, and here I was, totally sold out to this woman, and she didn't even know it.

I wasn't being subtle, that was for sure, but she couldn't possibly realize how far gone I was. Probably for the best.

My phone buzzed in my pocket, humming against my keys so it made a racket. I'd silenced all contacts except Kiley, so I whipped it out. I'd already made mention of this about twenty minutes ago when her first text had come through.

"She okay?" Nikki asked, fingers squeezing mine in what felt like both question and reassurance.

I read the text. *"I'm sorry I'm bugging you. I just had a really bad day."*

My stomach fell. The selfish jerk in me wished it hadn't been today, but that same instinct to solve her problems made it worse—not just wishing it wasn't happening but needing to fix it. I didn't want my sister to be in pain, and if my staying here and kissing Nikki like I wanted was going to prolong her bad day, I would forgo even that.

"Sounds like she's having a really bad one."

"Want me to come with you?"

The genuine concern in her voice, and the real offer to be there for Ki, shone brightly in her response.

I wished that was the right thing. But something told me it wouldn't be right now. Even though Kiley knew I was out with Nik and even though she'd essentially sanctioned our relationship, I couldn't push it.

A sigh escaped before I could stop it. "No. I wish you could, but I think maybe she just needs me a minute." I took her other hand in mine, gripping firmly. "I hope that doesn't sound arrogant, I—"

"Not at all. Please, I honestly get it. I mean, I have no

idea what's going on, but I get that *you* are her person, and she needs you. So go."

She smiled so sweetly and earnestly, it shredded me to have to leave her.

And I wouldn't just yet. I stepped in, releasing her hands so I could cradle her head in my palms, sifting my fingers into her hair and not stopping the momentum of the movement until our mouths met and pressed together like we were made for this. Like her plush lips were designed to curve to mine.

I shouldn't have made the sound, the hunger and relief taking me by surprise once again, and yet I did. There was no stopping it with this connection, this slide and release, press and nip, touch and chase. Good grief, how I wanted more, and yet, now was not the time.

"I do not want to leave," I said, resting my forehead against hers and taking in the sight of her hands fisted in my shirt.

"I don't want you to either, but one of the things I like most about you is the fact that I know you're going to."

I pulled back to get a look at her glorious eyes. "And one of the things I like most about you is the fact that I know you get it."

I stole one last kiss and released her so she could step to the door. She didn't play coy or fumble her keys—she went right in, not making me wait. I sucked in a deep breath and hopped into my car, drove the thirty seconds to my own garage, and parked.

I took ten seconds to breathe through the rapid change of pace and get my head right. The switch from Bruce, Nikki's date who wanted to devour her, to Bruce, legal guardian and big brother of Kiley, took a quick second.

A minute later, I climbed the stairs and knocked lightly

on Kiley's door. A beat after that, she opened it, a little heap of a person blinking back at me from a mascara-streaked face, then turned and plodded away.

I hooked a hand around her arm and tugged her back, all the way into my arms. Hers came around my middle and her head burrowed in, a guttural, pained sound emerging muffled into my shirt.

My heart rate spiked, and I clutched her to me. "I'm here. I'm here, Ki."

A thousand other things brimmed on my tongue. *I'm sorry. Tell me how to fix this. Tell me who to murder. Please tell me what's wrong. Please let me help you.*

The fact that she'd taken my hug and allowed me to comfort her might've meant she was letting some of that guard down, but my gut told me it was just that bad. Whatever had made this day so awful for her, the reason she'd said something about it in the first place raised the hairs on my arms.

"Ki, can you tell me?" I asked, urging her away a bit.

She pulled back, a ragged little raccoon with red eyes and a face that broke my heart.

"Marcus told me we needed to take a break." She sneered on the last word, then practically growled and pulled the bottom of her sweatshirt up to scrub her face with it. When she pulled it away, she looked just as much a mess, but her face wasn't wet with tears anymore, and she seemed bolstered by the move.

So often now, she seemed like a woman. She knew what she liked and had goals. She had a boyfriend—not that this made her a woman, but it was one more thing she had that she'd chosen. For a girl who'd only had so many choices, these things mattered. Class schedules and friends and a boyfriend and participation in things that interested her.

Right now, that movement seemed so childish, so endearingly *young*, and I was reminded again what a volatile little jerk I was at sixteen. I'd never stop being grateful I wasn't parenting myself at this age, even when things got challenging with her.

"I take it you don't agree?" I asked, keenly feeling the eggshell atmosphere.

She slumped onto a blow-up chair she'd gotten this past summer for her birthday, a "retro" piece of flair that'd been popular when I was not far from her age and therefore an item that made me feel the years between us vividly.

Arms crossed, dark hair sagging to one side in her ponytail with wisps coming out on all sides like little horns, she made another growly response before saying, "No."

I would've laughed, her grumpiness a weird relief to me after those tears, but her face crumpled. She opened her mouth to say something, then shut it.

A vise closed around my heart and cinched tight, tighter. She struggled for words, eyes welling with new tears.

"I just..." Her lip quivered and she choked out, "Why am I so easy to leave?"

Oh. God. Help me.

There is a kind of pain only parents feel, and I hadn't raised Kiley all her life but I felt it.... as close as I could experience, here it was, opening a pit in my chest, gnawing its way through every useless bit of flesh and bone into the very soul of me and ravaging.

This was more than grief over her idiot boyfriend. This wasn't a side issue, something we'd talk through and move past in a night. And if I stayed quiet any longer, if I didn't have a good answer, we might never talk about it again.

I moved to her, crossing the space in an instant and

dropping to a knee, silently cursing the blow-up chair for being the only place to sit other than her bed, which just wasn't close enough.

"You are *not* easy to leave. Anyone who leaves you is not only an idiot but obviously incapable of seeing how incredible you are." I swore violently under my breath, then internally berated myself for using those words in front of her. I'd worked hard to clean up my language, and it was something we'd encouraged in Saint Security—coming out of two decades of military life, the old habit died hard.

"Then *why?* Mom. My dad. My friends back in North Carolina. Now Marcus and..." She sucked in a breath, pressed her lips into a wobbly line.

My mind had taken on a muffled aspect, almost like how sound mutes after a flash-bang. Disorienting and gone, then distant, this moment had detonated on me.

But I had to know. I had to press into this, though so much of me wanted to tell her the truth—that I didn't know why people were so awful and there'd never be any explaining why our mom had failed us both in different ways. There would never be a good enough answer to take away this ache in her, and I hated that more than I'd ever hated anything.

"And?" my voice scraped out.

Her lips quivered with emotion as she whispered, "And you."

I'd never been shot. Other injuries, sure. But this, this...

"No. Ki. I'm never leaving you. I will never *ever* leave you. The reaper could walk in here now and I'd wrestle his scythe from his cold dead hands and beat him back until he surrendered. Until he understood what I need you to." I cupped her face and made her look at me, those pained, devastated eyes spearing me anew. I spoke slowly, every ounce of veracity and love for her pouring into each sylla-ble. "I. Will. Not. Leave. You."

Her brow pinched and she took it in—my words, my tone, the ferocity of everything in me crying out to her to believe this. To believe that she was loved and worthy of so much more than she'd been given in this life.

"It's okay if you do, you know. You and Nikki, maybe you'll want privacy, and—"

"No. I don't want anyone who doesn't want you, too. It's not a question. Not an issue. You will always have a place with me. I always *want* you with me. Do you understand?"

Her lashes fluttered, but she nodded.

I huffed, unconvinced yet knowing I couldn't force her into knowing something her life had taught her the opposite of. "We'll work on it. We'll *keep* working on it, okay?"

She nodded again, then sniffed. Something about her glance toward her bed, toward her phone, reminded me of where all of this had started.

"And I know this is probably the big brother talking, but I have to say if he doesn't get how lucky he is to be with you, then maybe it is a good time for a break."

She sighed, a watery, defeated sound. "It's not that. It's... he said I'm too closed off, or something." She mumbled the last bit.

I stifled a small smile at her eye roll, almost like she knew in some way he was right but was annoyed to have to admit it now.

"Well, I can't imagine that..."

She huffed and shoved my shoulder, a begrudging smile peeking out.

Relief hit strong and pure, like that first drink of coffee after a bad night's sleep. There she was, the girl who could see herself right. Who could see her imperfections, yes, but who got that he wasn't leaving because she wasn't worth being with. He was asking for *more* of her.

That little fathead better not be asking for too much, or he'd hear from me...

I stood, giving her space. "You know, if you want to open up to him, give it a try. As much as it pains me to admit, he seems like a good kid. But Ki, if you don't want to, then don't. Only give him as much as you're comfortable with..."

I cringed, the words clanging in my head. She waited, eyes brighter now, and I cleared my throat. "But not like, *give*. Just like, talk to him more, open up a little. But if he's pressuring you about physical stuff, you send him to me and—"

"Okay, that's enough of the sibling heart-to-heart for one night." She rolled her eyes, though the soft look she gave me told me thank you. Or at least, I'd snatch that expression and tuck it away as such.

I waved a hand, all casual, not-completely-in-over-his-head brother, and sauntered out of her room. "Fine, fine. But he better know if he—"

"Got it! Thanks, Boo! Night night!"

Her door shut practically in my face, and I laughed, shaking my head and moving down the hallway to my own room, where I sank to the bed and just stared at the ceiling, the gravity of the day and all its implications flooding me.

CHAPTER TWENTY-EIGHT

Nikki

At nine the day after my first official date with Bruce, Rosie bustled out of her room dressed to the nines in burnt orange and gold with a set of cerulean flats and matching handmade jewelry that somehow worked in a way I wasn't sure any other human could pull off.

"So?" Her eyes practically sparkled, and her bright lips curved into an expectant smile.

"Context?" I asked, feeling like I had a hangover from the night of tossing and turning I'd had once I'd finally surrendered to sleep.

She gave me a sour look. "Your date with the ex-special-ops lumberjack next door? What *else* would I be asking about?"

A laugh tumbled out of me. "I guess nothing." I smiled at her, a burst of love warming my insides. "It was really nice."

Her brows dropped low, disappointment etched into the bracket lines betraying her years of smiles at the sides of her mouth. "*Nice?*"

I ducked my face into my coffee mug, refusing to rise to her bait.

She waited another beat before acquiescing. "Fine. I know you came home at a *very* reasonable hour, and though I'm not surprised, since Bruce is a gentleman if there ever was one, there was part of me that was hoping..." She sighed out a wistful sound.

"That he'd keep me out too late and you'd have the closest thing to a great-grandchild on the way in approximately nine months?"

She shrugged a shoulder as she set a notebook and her keys onto the counter. "A girl can dream, can't she?"

The sip of coffee I'd taken nearly came out of my mouth, but I swallowed hard to force it down. "You're wild, Gram."

"I am who I am." She came to sit next to me on the couch. "And I need to talk with you about something."

The way her voice gentled and lowered a touch sent me back to my early twenties. Back to the heart-to-hearts we had every now and then.

"Is everything okay?" I asked, somehow sensing this wasn't about the birds and the bees.

She smiled, though it didn't look sneaky or happy. It was something almost sad, yet not quite. "I should've told you this sooner, but I wasn't sure how. I wanted you more settled. And now, you are. You have a job, you're making friends, and you have Bruce. I—"

I sat straighter. Rosie very rarely needed a moment to gather her thoughts. She didn't stop herself or second-guess her words. She was a woman who knew her own mind more than anyone I'd ever met.

"Just say it. Please."

She nodded. "I got word a few days ago that a spot opened up at Silverton Springs."

I blinked. "The old folks' home?"

She frowned. "Retirement community."

My thoughts swarmed, but nothing stuck. I wasn't clicking with this—couldn't parse it out. "Okay. Um, so... you're moving there?"

She took my hands. "I've always planned to eventually, but the stroke... I'm too isolated here. Bruce and Kiley are wonderful neighbors, but they've got busy lives. I can't expect anyone to look after me. If I hadn't had my phone, or..." She huffed, frustrated by something.

"I'm here, Gram. And I have no plans to leave. I came here with the intention of being here with and for you. I want to do that." Didn't she understand? Caring for her wouldn't be a burden.

"I believe you, Nikki. This choice has nothing to do with my faith in you—I know that if I asked you to, you'd make it your full-time job to see after me. But what I don't want is for it to become that. I want you to live your life, and it is my greatest joy that you're finding that you want to do that here in my little town."

I grinned through the ache in my chest. "*Your* town, huh?"

She winked. "I know I'm healthy, and I know my recovery was nothing short of miraculous considering what happened. I'd planned on waiting until I was older, but I've realized I don't want it to be something I do out of desperation. A few friends have gone ahead and moved in, and they're really happy." Her eyes moistened. "Can you forgive me?"

Seeing her tear up made me do the same. "Forgive you? What could I possibly have to forgive you for?"

"Because I lured you here to care for me and now I'm abandoning you. But I hope it doesn't feel that way. I understand if you're angry with me." Her lovely face looked borderline desolate.

"No, Gram. *No.* I'm surprised. But I've been feeling pretty useless on the caring-for-you front, and I'm just... readjusting. But you get to live your life how you want, too, you know? I want you to be happy, and if being with your friends will do that, then that's amazing. We'll be close by, and I'll see you all the time."

She reeled me into a hug, and I clung to her for a moment, inhaling a scent so familiar and soothing, I didn't want to leave.

That is, until she said, "I want you to have the house and—"

I pulled back, gaping at her. "No way, Gram. Sell it. I'll get something smaller and—"

"Sell this house I spent years painting and styling into the majestic wonder it is now? Sell the little walkway with my hand-tiled design? The bejeweled staircase and the personalized everything?"

Her humorous outrage had me smiling. "I think there are a lot of people who would fall in love with this house, but I see your point. If you want me to keep it for you, I will."

She shook her head. "No, honey. I want you to *have* it. It's yours. And if at some point in the future you don't have use for it, you can sell it and make off with the millions like a bandit." She winked.

My mouth dropped open. "But how will you... I mean, I don't want to seem disrespectful, but isn't

Silverton Springs very upscale? Won't you need a fair amount of capital for your stay there? Between us, I'm hoping you live at *least* another two decades. That's a long time for a residency." Numbers slotted into a cube in my mind, pieces into a puzzle and best guesses on what she paid for things at this house and what it might cost to move.

The smug little smile stopped me before her words did. "I don't think you ever realized it, but I was a bit of an artist in my heyday."

"I knew that. Obviously," I said, gesturing to the bursting colors around us.

She chuckled softly. "Well, yes, I went mad in my own home like a toddler with fingerpaints, but I am also a decently successful painter and tile artist in the public sphere. I had a shop here, but in my younger days, I had pieces in galleries in New York and LA."

"That's... awesome." I supposed I'd had the sense she'd made a living from her art, but she'd always been so modest about it. Or, if not *modest*, then at least unwilling to relive the artist glory days for me.

She laughed, pressing a hand to her chest, then shaking her head and gazing at me with this look that said I was such a sweet little ignoramus. "Oh, child. What I'm trying to say is, I don't need the money from this house. I have more money than I know what to do with. I could spend the next half century at Silverton Springs and still have enough to leave you a tidy nest egg. Please don't worry about me."

At this, my jaw dropped. "You... you're... okay. Wow."

She laughed again. "Don't act like it's *that* much of a shock. If you think back, I suspect you'll put some pieces together. But for now, what this means is you needn't worry about my finances. And for that matter, you really shouldn't worry about your own, but I know better than to expect you to cooperate when I try to give you money."

I frowned at her. My brain had started flipping through little moments from over the years—noticing the Chanel tag on one of her jackets, seeing one of her bracelets in a Cartier box, one of her friends mentioning a trip they'd taken years back that'd struck me as shockingly luxurious. And *holy crap*, I'd totally missed the signs, but Gram was rich. She was intriguing tax bracket rich.

But she lived simply. And knowing her, it made sense. She had a small house—a three bedroom on a decent plot of land that she'd cultivated into a little paradise. She lived how she wanted to live.

"Were you *off the grid* when my parents died because of the money?" I asked, the suspicion creeping in on me.

She frowned. "Ah, my nephew and his wife, your parents, had gotten to where they wouldn't stop asking for handouts and while I loved giving to them, I'd seen how it'd hurt them. By the time you came along, we weren't speaking —they'd decided I was the devil because, once I found out the kinds of things they were spending the money on, I refused to continue funding their habits, and I told them I wouldn't hesitate to call the police if I ever found out they were dealing or stealing or anything else I'd become concerned about. Once they cut me off, in a move I'll never stop regretting, I let them. I secluded myself in this place, and I didn't leave a trail they could follow, although frankly, it couldn't have been that much of a mystery considering I still had a house here and they knew I loved Silverton. I never imagined they'd have *you*. That I'd be missing out on you. If I'd known..." Her voice shook.

I didn't need her regret, though. We'd been over this before. At first, I could hardly stand to hear the truth—that she'd been here all along and it was ultimately no one's *fault*. Courts wouldn't be looking for next of kin in a great-aunt who had no verifiable attachment to my parents in years and who didn't especially want to be found. We'd covered that ground, and I didn't want her looking back with regret. I clutched at her hands and squeezed them gently. "We can't go back. The point is, you were there for me as soon as you found out, and I benefitted from that. I'm not sure you did, but—"

"I did, and I'll never be convinced otherwise. You might've given me a few more silver hairs, but you brought so much joy, even in the hard times."

Our gazes hung together, the memory of so many good and hard times while I processed the reality that I did have family and that I'd missed out on her, on the woman who had shifted from an unknown great-aunt to my Gram, for so long, even as I processed losing my parents.

The ache in my chest and sense of loss made me think of Kiley. My face must've changed, because Gram shook my hands lightly before she dropped them.

"What is it?"

"Bruce dropped me off and went home to talk with Kiley. She's having a tough time, and I was just thinking about how hard it was to accept the changes life threw my way when I was her age. I'm marveling at how healthy she is —reaching out to Bruce and talking with him."

Her mouth curved into a pleased grin. "She's lovely. Just like you were, for the record. But you had some sharper edges. I think Kiley... I think she has a little more people pleaser in her than you. I think in some odd way, being in the system for a few years made you unwilling to stop and do anything for anyone else—not in a bad way. Probably in a way that kept you safe. But Kiley..."

She trailed off, but I finished the thought. Because I recognized the truth as she was speaking. "Kiley doesn't know she's safe already. And as amazing as Bruce is, she's still waiting for him to leave her."

Gram's grim nod sent an arrow to my heart. I hated this confirmation—hated that this amazing child would feel unloved at any moment of any day. And then feeling so deeply grateful she had Bruce, because he wasn't going to give up on her. Whatever had happened yesterday wouldn't shake him.

That was the kind of love everyone deserved. The kind that *stuck*. Bruce's love for Kiley would stick. Gram's love for me and mine for her stuck, whether she moved to Silverton Springs today or next year or never.

And what Gram was giving me the freedom to do was to keep sticking with her, and also to find more people to love and ways to stick.

"She'll learn just like you did."

Gram's eyes pinned me, reminding me how hard it'd been to learn the lesson that she wouldn't kick me out or stop loving me, even when I pushed her away.

"She will."

After a beat, she cleared her throat. "Well, I'm glad we got that out there. Moving truck comes in three weeks, and until then, I'm off to meet my boyfriend."

I was nodding, accepting this information. Three weeks until the truck, and then—*wait.* "You have a boyfriend!? Who is he? When can I meet him?"

She'd already grabbed her book and keys and was cackling on the way to the garage door. "Have a good day!" she sang as she exited, door slamming behind her.

I blinked around the room, wondering what other little bombs she might've dropped on her way to see her boyfriend, then slumped back against the bright couch with a full-feeling sigh. Never underestimate Rosie Renwick.

CHAPTER TWENTY-NINE

Bruce

Nikki's gorgeous eyes flicked to the side to find mine as she filled a coffee cup. I shouldn't be standing this close, but I couldn't stop it.

I hadn't seen her in three days. I'd thought we'd snag a minute on Sunday, but we'd settled for a quick phone call thanks to a small fire I'd had to put out with work, and then I'd been out of the office Monday and Tuesday supervising security system installs in the ritziest neighborhood in Silverton known as The Ridge. Normally, Wilder did that, but he was on another op, so it fell to me. I'd planned to attend the all-hands, which we'd bumped to today thanks to so much going on.

So when I'd seen her get up and come to refresh her coffee after the meeting, I'd been drawn here. Never even made the decision to rise from my desk or zombie-walk in here—I just appeared.

"You have got to stop looking at me like that," she said, biting her lip in the way that made *me* want to do the same.

Although really, she didn't have to do anything to make me want to kiss her. That was my current perpetual state.

"Like what?" I asked, my voice almost gritty.

A breath whooshed out of her. "Like I'm a three-course meal and you're a man who hasn't eaten in a week."

I chuckled low. "It's a really bad idea to eat a big meal after that long without food, trust me."

Wide eyes turned to me, her mug now properly doctored and cupped in her hands. "Please tell me you've never gone a week without eating."

I shrugged like that particular week in my life was something small and not a time that'd taken a few therapy sessions to process and still sometimes made me wake up with a stomach ache. "Let's say I never miss a meal now."

She blinked, absorbing that information. "Okay. Wrong simile, then."

My smile stretched wide. It was a stupid thing to feel a little trill in my chest at her vocabulary, the book nerd in me reveling in her word choice. But that kid who'd given up his dream of going to college and getting a degree in English would never not appreciate a woman who knew her metaphors and similes.

"What's that smile for?" Her head tilted to one side in that way she had.

I chuckled at myself, but fessed up. "I was thinking how much I like that you know it was a simile, not a metaphor. The lit nerd in me is preening on your behalf."

She grinned but shook her head like I was a weirdo. And fair enough, I was.

"I suppose I knew you attend book club. Is that enough to qualify you as a lit nerd?" She stepped closer and spoke low like this was all clandestine. "Or is there more?"

The dip of her waist practically called to me, my fingers itching to rest there and feel her through the thin material of her white shirt, but I kept my hands to myself like a good boy. "There is more..."

Our eyes locked, and if we'd been anywhere other than the break room at work, I would've taken her in my arms and kissed her until we both forgot our names. Alas, the lure of her hadn't completely wiped my awareness of reality, and so I just gulped her in at this distance, only a few inches away and lit by fluorescent lights above casting her in an eerie glow that somehow made her hair look almost orange today.

"Tell me," she said, a whisper.

There were so many things I wanted to tell her, but I'd heard steps at the far end of the hallway and this moment between us would be over in a heartbeat. I dipped my head, lips millimeters from her ear. "Have dinner with me."

"Tonight?"

"Hey, guys. Anyone else eating out for lunch today? I'm going to try the new sandwich place if you want to join me in a bit." Kenny grabbed a mug from the cabinet and banged around.

Nikki and I had jumped apart when he'd started talking as though standing close and talking low was a crime. It wasn't, and I thoroughly disliked the feeling we'd apparently both had that said we needed to jump apart like we'd done something wrong. But we were just getting started. It felt like—it *was*—so much more than that, and yet I knew we needed to go slow.

"I'm all set, Kenny. Thanks." I raised a hand in a weird wave thing that I'd probably catch grief for later.

"And I've got other plans, sorry. Thanks for the invite." Nikki gave him a small smile that made a little flash of a dragon-like urge to hoard every smile of hers for myself arc through me, but thankfully I kept that under wraps.

Kenny shot us a cheesy finger gun and spun out of the room, miraculously avoiding dumping his coffee all over himself or the wall or floor. He had a tornado-like energy and most of what he did, even after his injury, felt like he was just *about* to get himself killed at any moment because of the risks he took.

Fortunately, he never took them with clients, so the rest was up to him.

We both watched the space where he'd left for a beat before I turned back to her. "Yes, tonight."

Her smile hit me then, and maybe it was the disappointment at how we'd both jumped apart like anything about this was wrong instead of being completely right, or maybe it was that I hadn't gotten to spend time with her, or maybe it was the way she'd been biting on her lip, but I did it. I slipped a hand to her waist and stepped close so our bodies were deliciously flush after being so close and so far at once. My free hand slid up her spine and into her hair, and I kissed her, mouths fused for a heartbeat, two, and then I stepped back, raising my hands like I was being held at gunpoint.

"Okay, sorry. That crossed a line. I'm sorry. I won't do that a—"

Suddenly, she was pulling me by the placket of my shirt, urging me back to her. She stole a kiss for herself, then shoved me away lightly with a low, disbelieving chuckle.

"I knew you were dangerous," she said, shaking her head.

"Me? Dangerous?" The smile on my face was practically vulpine, I could *feel* it. And it matched the feeling, the need to absolutely devour her. But again, not here.

She huffed out a breath and stifled another smile. "I'll see you tonight."

"Seven. My house."

She nodded and left me to lean against the counter and just breathe for a second before I padded out of the break room and down the hall to my office. Tristan was waiting for me outside it, propped against the wall.

"Been waiting long?" I asked as I entered the office and he followed.

"Just a few. Didn't want to interrupt."

I eyed him, catching the flicker of amusement that told me he'd probably heard every word of my and Nikki's interaction. I refused to blush, especially since Tristan already knew how much I liked her.

"What's up?"

Something about the set of his shoulders or the wrinkle of his brow hit me as off. I couldn't pin it down, because Tristan knew how well we all read body language and other cues, and so he was likely doing his best to act like everything was fine. His response to the question would be very telling.

"Remember Winnie?"

"The woman who's been writing you letters for like a decade? Yes. I definitely remember her." They'd never met in person but were close—maybe closer to each other than anyone else in the world, at least on Tristan's end. I wouldn't swear to that, but it'd be my best guess.

He nodded, like he was glad for my confirmation. *Odd.*

"She's coming here. Next month."

My brows rose high on my head. "Wow. Finally meeting in person? This is huge."

This could be really good for him. Already, my mind spun out into different threads of possibilities, different ways I could help make sure he didn't screw this up by being too shy or closed off. He had to do the work, be open with her, but I had to believe this was fate at work.

Maybe she's the one for him like Nikki is for me. I almost smiled at the thought but refrained for his sake since he seemed so serious and not all that happy about this.

In fact, his face had darkened considerably, and when he spoke, I had no more doubts.

"It is huge. It's also not good... at least, not under good circumstances. I'm going to need your help on a few things, and I want it compartmentalized if we can." He paused, exhaling enough that his shoulders moved. "She's in trouble."

All instincts in me went on alert. I'd never met this girl, but I didn't have to. She mattered to Tristan and Tristan mattered to me, therefore, she had my protection, my resources, and anything else I could offer. "Say the word and it's yours."

He nodded in thanks and ran through the first things he'd need. After hearing the whole story, I felt no better about the situation. All that initial glee over him finally meeting this woman who seemed like such a fit for him had drained away and left one thing remaining: Tristan was an even better man than I'd already known.

Ten minutes later, we'd gone through everything he needed, and I'd done my best to shoot holes in his plan. He'd shored up every edge, every possible issue, and when he left, all I could do was hope I'd done the right thing.

He'd specifically given me permission to tell Wilder and Sarah if I felt I needed to, but for now, I'd keep it close. And for whatever reason, this conversation had me aching to be near Nikki. I just wanted to touch her—just hold her hand and feel her palm warm against mine.

To make sure I could focus on her completely tonight, I got to work. There was only so much I could do for Tristan, and right now, Kiley was hanging in, managing the nonsense with her dad. My job at this point? Stay focused so I could leave on time and have no interruptions when I finally had Nikki to myself.

Nikki

Bruce's smile threatened to annihilate me.

Well, his smile and the whole thing he had going on—sleeves rolled to show his forearms, apron covering his chest and tied around his neck and slim waist. And *no*, I had not forgotten the fact that I knew exactly what he looked like under all of that. *Whew.*

He was making me chicken piccata. He'd been nudging hand-breaded chicken breasts around a cast-iron pan with a wooden spoon like some kind of hot ex-Army-chef, and the tattoos peeking out of his undershirt just under his collarbone, paired with how his hair looked a little messy after a long day... Honestly, I'd been gripping the countertop to keep from launching myself at him.

"So the Navy SEALs and EMU work together, but you don't like each other?" I asked, trying to focus on our conversation and broaden my understanding of both his past service and the US's current special operations assets and not admire all of Bruce's many, many... well, assets.

"I wouldn't say we don't like each other. It's just an interesting contention at times. But generally, we've got similar mission sets and we take turns. Also, not all SEALS are black special ops or SOF. Only SEAL Team Six and a few others. The bulk of Navy SEALs are akin to our special forces."

"And Special Forces are different from Special Operations."

He turned and winked. "Correct."

I squinted at him as he started plating our chicken over small beds of golden couscous. "But there's competition between you?"

He shrugged a shoulder, and his head rocked side to side in a *kind of* gesture. "Not really competition. I guess it's really stereotypes. The biggest one about our Navy friends is that they're hotshots. This isn't universally true, but how often do you read about EMU in the paper? Basically never. How often do you read about the SEALs extracting someone or whatever else? They're more likely to be out there, and we're just... not."

"Hmm. But why? It's not like people have never heard of EMU." I had. To be fair, though, I hadn't known exactly what it was.

"A lot more people had heard of it when it was Delta Force. They like to change the name and get fancy, but ulti-mately, anonymity helps with the job. And I should also add that it's not just news stories. The SEALs have an almost preprogrammed need to strip off their shirts at all times."

I tried to laugh but had to swallow the sip of wine I'd taken before I could let the sound escape. With a chuckle, I took the plate he offered me and followed him to the table. "Okay, please explain that."

He grinned, all free and gorgeous, and as always, it made my stomach flip.

"It sounds like a punchline, but it's just true. We'll do joint training exercises and it'll be fifty degrees outside but the sun's out, so those guys are stripping down and hopping on dirt bikes and running around like they're in a scene from *Top Gun*. It's honestly kind of wild the first time you witness it. Then it becomes a little concerning because you're thinking maybe all that time they spend in the ocean means they can't actually feel that fifty degrees isn't warm."

I was laughing *hard* now. Something about him tipping my image of all these tough SEALs on its head hit me in just the right way and I couldn't stop. Once I calmed down enough to take a full breath, I started cutting my chicken.

"Says the man who seems to lose his shirt anytime he walks into his backyard."

He coughed, choking on his own drink, then shook his head at me. "Touché, but also, says the woman who doesn't seem to mind the view."

My cheeks heated, but I shrugged and raised my wineglass. "To your perpetual backyard shirtlessness."

His breathy chuckle gave me a thrill as he touched his drink to mine. "May you ever be able to enjoy it."

We drank, gazes locked, and every inch of space in my chest was filled with the butterfly sensation I'd only ever experienced with him. I'd go mad from this feeling if I had to stay at arm's length from him.

As though he read my mind, and faster than I would've imagined, Bruce stood from his seat and bent, cupped my jaw, and kissed me. Just as quickly, he sat back down and picked up his utensils.

I blinked at him, the butterflies nowhere near abating now.

"Should I apologize? Sometimes, I can't help but kiss you, but if it bothers you, please tell me. I won't—"

"No. No. I just..." I cleared my throat, nervous energy washing away those flutters in an instant. "I've just never felt like this before." Nor would I ever have admitted such a thing.

In truth, he was potent enough, but the combination of *him*, my feelings for him, and the knowledge that all of this was a path I'd never walked had me a little anxious.

Attention on me, he just *looked* for a moment, his intense gaze so focused, it made me feel like I was the one shirtless and bared to him, before his grin spread slowly. "Good. Me neither."

Backflips. Cartwheels. Some weirdly victorious part of me standing up and cheering like a sports ball fan while that tender side worked with everything she had not to step back.

After a beat, he broke our connection, focusing on the food, so I made myself do the same.

"It's delicious. Thank you for making this for me." The chicken was golden brown, with a buttery lemon caper sauce drizzled overtop. He'd made fresh french green beans and a salad on the side.

"I was never very good, but I had Adam give me some lessons before Kiley came to live with me. Just felt like I needed to be able to give her something other than grilled meat and takeout."

And there it was again. One of the many reasons this man had me in his grip so tight and why I had no desire to get out of it. Yes, he was gorgeous and charming as all get out, but it was this part of him that'd learned to cook for his sister, who'd prioritized her over his own routines and comfort, that made me absolute mush.

"You know, you're a very dangerous man," I said, wondering how many times I'd thought it.

Those brown eyes hit me for the tenth time tonight and as usual, everything in me stood up and paid attention.

"Never to you, Nik."

Oh. How desperately I wanted to believe him.

We finished dinner and kept talking, moving to the couch in the living room. As the minutes passed, we inched closer together. Since Kiley was due any minute, the evening hadn't felt like a date in the way one might think, especially since the original plan had included her joining us for dinner. Instead, she dragged in through the door at just after nine o'clock looking exhausted and sad.

Bruce slipped his hand from where it'd rested on my thigh, warm and possessive and more than a little thrilling. He'd made no move in any direction other than just to touch me, to stay connected, his thumb occasionally arcing over the denim of my jeans and making me wish I'd worn a skirt just to feel his skin on mine even though it would've been chilly now that fall had officially rolled into Silverton.

"Hey, Ki, you hungry?" He stood and I followed not far behind, doing my best not to encroach.

She stopped, eyes finally flicking up to take in her brother, then me. Her face crumpled, then flattened out in an eerie way that hit me right in the gut.

"Sorry I missed dinner. Like I said, this calc is killing me, and Marcus was trying to help."

A ragged edge to her voice sent up another warning flare in my mind.

Bruce moved to her then, not stopping until he held her shoulders in her hands. "Is he being good to you?"

She swallowed but nodded. "It's not Marcus. He's trying to help me. It's just—" Her voice dropped out and her eyes flooded, but she gritted her teeth for a moment as she breathed, composing herself as though she'd decided she wouldn't cry and therefore would do *anything* not to.

"Tell me, Ki. It's okay. Whatever it is, it's okay," he said in a low, soothing voice.

I should go. I shouldn't be here to interrupt this moment even though seeing Bruce like this, being the wonderful man he was and supporting his sister, only made me fall harder. Kiley's eyes slid to me, and she blinked away the tears.

"I can go. I'm sorry for—"

"No, it's fine. I just... my dad's here."

Her attention shifted back to Bruce, and the energy changed. Something inexplicably charged, not in the way I often felt when I was close to Bruce, but in a heady and combustible way.

"Where? When? Where is he now? What did he want?"

The businesslike tone took me off guard, the soft solicitousness evaporating in the face of what he clearly determined to be a threat.

"When we were walking to the coffee shop. He pulled up, and Marcus tried to tell him to leave, but he ended up getting out. He bought us coffees and it was fine."

But everything about her said it wasn't fine.

"What did he want?" Bruce asked again.

She sighed and let her bag drop from her shoulder and *thunk* to the ground. "He said a lot of stuff. How sorry he is. How much he regrets getting put in jail. How he thinks..." She dropped her chin and mumbled something.

Bruce exhaled and stepped back, the expression on his face thunderous as he turned away. But when he spoke, it was with that same calm tone he'd managed. "Why don't you wash up? Let's get you some food and then maybe Nik can help you with the homework."

His gaze found mine, and I nodded because there was nothing else I could do, but I could help her with her math. Sign me up for a lifetime of that if it helped either one of them—this brain might as well be good for something.

She acquiesced and plodded up the stairs to go do her thing for a few while Bruce dished up her plate. I moved toward him, not sure what to do.

"What do you need?" I asked, hands finding his waist as he set her plate in the microwave.

He turned to me and hauled me close, body to body and heart to heart. "Just you. And maybe for that poor excuse of a father of hers to find his way back to jail."

I huffed a small laugh into his shirt, and we broke apart as Kiley came down the stairs. She slid onto a seat at the table after snatching something out of her backpack. Had to be her math work, and based on the tight expression, that hadn't been an empty excuse earlier.

"Can I see if I can help with that?" I asked, not wanting to push if she just needed time to wrestle with it, but more than willing to step in if it'd be useful.

"Yes, please."

It sounded more like a plea than a response, so I

beelined to the seat next to her as Bruce set down her warmed plate of food.

After she inhaled the delicious meal and we chatted over the assignment, I took a tack I'd used with students I'd tutored during college, and eventually, I saw the light come on in her eyes. It was magnificent on her, and the pride that welled in me felt pretty great, too. Since the first round with her, I'd been hammering out the details of the game I'd thought up that would hopefully help students just like her, and this moment gave me another little burst of anticipation that it really might.

"I've been overcomplicating it this whole time. I'm an idiot!" She sank back in her chair, a wobbly, wild smile on her face now that she'd finished the problem set.

I shook my head slowly, pinning her eyes. "You are so far from an idiot, Kiley. Don't say that."

She just rolled her eyes a little and shrugged. But this wasn't something I was going to let go.

"I mean it. You're an amazing woman, and you're learning this stuff much more easily than half the college kids I used to tutor. Plus, not understanding a concept is never what makes someone an idiot."

Her brow arched high. "What does, then?"

I chuckled, her stubbornness shining through and cracking me up. "A lot of things. The inability to learn things, especially due to thinking you know it all already. The refusal to change your mind when presented with new information. Treating people poorly because of the way they look or their background. A few others, but you get the idea. Not grasping a concept you're working to understand is never one of those things."

She nodded with a serene expression, almost like she was pleased with my answer. "That makes sense. I think I *was* being an idiot with Marcus, but he gave me time to get myself figured out."

Bruce materialized over my shoulder and plunked down two small bowls, each with a perfect round scoop of mint chocolate chip ice cream.

"Don't say that about yourself, Ki." He slid into the seat next to me and slipped his arm around my shoulders.

Kiley double blinked at his gesture but swallowed a bit of the ice cream and then explained. "But I was. He was trying to help me understand how he was feeling, and I refused to listen to him. It scared me, what he said, and I didn't like what it implied about me. But then after our talk" —her eyes tipped up to Bruce's, then refocused on her dish —"I couldn't ignore it anymore. He was right. He'd told me that because he cares about me, not to hurt me. And finally, I admitted it and it's much better."

"That's a sign of truly high intelligence. Your giant brain is serving you well." I winked at her.

She chuckled and shook her head, then stacked her bowl on top of her notebook. "Well, with that thought, I'm going to go let this giant brain power down and get some REM."

Bruce and I glanced at each other. Was that what kids said instead of just sleep?

"Sounds good, Ki. I'm taking you to school tomorrow, or is Marcus getting you?" Bruce asked as she started up the stairs.

"You, if you can. He has weightlifting early or something." She didn't wait for his response. She knew he had her.

And that was the beautiful thing here. She might still be struggling with her dad and everything else. I knew Bruce would have to address all of that, but he'd let it go because she clearly hadn't wanted to deal with it.

"You're amazing. You know that, right?"

His hand hooked around my waist and slid me forward in my chair. His legs were splayed wide and bracketed mine, those eyes boring into me like he'd hypnotize me if I didn't look away.

I stood and stepped closer into his space, sliding my palms against the curve of his jaw and leaning in to press my lips to his. He had a little roughness there, a five o'clock shadow I'd only seen once or twice, and it gave me an odd thrill to feel the bristles against my hand.

"Walk me to the door?"

CHAPTER THIRTY-ONE

Bruce

A week and a half after Kiley's dad approached her the first time, he had the foolish notion of doing so again when she and Marcus emerged from the training space we'd been building out about a half mile from the Saint Security offices.

I stood inside chatting with Quinn and her daughter, Cara, who were faithful attendees of the advanced self-defense course we ran on Saturday afternoons. Kiley and Marcus attended when they could, and I appreciated his support of her. I'd learned to accept that he was a fixture in her life, and especially after how he'd treated her these last few weeks, I had more and more respect for the kid.

Something caught my eye through the open doorway that let natural light and the cool late-October air filter in, and in an instant, I'd excused myself and moved outside in time to hear Carl Caruthers in the flesh.

"We had a nice time the other day, and now you're refusing to talk to me?"

Kiley had folded in on herself. "I'm not. I just don't want to go with you right now, okay?"

Carl practically spat his words. "If you weren't such an ungrateful little—"

"Hey now, Mr. Caruthers, there's no need to—"

Kiley's piece of trash father took a swipe at Marcus, who did a fine duck. Thankfully, Kiley was paying attention and she jumped out of the way or his fist would've connected with her face. He hadn't been aiming for her, but Marcus's reflexes might've made it happen. And all of that proved more than enough ammunition to send me into the fray.

"That's enough." I moved to stand in front of the kids. "You get out of here and you stay gone. You don't come onto my property and insult these kids. You don't treat them this way, ever. And you don't ever attempt to touch them, or I will call up my pal at the sheriff's office and make sure you're taken in for attempted assault. Questions?"

The sneer on his face was pure rage. "Always so high and mighty, like you didn't spring from the same trash she did." He notched his chin toward Kiley.

Disgust and something heavier laced through me. "Go."

His jaw jutted out like he might be thinking of resisting, but after he ground his teeth at me for a beat, he spat at my feet and sent foul expletives at me before he stalked off. The second he climbed into his rental and sped off with a squeal, I turned to Kiley.

"You okay?"

She nodded, eyes red rimmed but no tears. Marcus had his arm around her, holding her close.

"And you?" I eyed him, appreciating the way he'd instantly sought to protect her. Again, good kid.

"Yes, sir. I'm fine. I just... what's his deal?" He looked in the direction Carl had left, with a pinch between his thick brows, two angry spots of bright red coloring the light brown of his high cheekbones.

I brushed a hand through my hair, willing the fury bouncing around in my chest and just looking for an exit to calm.

"I'm not sure." My eyes shifted to Ki. "You guys want to go? I'm sparring with Tristan, but I'll be home in about an hour."

Marcus's gaze flicked to Kiley, then back to me. "Uh, if it's okay, I think we'll head to my house. My folks invited us for family dinner."

It made no sense, but that landed like a punch to the kidney. "Of course. Have fun. I'll see you by eleven?"

Kiley's gaze found mine and she nodded, then returned to her shoes as Marcus led her away.

We'd have to deal with this. If Carl was coming around bothering her, we might need to do more than just tell him to go away. She'd assured me he hadn't threatened her, that he hadn't been aggressive, when he'd talked to her last week. It was the only reason I hadn't hunted him down on the spot.

Everyone had drained out of the building, off to their Saturday afternoons and mercifully not expecting me to stick around and chat after that run-in with Carl. And Tristan would need an outlet as much as I did, which he confirmed with a curt nod when I walked back into the building. He wore sweats and a T-shirt, no shoes. I shucked the sneakers and socks I'd been wearing for class and raised my guard. I should've taped my wrists, should've grabbed my knee brace since our last time sparring had left me with a twinge I didn't like, but I couldn't be bothered.

"Ready?" I asked, knowing the man was practically always ready, but still needing the confirmation. The dip of his chin confirmed, and I moved.

Everything happened quickly—a jab to the ribs, an evasion, then a fairly dirty maneuver that left me on the ground. I let out my frustration in a growl, skipping up to standing and feeling particularly thankful I'd warmed up and stayed warm with the class this afternoon. Tristan was about as mild-mannered as any of us, but he was the close combat expert among us, too. Second only to the guy they'd hired at the unit and who provided full-time instruction to the best close-combat fighters in the world—including the men of EMU.

But Tris? He had it. And that patience, that usual calm, was slipping. He usually let me get out my angst before he took me out, but when he rolled me and pinned me a second time before I'd even made an attempt at him, I knew something major was happening.

"Wanna talk about it?" I gritted out as I returned to standing yet again.

"Aren't we?" he asked, attacking the instant I settled into my stance.

I blocked, blocked again, took a swipe at him and locked my arms around his head and *crap*. I'd been here before, thinking I had him, and he'd—yep. *Ouch*. We needed thicker mats in here. Even though I knew it'd hurt when I was a decade younger, I couldn't help but feel the reality of getting older in these moments. Tristan was only a year or so younger, and both of us had kept up our level of fitness since leaving active duty, but I'd be lying if I said I didn't feel every bit like I was closer to thirty-nine than twenty-nine.

"You recall I am not your actual enemy, yes?" I said, doing my best not to wheeze.

He made a sound more like something Beast would grunt out than anything I'd expect from the creature in front of me formerly known as Tristan, and then twitched his fingers in a "bring it" gesture that some idiotic instinct buried in my bones couldn't ignore.

And so it went. I attacked, he put me down. He attacked, he put me down. It should be noted that I was an expert in my own right. Some rounds had more grappling than others, but when Tristan was in control, there was no escaping it. He was so much better than the very best of us, it was almost frightening. The only person I'd ever seen beat him without a huge struggle was Kyle Croft back at EMU. A few guys could challenge Tristan pretty well. But again, when he let off steam like this, one merely accepted one's fate.

A half hour later, I was dreaming of a hot shower and an ice pack, and maybe seeing if Nikki would be willing to comfort my pathetic heap of bruises. But I did feel better.

Tristan gripped my hand and pulled me to standing, then clapped me on the back. "You're getting close on the arm bar."

The disbelieving sound that came out perfectly matched my face. "Right. So close."

He winced and smiled at the same time. Even after pummeling me and clearly working through something, he had humility.

And that was why he was one of the best. It was also why I hoped he'd let me in sometime soon.

"I appreciate the chance to be beaten into the floor. I'd also like to extend an invitation to grab a beer and use our words sometime."

He shook his head, but the thundercloud that'd appeared over him when I'd seen him earlier had dried out. "Maybe soon."

"What's up with Winnie?" I asked, guessing at the source of his rough mood.

He stared at me, neutral expression giving away more than he realized. "She'll be arriving soon. You good?"

Apparently, we were done. "Yeah. I'll lock up. You go on."

Fifteen minutes later, I'd cleaned the mats, locked everything up, and made it home. Times like these, I was grateful for the small town in ways I'd never realized mattered to me before moving here. Being able to leave work and be home within ten minutes felt invaluable after the brutal sparring session. Even in North Carolina, where I'd lived fairly close to my work, in the neighborhood where many of the operators had houses, it'd been a little over twenty minutes. Small difference, but I'd take it tonight.

I took a long, hot shower and let all the concerns of the day filter through my mind and slip out and down the drain. Or, I tried to. Tris would be okay. I didn't know what, specifically, had him tied in knots over Winnie's arrival, but I did know he had a solid plan to deal with it. Normally, that would be all he needed, but apparently not so in this case.

And Carl. I rested my head against the tile and let the water spray onto my back, easing the sore muscles there and soothing me. I should've stretched more, but hopefully, ice would help.

What would it take to make Carl disappear? Obviously, Kiley didn't want anything to do with him, and after the show of violence, her instinct, and my own, were correct. There was no way he was going to stay here and bother her.

It didn't even make sense that he was here—he should've been in North Carolina trying to find a job. I'd already talked to the sherriff's department about my concerns, and while they couldn't do anything just yet, they were aware of the situation. A lot of good that did at this point, since it didn't keep him from talking to her or upsetting her, but it was something.

And then there was the whole thing where I worked for a world-class security firm and we had our own methods. I'd only lightly mentioned it to Wilder and Tris, but after today's episode, I'd escalate it. I wanted everyone on watch for the guy. I wanted to know where he was spending his time, what he was doing to fund his little mountain escape, and I wanted to know what he was after. It made no sense that he was simply harassing Kiley for the fun of it. Anything I'd ever known about Carl pointed to the fact that he thought he could get something from her.

With one last inhale of the steam, I forced myself to move. After slipping on a pair of clean gray sweats, I grabbed a T-shirt and tossed it over my shoulder. I'd sit with the ice first before I bothered with it.

A light knock on the side door sent my pulse climbing. I'd texted Nikki that I was home and asked if she was free. We both had a lot going on, and with Rosie moving out the next week, she'd been knee-deep in packing duties this weekend. But I'd wanted to see her—needed it.

And here she was. In worn jeans and a soft-looking tee, eyes hooked into mine until they fell to my shirtlessness.

"I am always happy to be greeted by a shirtless Bruce Camden, but something tells me this isn't simply for my enjoyment." Her brows knit, and the concern in her voice had the oddest effect on me.

It made me want to sink to my knees and beg her. For

what? It didn't even make sense other than the reality that being near her made everything feel better.

"Hey, seriously. What happened? I'm here." She stepped into my space and slid her arms around me. Her hands were cold from the chilly fall air, but the press of her palms into the bare skin of my back was like heaven.

I ducked my head, nuzzling into her neck and feeling so oddly helpless, it nearly made me dizzy. Or maybe it came from the fact that I'd blown through the afternoon without any calories and was actually in danger of graying out.

"Thank you for coming, Nik." My words were muffled into her hair. If she found my neediness, the tight hold I kept on her, unappealing, she didn't show it. She just held me back, running her hands up my spine and out along my shoulder blades in calming strokes.

After a few minutes, she pulled back, fingers coasting along my shoulders and down my arms. "What do you need?"

"Just you."

She shook her head. "Very sweet, but I don't think that's all. Not tonight, anyway."

I grinned, more than a little delighted she wouldn't succumb to the line. "Fine. I need to eat and ice because Tristan schooled me so thoroughly, I should be given an honorary PhD."

She chuckled, beaming at me. "Go sit on the couch. I'll get you food *and* ice, and you kick up your feet before you pass out."

I frowned. "Do I really look that bad?" I padded through the kitchen and into the living room. When she didn't respond, I turned to find her watching me.

Her eyes locked with mine, and her smile flashed.

Appreciation shone in that gaze and sent my stomach to the floor, a new kind of need spiraling through me.

"Not so bad," she said, eyes flickering over me before she turned to the freezer to find the ice packs.

And I sat feeling old and yet oddly victorious that as battered as I was, she clearly still felt it. The way we were knitting together. We'd had our moments, and there was still some measure of friction between us and what might be ahead for us, but every bit of this felt right.

If only I could make the rest of my life line up like things were with Nik.

CHAPTER THIRTY-TWO

Nikki

Just shy of a week after tending to Bruce's wounds, I held Gram's hand and tried not to grip it too hard. The moving truck was unpacked, all her boxes and things piled into her new suite at Silverton Springs, and a decent amount of them were settled into where they'd stay. I'd be back tomorrow to help with more unpacking. All as it should be.

So why did it feel like my chest was caving in?

"Don't look so forlorn, honey. I'm ten minutes from the house, and you'll—" Gram cleared her throat, a thin smile pressing her lips as she swallowed. "You'll flourish."

I took her hands in mine. "You will, too. This place is great and I'm so happy for you."

I'd been anxious right up until I'd toured the facility and witnessed how luxurious it was. Comfortable, stylish designs. Friendly staff. A gorgeous dining room that put any other retirement home's eating arrangements to shame, I had to imagine.

Add to that how many people welcomed her like she was their favorite person and oldest friend—from staff to residents—and I realized she wouldn't be alone. That was the point of this, at least one of them.

"Need any help in here?" A handsome older man tipped his head in through the doorway.

It clicked—this was the man from the premiere! Had they been dating then, too? Had she kept it from me, or had it been a fledgling thing?

"Amir, come in. I want you to meet Nikki." Gram's light tone and the way her lashes fluttered the instant he spoke introduced him long before she said, "Nikki, this is Amir Adel. He's relatively new in town, like you."

I extended a hand, and he took it with both of his weathered but soft, dark hands, warmly shaking in a way that might've been odd if he didn't have such a genuine air. His graying hair was neatly styled, and thick eyebrows made his golden eyes look bright and open. He was at least half a foot taller than Gram and right around her age, give or take. He wore jeans and a plaid button-up shirt, brown shoes, and a matching belt.

"So lovely to meet you, Nikki. I believe I saw you at the premiere a while back. Rosie has told me so much about you." He grinned, a charmer's smile that made me return it.

"Nice to meet you and see you again, as well. I have to say Rosie's been a bit stingy with details on you, but I'm hoping now that we've officially met, I'll get to hear a bit more."

One glance at the woman in question revealed bright cheeks and a muttering of something under her breath. In all my life, I didn't ever remember seeing her blush like this, and it was likely the only thing that could've eased the shredded feeling in my chest.

Amir's attention caught on Gram, too. "Well, I hope so. Maybe you can join us for dinner soon?"

"I'd love that, thank you."

He nodded, then took a large step back. "Wonderful. I'll give you two a moment, then. And Rosie, see you at dinner?"

Her gaze steadied on him and she nodded. We watched him exit, and I had to give him points for reading the room and not lingering to chitchat.

"He's lovely, Gram."

She huffed. "Isn't he?"

The smile beaming from me at her consternation over this man came so naturally, it was a relief. I'd prepared myself to push through this afternoon, this goodbye, and then drown my sorrows in a two-thousand-piece puzzle and a tall glass of wine when I got home. I should work on my game, but I knew I wouldn't have the gumption. Actually feeling free to smile was a relief.

I had to tell her what I'd planned, though. I didn't want to bring down the lightness of my meeting her boyfriend, but I did need to get these words out. "I need you to know how much I appreciate you saving me again."

She gasped, then waved away my words. "Don't you say such a thing. I've—"

"You have to admit you saved me before. I don't know what I would've done without the time with you. And even though I know going back to California was the right choice at the time, being here makes me wonder why I needed to leave."

She closed in on me, pressing a warm hand into my cheek. "You made the best decision you could at the time.

And I didn't try to stop you, because it wasn't the wrong one. In fact, I think staying here would've been wrong in a lot of ways. You needed to forge your own path on your own terms. You needed to be able to choose being off on your own instead of being forced into it."

I nodded, the truth of her statements resounding through my head. That was exactly it. I'd never chosen to be alone. My parents had died and left me alone. I'd been moved from foster home to foster home, essentially abandoned each time I moved. I'd been left and left, and I needed to finally be the one to *choose* to leave.

"I just wish I hadn't needed that. I feel like I've lost a decade of time with you." The words squeezed out of a tightening throat, emotion cinching it closed.

She shook her head slowly, so calm. "No, my love. We've talked. We've visited. I may not have had as much of you as I would've wanted, but that's life. And now you're here, and I sincerely hope we've got many more years together."

The brutal hit of fear thinking we might *not* lanced through me, but I nodded, knowing I hoped so much for the same. "Me, too. Thank you for asking me to come, even if it was a sneaky way to get me to take your house."

She grinned, entirely pleased with herself. "My pleasure. Plus, it wasn't just for that. It was also to get you near Bruce." She winked.

My mouth dropped open. "Not even going to deny the matchmaking?"

She just shrugged. "Why? It's going swimmingly, from what I've seen. The man would propose tomorrow if he thought you'd say yes. Luckily, he's too smart to rush you."

Her words sobered me, and before I could check myself, the words sprang free. "Really? You think he's that serious?"

She studied me. "You don't?"

I started to say no, or I didn't know, but could I even pretend I didn't? He'd been so forthright and clear, so completely sure of things. Steady. And I'd been right there with him—at least, I'd willed myself to be. Hearing her say it had shocked me, but not the thought of a life with him.

"I guess I do. I just..." I wasn't sure I knew how to verbalize the confusing clutch of emotion and reaction hitting when I stopped to really think about things with him.

She took me by the shoulders and pinned me with her gaze. "I won't tell you how you feel or what you want. And I want to be very clear. I love Bruce, I truly do, and I love Kiley, but *you* are my blood. If you decided to never speak to the man again, I might question why, but I wouldn't fault you for not moving ahead with him for whatever reason. *You* get to choose. He is a man who will stick with you, if it's right between you, but if it's not? That's okay."

I dipped my chin, showing I understood. Showing I heard her, and I did. And the truth inching its way closer to my heart struck its chord louder than ever. The theorem floating around, waiting to see where all of this would go... it didn't need anything else. The proof had been written, the theorem proved, and there it was.

A man like Bruce would love his woman, his future wife, like that—he'd stick. But the fear I'd battled for a lifetime cropped up, right on schedule.

"What if I don't know how to do that for him?" I said it so quietly, I wasn't sure she actually heard me.

She squeezed me gently, then pulled me in for a hug. When we stepped back, she had a soft smile on her face. "If you choose to, honey, then you will. There is nothing you can't do if you decide on it."

I chuckled, her unwavering faith in me almost painful at this point. I didn't want to be sobbing as I left, and I knew she wouldn't want to part on a sad note even if I would be back in twelve hours to help her get settled. So I shifted gears and took her with me.

"Thank you, Gram, truly. Now, should I be worried you're practically living with your boyfriend after only knowing him a few months?"

I'd just finished showering and changing into my comfy clothes when the knock came. My heart leapt, and I didn't even pretend not to run on tiptoes to the door. When I opened it, Bruce stood there like the paragon of male beauty he was. *Pythagorean theorem, he's beautiful.*

"Hello, neighbor."

I bit my lip, savoring the rich rumble of his voice. "Why, hello."

He held up a bag. "I hope this isn't presumptuous, but I thought you could use some company."

My heart did a complex tumbling pass across my chest. I should really probably get that looked at. "I am always glad for your company."

Other than Rosie, I didn't think I'd ever actually felt this way. I'd cared about friends and people I'd dated, but I hadn't ever felt this potent mix of relief and expectation when I was around someone. And not like Bruce had to do or say something amazing to keep me interested—simply being around him was something to look forward to.

A few minutes later, we'd set up clamshells of pie from

Diner, and I'd poured him a glass of wine and grabbed forks for us. He sat next to me on the couch, socked feet looking startlingly pleasing on my rug.

My rug. I didn't like the thought, and yet, I'd seen the look of relief in Gram's eyes. She'd miss this place, but it felt like she'd been planning this and preparing for the move for a while now. Bruce's large hand on my thigh pulled me from those worries.

"Do you want to talk about today?"

I finished chewing a slice of the apple pie I'd just tasted —tart-sweet apples and cinnamon and buttery crust. "We can. I think I'm still processing it. I guess that'll take a while."

He squeezed lightly, then released me and took up his fork to spear a slice of the blackberry pie. "You don't have to. I can just see your mind running, and I'm here if you want to process externally."

I sighed. "I'd planned to drink this wine and do a puzzle and try to ignore my feelings, but if you're going to make me confront them, I guess I can."

His mouth twitched, clearly sensing the humor in my words. "Like I said, I'm here for whatever you need."

It was the earnest way he said it that plucked at the heartstrings already pulled taut in my chest. Where in the past I would've hoarded my feelings, maybe buried them and only taken them out to examine when I was feeling particularly capable of handling heartache, I wanted to share this. I wanted someone here with me, even if it meant him seeing me fall apart.

And if that didn't show me what Gram had said was true, I didn't know what would.

I steeled myself with a slow inhale, refusing to let the restless bounce of my knee or the clammy palms that'd appeared out of nowhere stop me. "I'm good, I think. Sad, but not devastated. It feels like sore muscles or a bruise, maybe. Like I know it'll get better, but it'll take time."

He listened with an open expression that said I could keep going—that he was in no rush for me to package up these feelings and tuck them away if I didn't want to. But the realization plaguing me all evening as I paced around the empty-feeling house was less that I missed Gram and more that I missed *him*. We hadn't seen much of each other lately—not nearly as much as I would've liked, and I felt the intense truth of my feelings for him rising in me with every minute that'd passed.

"I know she'll be happy there. And I—" I cleared my throat, willing myself to be brave. *I can do this*. I could.

Right?

Or, if not completely. If not all the way, I had to try.

"I think I'll be happy here. I know I can see her whenever I want. I know we'll still do things together—she'll even still come here to the house, if she wants. I think what has me so wrapped around myself is actually less about Gram's moving out and more about my feelings for you."

All movement in the room ceased, though I couldn't have said what had been moving prior to that moment. Maybe the heater buzzing upstairs or his chest rising and falling with barely detectable motion. The intensity of Bruce's gaze on my face multiplied exponentially. It extrapolated out to the farthest reaches of measurable possibility until it mirrored infinity and I suspected something akin to what reflected on my face, too.

"And what are they?" he asked, voice low and unmistakably hopeful.

I took a wobbly breath, my entire body alight with

adrenaline so violent, my hands shook. "They are... substantial."

His face split open with a gorgeous smile and a laugh. Then his arm shot out, fingers slipping into the hair at the back of my head to urge me forward. He pressed a searing kiss to my lips, then released me, his eyes practically sparkling back at me. "That's good news."

"Is it?" Even these words seemed to tremble. So much of me shuddered in the wake of my confession. It was all I could manage, and there was a kind of inverse effect—the words had run out of me, but now I waited. A vacuous hole waited to widen or shrink, all depending on *him*. And what a truly gargantuan amount of power I'd given him.

"Yes, Nik. Because my feelings for you are life-changing. They have already changed things for me. I don't want to rush you, but I do want you to know I am ready to talk about this, ready to tell you whatever you want to know, when you're ready."

Pulling him to me, I wrapped my arms around him and hugged him close. He was so solid and warm and wonderful, all of him gently handling those bruises and aches from the day. But as we sat there holding each other, some of the hurting places eased off and it was like some part of me took a breath. That hole shrank, and shrank, and though it didn't disappear, the edge of terror did, at least for now.

"Thank you," I finally said, whispering into the long column of his neck. I pressed a kiss to the base of his throat, chasing after the words like I could write them into his skin.

His chest rose, and his fingers flexed where they rested on my back. I kissed him again, along his collarbone, dipping to the top of his tattoo, then up his neck. I followed the sharp cut of his jaw, savoring the warm, masculine scent of him and the bite of his five o'clock shadow against the soft skin of my lips.

"Nik," he said on an exhale, like a question or a plea. Either one sent a heady shot of desire and need throughout me.

I wasn't ready for the bold confession I needed to make with words—that someone more adept at feeling would say. But I could try to show him. I desperately wanted to show him how I felt. So I pulled back and answered what I thought he'd asked with my own question.

"Will you stay with me tonight?"

CHAPTER THIRTY-THREE

Bruce

She needn't have asked, but I loved that she did.

I loved that she'd been sitting here sipping wine and doing a puzzle instead of watching TV. I loved that she wanted me to know she felt something big for me but wasn't quite ready to say whatever that was, exactly.

And I definitely loved that she wanted me to stay.

Instead of responding with words at first, I took her lead and knit our fingers together, delighting in her short, neat fingernails and the soft skin of her palm. "I can't think of anything I'd like more."

She grinned and laughed, like the cheesy yet truthful line both charmed her and made her want to roll her eyes. I joined her, enjoying the lightness of the moment despite a lot of heaviness that came before—both this moment and earlier in the day. The last few weeks, in truth.

I reveled in the crease in her cheeks bracketing her

smile and the way her eyes lit up. She was gorgeous and she was mine. *Mine.* I'd never felt it for anyone else, not ever, but sitting here, laughing together before we took this step, it was written on the stone of my heart, and no amount of time would ever wash it away.

And I needed her to understand that. Maybe we wouldn't say *all* the words now, but I desperately needed to make sure we were on the same page. I'd learned both in my professional and personal life how assuming often led to disaster. Her "substantial" feelings for me might simply be that she felt anything at all in my direction, while I was ready to tattoo her name across my chest and put a ring on her finger.

Okay, well, at least one of those things.

Well, in truth, both.

So I pressed her hands between mine, stilling my own laughter and sobering a bit. "But..."

That did it. She straightened and her face fell. "But?"

Nerves clawed at me, but I pushed them away. No amount of anxiety would keep me from honesty with her. "I need you to understand that for me, this means something. It means *everything*, honestly. I know the words will come eventually, but I have to make sure you know you're it for me, Nik. And I don't want to stay and assume we're on the same page if you're not at least in the same book."

Her gaze stayed hooked into mine and she nodded. "I—I understand."

I swallowed, waiting. Internally begging her to say more, to say *anything* to appease my need for more of her. But looking at the cruel mix of desire and fear in her eyes, I could see that any more words would be too much. It would break this moment wide open and potentially push her too far, too soon. So I nodded, accepting what she gave and not asking for more.

It would come.

I had to believe it would come.

Her eyes fell to my mouth, her lips parting and spearing through the ache. I wanted her words but right now, I needed *her*—her touch, her body against me. I needed to show her the page, let her read the chapter, and look forward to writing the ending together.

Waking next to Nikki felt like something out of a dream, except I'd never had a dream this good. Nothing that would compare to the last twelve hours we'd spent together, some restful and some far from it and absolutely more than I'd hoped for when I'd showed up with pie last night after Kiley went to her friend's for an overnight, ready to comfort Nikki and help her not feel so alone.

But like she had every day since I'd met her, Nikki kept me guessing.

In an easier version of this story, she would've laid out her feelings right there before we made love. I wanted to see them in her eyes, feel them in her touch, but she couldn't say them.

It hurt. Man, but it did, because I was ready to fall to my knees and beg her for them. Fortunately, I had a brain and it read the signs she was giving me. She needed a little more time, and I wanted to give it to her. We *had* time, after all. She was here and planning to stay. I didn't like thinking about what would happen at the end of the year when she moved over to the accountancy and away from Saint, but we'd handle it. Together.

I hope it'll be together.

The problem with this heart of mine was that once someone owned it, they owned it. I didn't give it all that freely, but once given, I'd never have it back. Wilder knew it, Kiley was learning, and Nikki... I had to believe she'd know it eventually, too.

I was a patient man. I could be patient for her.

"Morning," she said, eyes still closed on the pillow next to mine. Or, hers, but which had become mine last night.

"Morning. How'd you sleep?" She'd warned me she didn't often sleep very long. I could relate, though from what she described, I got more than she did.

Her eyes finally opened, the glorious light brown of them better than any view I could fathom.

"Very well. I worked on my game a bit."

I startled at that. "You did? I didn't hear you."

She grinned, the genuine smile sending my stomach straight to my toes. "You were out cold."

"I'm sorry. I would've kept you company." I didn't love the idea that I'd slept through her waking and doing whatever she needed to, though more than anything, it surprised me. I didn't often sleep so soundly.

She ran her fingers through my hair and tugged, sending a sense-memory of the night before crashing through me. "I'm not sure I would've gotten much done if you'd been awake."

Heat filled the space between us, and the impulse to haul her into my arms and make love to her again hit me like a slap, but she chuckled and pressed a lightning-quick kiss to my lips.

"I don't think—"

The house phone rang, and Nikki froze. I didn't know how often she got calls on that line, but from her expression, it wasn't often. She scrambled out of bed and bolted out into the hallway, thundering down the stairs and reaching the phone just after the third ring. I followed close behind, lightly regretting not pulling on pants over my boxer briefs, but the look on her face had sent alarm rattling through me and I'd known before her face blanched entirely once she answered that something was wrong.

"Okay. Okay. Can I talk to her? Okay. I'll be right there. Yes, thank you for calling. Yes, that's the number. I'm so sorry. I'm so sorry. I'll be right there." She hung up and turned to me. "Gram. She passed out. They don't know if it was another stroke or what, but they're taking her to the hospital. They—" She swallowed, eyes staring blankly at my chest. "They called my phone earlier. It's on silent. I didn't hear it."

I took her hands, urged her chin up so she'd see my face. "Let's get dressed. I'll take you over there, and we might even beat them if they're just getting her into the ambulance."

She still looked ill. "I should've answered."

I held her a little tighter. "You did. You just did and now you know. She's in good hands and we'll get there. Let's get dressed."

She nodded, then seemed to finally switch gears into action. She sprinted up the stairs two at a time, and in minutes, we were both dressed and loading into my car. I checked my phone as we walked to the door. No word from Kiley, but she and her friend were likely sleeping late after staying up all hours. I'd sent her a message last night, one last thought before I came here, and she'd given it the obligatory thumbs-up. We'd had a long talk a while back about acknowledging my messages in some way, even if she didn't *want* to, so I knew she was okay. She'd given me that, at least, and so I'd give her a little more time before I checked in this morning. Marcus would be picking her up so I had plenty of time to be with Nik and see to Rosie before I needed to be home for Kiley.

After another few minutes of tense silence, I dropped Nikki at the emergency entrance and parked the car. Fifteen minutes later, we were seated in the ED waiting for word from the doctors.

"She's awake. This is good. I guess she said she's fine. They just wanted to figure out if she'd had a stroke, so they are doing the test now and then I can see her." She'd repeated this update a handful of times in different words, her knee bouncing as she sat and tried not to crawl out of her skin.

I didn't want to give her false encouragement, but I had to say something. "It sounds like they were right there and that the staff did everything right. There's nothing you could've done by being there, and now she's getting checked out. This is a good hospital, and if she needs something they don't have here, they'll transfer her. I promise you she's in good hands and they are going to do everything they can."

"Nikki? Oh, I'm so glad you're here." Dove pressed a hand onto Nikki's shoulder, and Nik jumped up and accepted the hug her friend offered.

Such an odd moment to see her take comfort in someone else, and yet, it wasn't jealousy I felt, but relief. The more people Nikki had here, the more support and people in her corner, the more likely she would be to stay. And even though we'd had an amazing twelve hours, I worried what something like this might be doing to her.

The half hour proceeded slowly, even with Dove there

to keep up conversation. Something was nagging at me, a worry that wouldn't stop even now that we were here and were learning more. But I figured it would dissipate any minute—certainly once Nikki got to go back and see Rosie.

But then my phone buzzed with a text from Marcus. "*Is Kiley with you? I just got to Tara's house and they said Kiley got picked up an hour ago.*"

"I'm going to step outside to take a quick call. I'll be right back." I kissed Nikki's temple and kept my expression as placid as possible when she checked my face for clues. Appeased, she squeezed my hand and released it, turning back to Dove while she spoke.

I exited the building as quickly as possible without arousing alarm and dialed Marcus as I went. "She's not with me. Last I heard from her was about eleven last night."

"I swear I was on time. I called her and texted, but she isn't answering."

Crap. "You guys are good, though? I know it's been a little up and down. I hate to pry, Marcus, but I need to know she doesn't have any other reason for screening your calls."

"No, sir. We're good. Really. I know we've had our stuff lately, but we've been good."

"Good." And *crap.* Because this was *not* good. *This* was what had been niggling at me since this morning. I'd chalked up the no-contact to Kiley being with her friend and not being worried about me. That was all normal. But things around here hadn't been normal. She'd been on guard against me and likely Carl, too. She seemed to move from curious but upset with the situation a few weeks ago to most recently disgusted and disappointed.

Would she go with him if he showed up? I didn't think so. She might agree to talk, though, and maybe he'd know he shouldn't stick around somewhere a responsible adult would see it and let word get back to me.

Maybe they were sitting at Diner sipping coffee and eating pie for breakfast like Kiley loved to do. It could be that simple.

"Can we call the police? I have a really bad feeling about this, Mr. Camden."

The way his voice edged with fear made me want to shake him and hug him at the same time. He might've been seventeen, but he was just a kid. Fortunately for me and Marcus and Kiley, this was what I did best. I stayed calm, made a plan, and executed it with precision. If we needed reinforcements, I happened to know some guys.

If I had a black pit opening inside me and threatening to swallow me whole with a senseless fear like I'd never known? Well, that was just the reality of being a parent, I guessed. And for now, that hole could shove it. I didn't have time to get taken alive by the what-ifs. I'd find her and it'd be just fine. Everything would be fine.

"I need to wrap something up, but I'll call my guys. We'll start looking. If we can't find her in town, we'll get the police involved. We need some kind of evidence that Carl has her before we can justifiably send out an amber alert. Keep trying her phone, and if you've got any friends who might know where she is, call 'em. This isn't the time to be shy." This was the more the merrier.

"Okay. Yeah. I'll start calling and check with everybody. I'll run over to the school just in case she was going to work on the chem lab she needs to make up, but I don't even think it's open yet."

He was babbling a bit now, but he stayed focused. The kid was handling the situation remarkably well.

"Good plan. I'll check in within the hour." I hung up

and immediately fired off a text to Tristan and Wilder, then jogged back in but slowed my pace before reaching Nikki.

A nurse was talking, smiling and nodding like she was giving good news. As I got close enough, I could hear, "You're welcome to come back and see her. She's been asking for you."

Nikki turned to see me, and I slipped a hand behind her back and kissed her head. "This is great. I've got to run and deal with a work thing really quick, but you can get me on my phone, and I'll be back as soon as I can."

Her brow furrowed, but the nurse piped up. "Unfortunately, only one person can visit at a time right now."

"I guess it's good you don't have to sit around in here anymore. Is everything okay?" Her amber eyes tracked between mine.

I had never lied to her, and I didn't want to now.

"I think so. I hope. Should be." Less confident than I would've liked, but there was no chance I was going to tell her Kiley was missing. She didn't need more stress, nor did Rosie, and so for now, I'd keep the details sparse. "I'll be back soon. Love you." I kissed her lips and turned, only realizing what I'd said and the startled look on her face as I went.

But looking back would mean seeing her face and wanting to run back and explain myself, or do a better job confessing my love than tossing it out there on a stressful morning in front of two other women I didn't particularly know when I didn't have time to let the words unravel between us.

That said, I'd been thinking the words for days, feeling them for weeks. I'd wanted to share them a hundred times in the last twelve hours, and this moment, when she was going to see Rosie in a hospital bed, and I was about to go hunt down Kiley and hopefully not have to maim her father... I'd had to say it. I'd needed to let them out. I just hoped she'd forgive me for flinging them out there and not sticking around to let her respond.

Time mattered now. Internally, I'd delineated the best courses of action, marked my best plan, and I had texts from my entire team. We'd find her. It'd end up being nothing, but in case it wasn't, in case Carl had abducted his own daughter?

Saint Security was behind me, and we would find her. Whatever it took.

CHAPTER THIRTY-FOUR

Nikki

After Bruce's abrupt goodbye and that "Love you" sent out so casually it knocked the wind out of me, it'd taken a full minute of fumbling around not being able to figure out what to do before I'd shifted into gear and managed to follow the nurse.

Through the doors and down a long hallway, I finally ended up in Gram's room, and mercifully, my frazzled brain had let me focus on the immediate issue.

I'd prepared myself for her to look small in her hospital bed. I'd braced for bad news and tragedy, for timelines and regret over lost time and even the idiocy of her moving out. I'd mentally convinced myself to do whatever it took to stay strong and not break down sobbing and begging her not to die and leave me alone in this world.

I had not expected *this*.

"Dehydration," I repeated for a third time.

"Yes. And perhaps a bit of exhaustion. But no evidence of stroke." Dr. Daniels seemed to be fighting a grin, her expression one of patient amusement.

"I told the staff I didn't have a stroke. I felt weak and tired but not confused or upset, not disoriented. Just... bad. And they've had an IV in me for hours now. I just need a good nap and some lunch, at this point."

Gram's voice had an edge of impatience, and I couldn't blame her for it. She'd not wanted to come in, but due to her medical history, when Amir had found her with very low blood pressure and weakness this morning when he'd popped in to ask her to breakfast, they'd all flipped.

I kind of loved him for it, even though I understood why she wasn't pleased. That said, this was exactly why she'd moved in there—to be monitored. To not be alone if something happened.

"I've been bracing for terrible news. This is very... solvable, right?" I asked the doctor.

She nodded, her deep tan hands clasped in front of her a stark contrast against the white coat. "Absolutely. As I told Ms. Renwick, it sounds like she'd been overdoing it a bit and had lost track of hydration. We've had a heart-to-heart about such things, and I expect she'll be on top of it from now on."

"Of course I will," Gram practically scoffed.

"Gram." I widened my eyes, a little surprised by her surliness.

But Dr. Daniels shook her head, waving off the attitude. "No worry, Ms. Hastings. Your grandmother is going to be fine. I'll get the nurse to finish up the discharge paperwork, and we'll get her out of here as soon as we can."

"Thank you, Doctor."

"If you need anything else, let us know," Dr. Daniels said, then turned to Gram. "It was nice to see you, Ms. Renwick. Please take care of yourself."

"I'll do my best to *not* see you again soon. Unless it's at the market, Larissa." Gram winked, and I chuckled.

Of course she knew the woman well enough to be on a first-name basis. How I'd forgotten we were still in Gram's small town and not somewhere else where there was anonymity had to be due to the stress.

As Dr. Daniels bustled out of the room and off to save someone else, Gram clucked her tongue at me. "Where's your man?"

My stomach flipped and dropped at that, tumbling down a hill and off a cliff it'd been narrowly avoiding since last night. "He had a work emergency come up."

I frowned, a fresh round of worry wedging between my ribs.

"Oh, I'm sorry. But he was here? He came with you?" Her brows were high with expectation, almost hopefulness.

After the morning she'd had, it was the least I could do to put her out of her misery. "He was. He drove me, actually, so I can't give you a ride home." I hadn't even thought about that until right now. I sent Bruce a text to ask if he had an ETA and sat on the edge of Gram's bed.

"I'm sure Amir could drive us. Or we can get the Springs to send a shuttle. We'll be fine. I bet you it takes at least another hour until they'll discharge me."

"Okay. Yeah, it should be fine," I said absently, staring at my phone and willing him to respond. Silly to expect a response immediately.

But after that hour and another half hour had passed, after the nurse had brought the discharge paperwork and

Gram and I had walked arm in arm to the front where the shuttle picked us up, complete with Amir acting as host of our ride and fussing adorably over Gram, I still hadn't heard anything, and my nerves had notched up with every passing minute.

Once she was settled back into her room in her velvety chair she'd had the movers install at an identical angle to her TV as she'd had at the house, she snuggled down into the chair with a blanket on her lap and gave me the look. Amir had left us to see if they were still serving lunch, and I knew I was in trouble.

"Stop your fretting. He's going to be fine."

I shifted on the love seat she'd taken from her room and now sat at a right angle to her chair. "I know. I just have this sense of dread. I mean, we just had this amazing night together and—"

The Cheshire cat grin eating Gram's face should've been criminal. "Did you now? Tell me everything."

I couldn't hold in the laugh that burst out of me. "Not likely."

She shrugged. "Had to try."

With a sigh and relief at the moment of levity, I slumped back. "I don't know why I'm freaking out. I'm not used to not being able to get ahold of him, but I'm also realizing there's never been anything like this. When he left, he said he loved me, just kind of tossed it out there, and I—how can he love me? I mean, we barely know each other. We met, what, three months ago? That's insane. That's foolish, frankly, and—"

"Now, now. Let's calm that runaway train and think about this with your very favorite thing—logic."

Her words should've soothed me, but the thought of

using logic when I'd been letting emotion rule the day and lead the way sounded terrifying.

Because logic would tell me this made no sense. Bruce was a guardian to his sister and had his own business he needed to focus on. Logic would remind me that a mere ninety days wasn't enough to know someone, let alone fall for them. Logic would point out that half of marriages ended in divorce and the odds got higher if you came from a background like mine and Bruce's. *Logic* would absolutely show that history would repeat itself like it always did, and I couldn't get to have Bruce just like I hadn't had anyone else but Gram.

On reflex, I touched the stone I'd somehow managed to slip into my pocket in the midst of things. And yet, sliding my thumb in soothing arcs over the path I'd mapped thousands of time on the stone's surface, it occurred to me I hadn't done this in days. I hadn't needed this touch point, this tether.

Because here I was. With Gram. And... more.

"I see the spiral, Veronica, and I'm telling you to quit." She held out a hand in silent command.

I took it obediently, her soft, warm hand instantly bringing me a measure of comfort even as her use of my full name set me on alert. "If it was that easy, I would've."

She tugged on my hand, drawing my attention to her face. "I want you to hear me when I say this. Okay? You ready?"

I nodded, bracing.

"It's okay to trust yourself. If I were a betting woman, I'd put all the chips on you and Bruce if that's what you want. If that's what *you* choose."

Throat tight, I worked to clear it, even as molten fear

and doubt swirled in my gut. "I do trust myself." After a beat, I added, "Or, I thought I did."

"Sometimes, we can fool ourselves, especially when things are going well. I don't think anything is actually going wrong, but I do suspect that you are worried about *that* more than anything else."

"Maybe," I admitted.

Too true, though. Nothing was wrong. Everything here was right. New friends who were supportive and kind. Loving Gram, who had not only been fine today but had just given me her amazing house and a sense of financial security I'd never felt I had a right to. And Bruce...

She smiled before smothering it with a serious gaze. "I'm sure you just ran through statistics and the like to help bolster your concerns over a future with him. I don't need to hear those recited. What I want to know is whether you love the man."

I exhaled, that shakiness in my gut stilling as the answer practically glowed in front of me. "I do. So much."

I'd avoided admitting it to myself, and I foolishly hadn't said the words to him, but I did.

"Good. Then that's what you need—at least to start. No one's saying you have to go propose today. But let it unfold. Let yourself be fully known and loved. Let him know how you feel and see what happens." She patted my hand and released it.

"I want to do that." I swallowed. Exhaled. Shoved iron and pure will into my spine like I had for lesser challenges. "I can do that." I huffed out the nerves banding around my chest and added, "I think."

She chuckled. "You can. I have faith in you."

Something about that hit me, and before censoring it, I

asked, "Why? How can you have such faith when I left you?"

She gave me a soft smile that had my teeth gritting against tears.

"You came back, Nikki."

I was already shaking my head. "Because it suited me. Just like my parents. I only came for you because it was in my best interest."

There it was. The fear I barely dared speak aloud.

Her steady gaze didn't waver, but her voice shook with vehemence when she spoke. "That's a crock and you know it. You came because I asked. Yes, the timing worked. That was the only reason I asked because I never would've taken you from a life you loved. But I could've called years ago and asked and you would've come. I know that like I know the back of my hand. I know it the same way I know you probably have a piece of the sidewalk in your pocket right now."

My hand had migrated to it, pressing it against my leg from the outside of my jeans pocket even as surprise hit that she knew about it. "What if you're wrong? What if I hurt them?"

More than the fear of trying for myself and failing, more than the terror of him leaving me, it was this. The fear that I'd hurt Bruce or Kiley. That somehow, my inexperience and the blood of my parents flowing in my veins might sabotage anything good. I'd never allowed myself to consciously admit that, but there it was, out for both of us to see plain as day.

"That's for them to decide. Only they can tell you whether you're worth the risk in their minds, but let me make one thing clear. You are worthy of love, Nikki, and you are capable of great love. In fact, I believe you, like all of us, were made for it. Don't let your past or your big brain fool you on that count."

She grinned when I chuckled reluctantly, silently praying I could do that.

"I'll do my best."

She nodded, approving. "Well, then, I think we can consider it done."

CHAPTER THIRTY-FIVE

Bruce

Oak, Beast, Barbie, Doc, and even Stone, all stood with weapons on their hips, hands itching to draw. I'd forbidden them to until we knew what we were up against. We weren't on a mission in another country, and civilians, even highly trained former operators, couldn't just go storming into a hotel room with weapons drawn. No better way to get someone killed.

Carl might've taken Kiley, but I had to assume he didn't want her dead. That'd been real hurt underneath all that fury the other day—he'd thought he'd made progress with the coffee encounter, apparently, but Ki still had reservations. Of course she had. But he'd been both enraged and upset. He'd handled it all wrong, but I'd seen the gamut of human emotions play on faces in the course of my life and, unless all those senses were failing me now, I didn't think he wanted to harm her.

What he *did* want with her, we'd find out soon enough, but bulldozing in without much awareness wouldn't do us any good.

I knocked on the motel door, adrenaline firing through my veins so much, it should've had me shaking if I hadn't trained for decades to maintain calm in situations just like this.

Except no. There'd never been a situation like this. We'd spent an hour combing through Silverton, checking every business. We'd called the police once Marcus had reached all her friends and they, too, had attempted to help by suggesting places she might be. Ultimately, she was nowhere.

Her phone had to have been off, but just as I was about to lose it, we got a ping on her cell. She must've turned it on, and we tracked her thanks to the location sharing I had for her—right to where we'd planned to go next. I hoped she saw I was coming for her—that we'd be there soon.

He'd taken her an hour down the canyon to a motel. The dive of a place Carl had been holed up in for weeks now and that Wilder had tracked down in a half hour after Carl's last ill-advised visit to town, somehow flouting his bail and setting himself up for a nice little trip back to jail.

"Open up, Carl. Let me see that Kiley's okay," I said loud enough they had to be able to hear me through the door.

After another minute and another knock, but before I threatened to bust it down, Carl pulled it open. His eyes were red rimmed, and he had that strung-out look I'd seen too many times to count. He hadn't been high the last time I'd seen him, but no surprise he'd fallen off the wagon.

"Get outta here, Camden. I don't need you meddling in

my family." He spat at my feet yet again. Such a charming signature move.

"Carl, I need to see Kiley. Once I see that she's okay and you let her come out here, then we'll talk about what you need."

An ignorant observer might've heard the calm in my voice and thought I *was* calm. That my words meant I didn't have violence coursing through my veins.

That observer would be an idiot.

"She ain't comin' out, and she ain't comin' with you. She's *my* daughter."

A banging sounded from inside, and instantly, I knew she was either in the closet or the bathroom. That confirmed she was here against her will, though it hadn't taken a genius to figure that out, but I'd needed it confirmed.

I leaned in like I was going to tell him a secret. "Carl, I'm going to give you to the count of three to show me Kiley, and then I'm going to have to come in and see for myself."

He hurled expletives at me like it'd make a lick of difference.

"One."

"You ain't got a right to come in here. She's *my* daughter and she'll do as *I* say. You're just her trash-mother's leavings from another man. I—"

"Two."

"—don't even know why you're tryin'. Nobody's got a right to her but me. I might've messed up before, but I'm on track now. I can't believe you—"

"Three."

Then it all happened fast.

Gripping the side at chest height, I shoved the door and hit him in the face. He swiped at me and caught me in the ribs—I'd have a bruise. Oh, well. I pushed with every bit of adrenaline against the panel between us, and he finally lost his footing and stumbled back. I moved in, Doc and Oak behind me. Barb stood a few steps outside, and I figured Beast and Stone were looking for another way in to get Kiley in case things went south. Doc and Oak grabbed Carl as I rushed to the closet door and found it blocked by the cheap but oddly heavy sitting chair.

"I'm here, Kiley. I'm coming."

I could hear her frantically clawing at the handle, shaking it and trying to get free. I tore the chair away from the space and yanked open the door. She came tumbling out, and I caught her, dropping to one knee with the momentum of her crashing into me.

"You're okay, you're safe." I hugged her to me, and she held on so tightly, I started to see spots. I stood and carried her out into the sunlight, out of the trashed room that smelled like something had died.

She was sobbing and saying something I couldn't understand. I set her on the bed of Doc's truck and held her for a few minutes as the guys called the police and zip-tied Carl. Eventually, I eased her back, literally prying her arms from around me and held her shoulders, capturing her eyes.

"You're safe. You're safe, Ki."

Her lashes fluttered and more tears tracked down her face. "He said he wanted to apologize. Wanted to try to make up for all the ways he'd failed me. Take me to breakfast and then I could meet up with Marcus. I didn't want to, but he just kept begging. I thought if I did it, he'd leave me alone. It'd be closure, you know?"

I nodded, understanding her logic, though I wished I'd made it clear she didn't owe him anything.

"He just kept driving, right out of town. I started

freaking out, and he told me he'd wreck the car. I tried to text or call, but my phone died in the night and I couldn't even get it to turn on. So I just stayed quiet and told him I needed to plug it in—that Marcus would be worried and report it to the police if he didn't hear anything from me."

"That's good. That was smart."

Her chin wobbled. "I was so scared. I just kept thinking what if you didn't find me? But I knew you would."

I pulled her in, holding her tight.

"I knew you would."

She said it again and again, and I held her for as long as she needed. Time stopped meaning anything because what else mattered in this moment?

"I wouldn't have stopped looking, you know that, right?" I pulled back to see her face.

"He said you have your own life. That you're going to marry Nikki and you won't want me bugging you while you're starting out. I know I shouldn't have believed him. I'm sorry I did, but—"

"You don't apologize for anything. He's someone you used to trust, at least a little, and he played on the exact thing you're scared of. I never would've thought he was smart enough, but he manipulated you. You're brilliant, Kiley, but you're a kid and he's your dad. You can't ever think you did anything wrong here."

"But you're my brother. And I know you love me."

My heart squeezed painfully in my chest, victorious at hearing her say it so plainly. "I do. So much. And yes, I want Nikki in my life, but not without you. I hate to tell you this, but you're stuck with me. We're family by blood *and* by choice. I'm going to be there when you graduate high school and college. When you get your PhD if you want, or when you become the youngest person in Congress, or when you start whatever small shop you want with some silly single-word name on Main Street."

A watery chuckle snuck out. "So you're not going to kick me out when you marry her?"

I grinned. "You'll wish I would. We're going to be so disgustingly in love, your eyes will probably get stuck in the back of your head from all the rolling they'll do."

Right on cue, those eyes rolled, and a minuscule smile crept over her lips. She shoved at my shoulder and I stepped back a bit, then noticed my shirt sticking to my side. I glanced down, holding the shirt out enough that I could see the deep blue color had turned a darker hue.

"Boo! You're bleeding!"

Her words hit right as the realization did, and I yanked up the shirt. Sure enough, my stomach was covered in blood. Someone gasped, likely Kiley, and Doc's hand came to my shoulder.

"Sit down, Jaws. Let's have a look." His voice seemed far away, which made no sense since he was right next to me.

"I'm fine. I'm just... It's a flesh wound." It must've been when Carl had hit at me, but I'd never seen a knife. I'd been so focused on getting to Kiley, I'd thought he'd just punched, not stabbed. Now I was graying out. I hadn't eaten today, like an idiot, and between the adrenaline and stress paired with blood loss. *Crap.* "Actually, I should sit down."

Doc chuckled as he lowered me to sitting right there. My muscles tightened, and searing pain burned through me like I'd been stabbed again, but this time with something on fire. "He got me deep, but I don't think it hit anything major."

"That's a fun theory," Doc said, his voice that familiar

matter-of-fact tone he took on in times like this. And yes, he'd examined me more than once, including after being stabbed. I trusted him with my life, which was one of many reasons he worked at Saint now.

"Should we go to the hospital? Do we have time to get back to Silverton, or do we keep going to Ogden? Is he bleeding out?" Kiley dropped to her knees on the side of me Doc wasn't occupying and leaned over me, eyes huge. "You can't die, Boo. You can. Not. Die. Okay?"

I reached up and grabbed her neck, hoping my touch would steady her. "I'm not dying, okay? This man here is the best there is, and he's not going to let me die, are you, Doc?"

"Not a chance," he said, sending a wink to Kiley as he finished bandaging the section of stomach. In the field, he might've packed me with quick-clot and we'd deal with the fallout later, but we were an hour from home and good doctors and likely a CT scan to make sure Carl hadn't nicked my intestine or liver.

Kiley blinked at Doc like she was seeing him for the first time. "Okay, good." Her brow furrowed, and she eyed his busy, gloved hands, then turned to me. "So I can call Nikki and tell her you're gonna live?"

CHAPTER THIRTY-SIX

Nikki

I'd left my phone in Gram's room during dinner. It'd been hours since I'd texted Bruce, and I'd heard nothing back. Instead of fretting over the huge decision I'd made this afternoon—the choice I'd made to choose Bruce and let him choose me and see what happened—and the additional worry of *not* hearing from him all day, I let myself be swept away by Amir and Gram and meeting all their friends. It'd been lovely.

Not so lovely? Returning to the room to find a dozen texts from Kiley letting me know that Bruce had been stabbed while rescuing her from her dad's kidnapping attempt but that he'd be fine.

Pretty sure my skeleton bolted out into the night and attempted to run to him that instant, but the rest of me turned sluggish and threatened to sink into a puddle in the middle of Gram's brightly colored new suite.

A half hour later, Dove and Catherine had come to get me from Silverton Springs, bless them. Catherine had answered instantly when I called and though, yes, I could've probably walked to Bruce's house in the time I waited for them, I didn't want to leave Gram or be alone. I was too frazzled, and I didn't have to face things on my own anymore—imagine that.

As we drove, I talked to Tristan, who filled me in on the details now that he and the others had finished up with the police, and my mouth had hung open even as my heart raced. I couldn't stand waiting any longer to hear what had happened, and Kiley or Bruce must've known that and had Tristan call.

I needed to get to Bruce, and frankly, I needed to get to Kiley. She must be traumatized.

When Dove pulled into Bruce's driveway, I was out before she'd fully parked, jogging inside to find Adam, Wilder, Beast, and Dorian all milling around, and finally, Bruce splayed out on the couch.

I'd never crossed a room so fast. In an instant, I was by his side, kneeling next to him and cupping his face in my hands. "Are you okay?"

His smile grew the instant he saw me. "I am now."

With a shake of my head, I leaned in to press my lips to his. Relief coursed through me even as a hundred questions bubbled up. "I'm so sorry I didn't know. I'm so sorry I wasn't there."

I'd just spent the afternoon reflecting on how I was going to stick with Bruce, that I'd be there for him and Kiley and figure out a way to be the person I thought I was instead of the person I feared I was, and yet here we were. *My person* had been gravely injured, and where had I been?

Picking at a piece of Boston cream pie and chatting up Gram's gal pals.

But Bruce was having none of it. "No, Nik, I'm sorry I didn't tell you what was going on. I didn't want to pile any more worry onto your day. But I realize how upsetting Kiley's texts must've been."

A breath whooshed out of me. "Bit of a shock, yeah. Are you really okay?" I let myself touch him—palm his cheek, then pass a hand over his muscular shoulder.

"I am. They ran all the tests to make sure. Fortunately, Carl was just making his last stand and wasn't trained. If he'd known what he was doing and had any aim, I'd be in surgery right now."

"What was he thinking?" I wondered aloud.

He shook his head, genuine regret on his face. "I think in a very messed-up way, he thought he was doing the right thing. He wanted a connection with Kiley, wanted to make up for giving up his place in her life. I think it hit him hard that she's doing so well without him and wasn't sitting here waiting for him to rescue her or something. It was rooted in the selfishness that had him signing away rights and landing in jail, so it was completely messed up, but I think I can see a thread of Carl-logic in there."

"What happens now?" I asked, already knowing the primary result of Carl's whereabouts.

"Carl is heading back to jail. He was using, and he shouldn't have ever left North Carolina. It's a mess. But Kiley will have time to sort out how and when she wants to talk to him on her own time, without him pressuring her."

I sighed out my relief that Carl's motive was something less outright malevolent than I'd feared and the ending to this gave Kiley safety, even if it had done more than enough damage, and bent to hug him. Awkward with the way he was lying, and I was positioned over him, but I needed my arms around him. He held me close, breathing me in as much as I did him. "I'm so glad you got her back. You're a literal hero."

Snickers behind me reminded me we weren't alone, and I leaned back, but Bruce kept an arm hooked around me.

"He is a hero, probably a hundred times over, but don't tell him I said so." Adam winked at me, and I chuckled as Bruce's arm tightened.

"I think that's enough, guys. Thanks for being here. And thanks for calling her, Tris."

The quiet man nodded from where he stood in the kitchen, and they all said their farewells. Dove and Catherine had stayed just inside the door to give us space, and they waved at me as they exited with the Saint men. As they let themselves out, since Bruce apparently had no plans to let go of me, I turned back to him.

"Is Kiley okay?" I traced his thick eyebrows with my fingertips, grateful for every hair on his head.

"I think so. I'm sure there'll be a period of coming down from all of this, and I really don't know how to help her process it, but we'll get her some professional help. I'd already been thinking maybe it's time to find someone here, and I suspect she'll be more open to that now."

I pressed a slow kiss to his lips. "I'm so glad you're both okay."

He hummed, eyes shutting as I ran my fingers through his hair. "Me, too."

Knowing I should wait but unable to hold off any longer, I spoke up. "You said 'love you' before you left the hospital."

His eyes popped open. "I did."

"Accidentally?"

He chuckled, then grimaced as the movement must've tweaked his injury. He exhaled slowly through his nose for a moment, then pinned me with his gorgeous dark eyes. "I said it because I meant it. I love you, Nikki. I'm in love with you, and it might seem soon, but I can't pretend I don't feel it. I shouldn't have said it then, but it came out and I didn't have the time or desire to reel it back in. I'm sorry if it surprised you and that it happened when we couldn't hash it out. And when you didn't have a chance to respond."

I bit my lip, attempting to hide my smile. "You think I'll have a response of some kind, huh?"

His lips slid up into a half-smile. "I hope. But there's no pressure here. I don't want you feeling obligated or anything other than just happy knowing I feel that way about you—knowing that you deserve incredible love and I want to be the one to give it to you."

This man was unbelievable. Such a tender soul inside of a literally heroic body, and he was mine. "I am happy. I love you, too, so it works out."

The gorgeous, beaming smile that hit me was like an arcing parabola of beauty, perfect curve, and symmetry. He was so handsome and so unafraid to show me who he was. It was amazing and overwhelming and thrilling.

"You do? You sure? Because you don't have to say it back," he said, eyes glittering and cheeks creased with his smile.

I returned that grin. "I am sure. I love you. I don't know how to do this—fair warning—but I've never wanted to try. Not until you. And I'm going to give it everything I have because you deserve incredible love, too." I swallowed, so much emotion overwhelming me and triggering tears. "And I've been worried it's too soon, like you said, but I've had some encouragement from certain meddling elders to just enjoy it."

"Very sound advice," he said before closing the gap between us.

We kissed just like that, me bracing myself with one hand on the couch over his shoulder, his hand at my waist, until we heard footsteps on the stairs and pulled back.

But Bruce didn't release me completely. He held me fast, gaze locked with mine, and said it once more. "I love you."

There was no sense in trying to stifle my reaction. I stole another kiss and echoed him. "Love you, too."

"Okay, well, you guys are precious." Kiley bustled into the kitchen, apparently unfazed by finding us huddled together and kissing on the couch.

I jumped up and ran to her before throwing my arms around her and squishing her to me. "You're getting hugged whether you like it or not."

The eye roll was practically audible, and yet she broke free only to return the hug a second later.

"I'm so glad you're safe," I said, squeezing her tighter.

"Me, too. I'm glad Ms. Rosie's okay," she said, her words muffled in my shoulder. We pulled back after a minute and smiled at each other. "You know, I hope you do marry Boo. You guys would be adorable together."

Bruce coughed and choked on a swallow.

"What? Like that's not where you guys are headed?" She shrugged.

"Kiley."

Bruce's tone was a twin set of amused and chagrined. It gave me the sense that he liked the idea, the glimpse of a future together, but didn't want to spook me. And I'd real-ized over the last few days, especially since last night, that he'd done exactly that. He'd been feeling these things for me for weeks, he said, and yet, he'd held himself back for my sake.

"Are you going to be the flower girl?" I said, winking at her.

Her eyes lit up with delight. "Oh, definitely, but only if I get to have a flower crown and a special dress."

"Done and done."

We glanced at Bruce to find him staring at us with a stunned expression.

"Don't look so shocked, Boo. You know you want to marry her. I bet you'd propose today if you thought she'd say yes."

He barked a laugh but smiled. "You're not wrong."

My stomach flipped, and a kaleidoscope of butterflies winged around in my belly. A twinge of nerves, but not that flare of worry, not the sense that if I said yes, it'd all end in disaster.

We'll stick. Somehow, the more I dove in, the more certain I became.

Kiley's phone rang, and she held it up.

"It's Marcus. Mind if I take it?" She was looking at Bruce.

"Go right ahead. Tell him thanks again."

She mouthed, "Okay" and bolted up the stairs as she answered.

I filled two glasses of water and returned to Bruce's side. He'd somehow managed to sit up so his legs were extended on the couch and he sat upright against the pillow on one end.

Now that he'd repositioned, I could sit on the edge of the couch next to his thighs. Just being close to him like this sent heat racing through me. Since the relief had worn off and I knew he wasn't on death's door, the usual physical effect he had on me had taken hold yet again.

"So you want to marry me?" he asked, completely pleased with himself.

My turn to bark out a laugh. "Eventually, I think."

His mouth dropped open, then he laughed. "Yeah? Really?"

Happiness flooded my every sense. "Yeah. I mean, I think like Gram said, let's enjoy being together and being in love." I twined our fingers together and snuggled closer to him. "But I like the idea of Kiley in a flower crown. Maybe a junior bridesmaid instead of a flower girl, though."

He huffed out a disbelieving sound but lifted his chin to capture my mouth with his. Too soon, he pulled away, but it was worth it when he did.

"Well, then. You let me know when you're ready, and we'll get the party planning started."

I chuckled, then sobered when I saw just how serious he was. Those butterflies winged around so viciously, they had to be deranged by now, dizzy and love drunk.

"How will you know? How do I signal that?" I traced the jut of his collarbones through the thin shirt he wore.

His eyes flickered around the room as he thought, that beautiful mind working to come up with something that would no doubt delight me.

"How about something mathematical? Like you give me a formula for love or something? That's a thing, right?"

I laughed, thinking of something cheesy like saying "143" indicating the number in each representative equation for the letters in the word, but then an idea hit, and my heart rate ticked up. "Actually, how about Euler's formula?"

He pinned me with that dark gaze long enough, I worried maybe he'd forgotten our conversation until he nodded. "Still no idea what it is, but yes. That's it. Flash me the formula and I'll know."

I beamed at him, happiness barraging me so viscerally, it had to escape through a laugh. I loved how unafraid he was to admit he didn't understand. It struck me as such a rare quality in a man who had so much confidence, and yet didn't that explain it? He had confidence in himself and what he knew, so admitting he didn't know something wasn't a matter of fear or embarrassment. It was simple fact, and he wasn't daunted by it.

One more thing to love about him.

"Let's just say it gives us the reason for two different things to exist in one space." I looked at him meaningfully. "And even though we're actually a lot alike in some ways, I like the image that reflects."

His eyes hooded, and he got that particular look that made my blood heat.

"I love it when you talk about stuff I don't understand. It's so freaking hot."

I burst out laughing. "You're a very odd man, you know that?"

He feigned confusion. "Why, because I find my future wife to be attractive? I'd say I'm a very lucky man."

This man. "Well, if you're lucky, then so am I. The odds might've been against us, but I think we've got a chance."

His large, warm hand slid along my arm and up to cradle my jaw. "We've got more than a chance, Nik. We've got each other."

EPILOGUE

Bruce

Six months later

Six months after the day Nikki told me she loved me, I got the first clue. She'd tucked the symbols—letters?—into an envelope with nothing on it. Nothing remarkable. White security, sealed with the pull-tab sticky stuff along the edge, no words, no trace of explanation.

But she knew I didn't need it. I'd memorized Euler's formula, and I knew its parts even if I still had only a vague sense of how someone would use the thing. What it meant to me was I'd just gotten the green light to propose to Nikki Hastings. I'd gotten, at least in part, the sign that she wanted to go to the next step.

I blew out a breath, anticipation making my lungs tight.

"Okay there, Jaws?" Adam strode in with a stack of papers and eyed me. "Your incision bothering you?"

"No, no, Doc. I'm good. Just... I think I got the go-ahead from Nik." Just saying it out loud made me feel a little ill from the way the adrenaline cranked through me. My body's response to the plain envelope and simple black letters cut out of printer paper was far more than I'd expected, and yet, I couldn't blame it. This was it. *This* was it.

Adam's game chuckle had me grinning even harder.

"Glad to hear it. I think we're all ready for you two to tie the knot."

I raised a brow. "Yeah? Am I that bad?"

"Beast told me he was going to quit if he had to walk in on you guys sneaking around and whispering sweet nothings in the break room when she drops by again." His face showed incredible amusement, as I would expect.

"Beast said the phrase *sweet nothings*? It really must be dire, then."

We laughed together and I couldn't stop smiling. "Guess there's only one thing to be done."

He nodded and patted the doorframe on his way out. "Guess so."

The next bit of the formula came an agonizing three days later. Ki walked up and handed me another envelope.

"This is for you. Also, I approve, obviously. Let me know how I can help." Then she stalked away but kept glancing back like I wouldn't notice.

Even though I knew what I'd find, my heart thudded in my ears and my pulse shot through the roof. I fumbled with the seal and removed the letters. Not the rest of it, though—there'd be one last envelope if I had to guess, unless she intended to torture me by doing one letter at a time.

I doubted it. Because she'd seemed anxious to know I'd received her envelope the other day, and when I'd played it cool, she'd been the one flustered. I loved that she was as excited about this as I was. I also loved that she'd made it a bit of a puzzle—no surprise there.

"You know, you could just go ahead and ask her." Rosie hollered this from her old driveway where she and her boyfriend Amir had just exited her car.

"Do I need to report an attempted B and E? What are you doing here?" I crossed the space and extended a hand to Amir, who shook it, then accepted Rosie's hug. Kiley, Nikki, and I saw them weekly for family dinner—an event I wasn't sure which one of us loved more—but they still liked to stop by. Now that spring was coming on, Rosie liked to pretend she needed to check on her flowers, but really, I think part of her still loved the house and just liked being in it.

"Oh, go on and talk, Bruce. But I'm not the one stealing hearts." She winked, then wiggled her brows.

The laugh came out like it often did with Rosie, and very often these days. I hadn't exactly sewn up my *doer* tendency, but I'd made progress in that direction. At the new year, we'd had new staff come in—a new admin to replace Nikki, who only did our accounting and payroll now that she'd gotten more focused on launching her math app—and a few new positions elsewhere in the lineup, too.

But mostly, I'd started letting myself rest. Relax. Enjoy Nikki and my time with her, which in turn helped me enjoy Kiley and my time with her. Ki seemed happier than ever, and while I didn't think she looked at Nikki as a mother, I think they did have a kinship forged by similar life experiences that was unbreakable. Plus, the whole math nerd thing. Paired with therapy she'd been devoted to since the Carl mess, Ki was flourishing.

"I'm not stealing hearts. If anyone did that, it was your great-niece, and I think you know it." I winked right back.

Amir chuckled, and Rosie smirked. "Oh, I do. And I can't wait for the wedding."

No one had been shy about their expectation that Nik and I would end up together, least of all either one of us. But because of Kiley, and because of both of our histories, and despite the complete abandon with which I'd fallen for her, we did our best to move slow. And I did my best not to hint or pressure. We had a plan, and here I was, holding the second piece to a puzzle that meant I could ask a question I'd only ever wanted to ask her.

"You know how I feel about it. Y'all go on in and I'll see you Sunday, right?" I waved as I wandered back to my yard, wondering how I'd manage to think about anything else until she delivered the next one.

Nikki came home late on Friday night, just like I did. We'd maintained our tradition of girls' night and Saint staff at Craic. I'd seen her from afar. I'd stolen a kiss and had to convince myself to leave her be instead of hauling her over my shoulder and taking her home early, but I kept it together.

Until we both pulled into our respective driveways and she walked toward me. Kiley was out with a friend. Nikki and I had planned to have a late dinner and watch a movie at her place, and I wasn't sure how I'd contain myself, but then she surprised me.

She reached into her purse and pulled out another white envelope. "Go ahead."

I swallowed hard. "I thought you'd make me wait on this one."

She quirked a brow. "Who says that's the rest of it?"

Our eyes hooked, locked, and I took it from her hands and tore it open without glancing down. "Because I know you. You'd want a prime number, and you're impatient."

She lit up, a brilliant smile covering her face before she shook her head. "Any time I worry you don't know me well enough, then there you go."

"So I'm right?"

She grinned again. "I couldn't stand to wait any more. I'd planned it for tomorrow but... couldn't do it."

Gazes still entwined, I pulled out the pieces and finally glanced down to see the last parts of the formula.

"Here I go." And I got down on one knee.

Nikki

My mouth dropped open as he took my hands. "Wait, what? What are you doing?"

Half of that gorgeous mouth pulled up. "What do you think I'm doing, Nik?"

I'd been so smug about surprising him with this last piece even though it was all due to my own impatience, and yet here I was and I couldn't find a word. Not a *single* word would come out of my mouth because *is he really doing this!?*

"Is it too soon?" he asked, the genuine concern written in the lines of his brow.

That did jump-start me enough to eke out a "No, sorry. I just... I never imagined you'd be, I don't know... ready."

He gave me the full heart-stopper smile then. "Nik, I've been ready since a few weeks after meeting you. I know that sounds insane, but you know it's true. I could not be happier to have this envelope in my hand. And if it means what we planned for it to mean, and you are ready, then I have a question for you."

Everything in me shimmered, and my blood pulsed wildly through my veins. My mouth had gone dry, and the crisp spring air did nothing against the flash of heat that'd come on the heels of the crash of adrenaline.

Was I ready for this? Really?

Yes.

Yes, I was ready. There was no hesitation now. In truth, I would've been ready six months ago when I'd told him I was in love with him, but I'd needed time. I'd needed to trust myself and to trust that trust, as meta and overdone as that sounded. I'd needed to know that my love for him wasn't going to fail him.

I would fail him. I would hurt him. We'd already had a few arguments, like all couples were wont to have, and I'd hated it, but working through those things had shown me that yes—I'd already known Bruce would stick with me no matter what, but it'd shown me that yes—I'd stick with him, too.

So I took a deep, steadying breath, and told the most wonderful man I'd ever known the truth. "Yes. I'm ready."

He squeezed my hands and pinned me with those dark eyes now glittering in the moonlight.

"This is where it started. This space between our houses is where our worlds collided. It's where we had our first kiss and so many conversations that made me fall for you. It's where we learned each other and figured out we were meant for each other."

Throat tight, I swallowed and nodded. I couldn't disagree with any of that.

"I know we'll have a lot to learn, and life will likely hand us more than we think we can handle. But together, we can face those things. We'll solve the problems as they come, work out the proofs together."

A watery laugh came out, loving his word choice. "I think we can, too."

The smile around his eyes sobered, and he had that earnest, intense look that made my stomach drop.

"Veronica Hastings, I love you with everything that I am. Will you marry me?"

The stars seemed to glitter even more brightly, the moon glowing like a showoff and lighting up the mountains in an almost heavenly-looking white, but the most beautiful thing was this man in front of me. I tugged on his hands so he stood and shifted so my hands were around his neck.

"I love you, too, and yes, Bruce Camden, I will."

A kiss sealed the moment, so perfect I could hardly breathe through the excitement and amazement that this sweet, wonderful, brilliant, gorgeous man was *mine*.

He pulled back and one of his hands dropped away and he reached for his pocket, instantly producing a small black velvet box. I let out a chuckle-huff sound of disbelief at the sight.

"You thought I'd propose without a ring? Come on now,

Nik." He gave me a dashing little frown and flipped open the box.

The moonlight glinted off a stone—not huge, but not small either.

"It's platinum and conflict-free. I thought about getting something fancier, or just gigantic so everyone would know you're my wife, but I restrained myself."

I giggled, his excitement tangible as he took the ring and slipped it onto my shaking finger. "I love it."

He huffed out a relieved breath. "I love you."

Thank you so much for reading Bruce and Nikki's story! You can catch Tristan and Winnie in Safe with You—keep reading for a bonus epilogue from Tristan! Or, if you'd like to see where Wilder and Saint Security's story began, check out Almost Home. To see Eddie and Bri's story, don't miss Love Undercover.

BONUS EPILOGUE

Tristan

NOW

Fourteen and a half years.

I'd been talking to this girl for fourteen and a half years.

Woman. She was a woman now. But when she and her family had adopted me as their soldier through the aptly named Adopt a Soldier program, she'd just celebrated her sweet sixteen.

She'd gone on and on about how excited she was to be sixteen, finally, and how it'd only be two more years until she could graduate and head off to college. As a soldier six years deep into what I'd already known would be a lifelong career, I remembered the excitement of being able to leave home and start my own life. In the utter wasteland of my current deployment at the time, her palpable enthusiasm had charmed me, and oddly enough, given me hope.

What a precious thing in the bleakness of war. I'll never

forget how her rambling, self-deprecating e-mails had given me space to breathe. How I'd looked forward to the care packages her family had sent that included little hand-written notes from her. And they'd all bubbled over with looking ahead to what came next—to launching out into the world and figuring out who she really was.

But Winnie hadn't done that like I'd thought she had. Somehow through all our e-mails and letters over the years of her college, my deployments and moves, and ultimately settling into special operations in North Carolina, I'd never grasped how close she'd stuck to her family.

Not until very recently.

And now, as I navigated the drive from Silverton to the Salt Lake City Airport, I couldn't have verbalized my thoughts for anything. My mind had been slower to filter through and release them into words these last few weeks since making this plan, and today proved no different.

With a sharp exhale, I steadied the tipping sensation slithering in my gut. Whatever my feelings were on the matter, they didn't get a voice in the discussion anymore. We were doing this.

Winnie, a woman I'd known for fourteen and a half years but whom I'd never met in person, a woman I'd mentally clung to more than once in that time, was finally going to be here in the flesh. But worry had stifled any excitement or anticipation over that reality.

Because Winnie was in danger. And she was coming here because she'd run out of options.

And we were getting married as a last resort.

Thank you so much for reading. Don't miss Tristan and Winnie in Safe with You.

AUTHOR'S NOTE AND ACKNOWLEDGMENTS

Thank you for reading Made for You! I'm so excited to be starting this series, and I can tell you that ALL of the single Saint Security personnel are clamoring for their stories to be told.

Huge thank you to my husband for cheering me on and working to give me space and time to write this book in the middle of our PCS (permanent change of station). The Army life is a wild ride and I'm so glad to be on it with you and our amazing, weirdo kids.

Thank you to Zee Monodee for her consistent and persistent help in refining this book until the characters were all ready to meet you. Thank you to Amanda Cuff for catching so many unnecessarily hyphenated words, and much more. Thank you to Jamie McGillen for her close read and finding all my un-curly apostrophes and missing words.

Thank you to my amazing beta readers Amanda, Genny, and Ashley. Your questions, suggestions, and insights always make the books stronger!

Thank you to my Facebook group for helping me determine Kenny's name. I know you were rooting for Matty — I promise we'll have a Matty! I swear! :*

Thank you to Suzan, who will read this before any other ARC readers because she's awesome. Thank you for being willing to read my books, catch those last lingering typos, and to champion the books on social media. You are truly a wonderful human and you do so much to support indie authors. Thank you!

And finally, many thanks to *you*. I'm honored you've spent your time reading my book.

Now, off to go see about Tristan and his woman...

ABOUT THE AUTHOR

Claire Cain lives to eat and drink her way around the globe with her traveling soldier and three kids, but is perhaps even happier hunkered down at home in a pair of sweatpants and slippers using any free moment she has to read and cook. Or talk—she really likes to talk. She has become an expert at packing too many dishes in too few cabinets and making houses into homes from Utah to Germany and many places in between. She's a proud Army wife and is frankly just really happy to be here.

You can also join Claire's facebook reader group for exclusive content and fun: https://www.facebook.com/groups/clairecain/

Website: http://www.clairecainwriter.com

E-mail: Claire@ClaireCainWriter.com

Newsletter sign-up for new releases, exclusives, and freebies, including a free book:

http://www.clairecainwriter.com/newsletter

amazon.com/author/clairecain

bookbub.com/authors/claire-cain

instagram.com/clairecainwriter

facebook.com/clairecainwriter

goodreads.com/clairecainwriter

pinterest.com/clairecainwriter